# Gwyneth Arriving

# *Also by Reg Quist*

*The Church at Third and Main*

*Hamilton Robb*

*Noah Gates*

*Terry of the Double C*

Danny Series

Just John Series

Mac's Way Series

Reluctant Redemption Series

The Settlers Series

# Gwyneth Arriving

FRONTIER DREAMING

BOOK TWO

REG QUIST

**Gwyneth Arriving**
Paperback Edition


CKN Christian Publishing
An Imprint of Wolfpack Publishing
1707 E. Diana Street
Tampa, FL 33610

cknchristianpublishing.com



Paperback ISBN 979-8-89567-865-7
eBook ISBN 979-8-89567-864-0

# Gwyneth Arriving

#### Acknowledgments

Much thanks to my good friend, Dr. W.D., MD, FRCSC. TX.

# PART ONE

# *Dr. Gwyneth Wycome, Md*

CHICAGO

# Chapter One

THE BIG OAK DOORS OF THE MEDICAL COLLEGE BURST open. A gaggle of boisterous men, some young, some much older, surged out into the late spring Chicago sunlight. It had been a long, sometimes tedious, sometimes enlightening two years. Some had found the studies to be more difficult than they had imagined or were prepared to work through. Fewer men emerged on the final day than had entered on the first day, but there was the same number of women, just one, born Gwyneth May Scanlon, now Gwyneth May Wycome, M.D.

Each graduate was relishing the dream they had fostered since before entering the school. Doctor. The right to open a medical practice anywhere of their choosing. But first, a one evening celebration. There had been many an evening spent at the Turf and Suds. And many a morning of regret. This would be the last. Tomorrow, it was off to show the world their learning.

Gwyneth purposely hung back, her dormitory room door closed. There would be no pub time for her. There never had been. The men had even quit inviting her. For the last time, she straightened out the compact space the college had set aside for their first and only lady student. Her presence represented a new era for the school, and a challenge to the men, most of whom had never seriously considered the idea of a female doctor.

Gwyneth had mostly kept to herself, studying and going for long walks when opportunity allowed. Although time had dulled the pain, she still had no interest in replacing the love she lost with the death of Trent, her husband. They had struggled through their ranching years together, building the Mirrored W into a frontier ranch to be proud of. But when the rattle-brained animal Trent was riding broke into a fit, it was as if two people were thrown to the rocky ground and killed. The deadness in her heart would not be lessened by an evening of celebration at the college pub. No, she was used to being alone, and alone she would remain.

When the raucousness that had reverberated through the school's hallways faded, to be replaced by a welcome silence, Gwyneth took one last look around her room, picked up her suitcase and her medical bag that she had carried over so many wagon and horseback miles, moved into the hallway, made her way to the oak doors, and hesitated. As she had done so often, she again thought of the long trail that brought her to this moment.

*Trent, you would have been so proud to see this. Thank you, my husband. Can you see it, Trent? Right there in my medical bag, safely tucked away. There's a piece of paper. Just a small piece of paper. Hardly anything at all, when you think on it that way. But if you could unroll it, Trent, you'd see that it says Gwyneth May Wycome is qualified to serve as a medical doctor and surgeon. Just a piece of paper, Trent, and so few words. But it's all the world to me. Stay with me, Trent. I need you so.*

With a small, satisfied, yet somehow sad smile on her face, she pushed the door open and stepped into her new life.

# Chapter Two

THERE WAS A TWO-MILE WALK ON THE DUSTY STREETS of the city between the doctor's college and the Lakeside Women's and Children's Hospital. Not all the streets were perfectly safe. Anyone advising Gwyneth would have said to take a cab. But comparing the danger of those streets, where poverty and want and hopelessness often drove people outside, sitting pointlessly and aimlessly on their front stairs, seemed almost trivial to Gwyneth when compared to her years on the western frontier.

When thinking about what she was exposed to during her walks, she couldn't help remembering her father-in-law's words. Abe had said back in Bessie Creek, Colorado, a tiny, struggling gathering of shacks and half canvas buildings. *"I'd rather be poor here, in the Creek, than in some big heartless city. Here, at least a man might do something about it. In the cities he's just run over and cast aside."* She had doubted the words when she first heard them, but with the evidence all around her, she'd had to revise her thinking.

During her evening or Sunday afternoon walks, she often stopped to talk with folks, especially young mothers. The tenements were peopled with whites of many cultures and languages, immigrants from afar, along with freed blacks still hoping to find a way through the mysteries of life.

Signs of disease and malnutrition were everywhere. Gwyneth advised on medical issues when she thought it wise. Settled for a bit of quiet encouragement when that was needed. She had nothing else to offer.

Even the groups of hard-looking young men, staring into hopeless futures, were attentive to her talk of hygiene and self-care. These were the same men and boys who might rob and beat a stranger on a moment's notice, with little provocation, but she had gradually gained their trust. She avoided drunks and the older, harder-appearing men.

After leaving the college and tuning her mind and steps toward the hospital, she wasted no time, simply smiling and waving at the folks along the way, sometimes greeting them by name. She had been negotiating with the hospital for the past two months, appealing for a position as a doctor, which she would turn into a deeper training and learning opportunity. That she had been successful and now had a job to go to was proof enough that she had won them over. Her goal today was simply to say hello and to advise that her college days were behind her, and that she would report for work on the schedule the hospital set for her. She knew there had been objections to putting her on staff, but the very determined Mrs. Gladys Pierpont, who was in charge of the charitable organization that raised money for the institution, would brook no argument.

~

"I WON'T HAVE IT," shouted Dr. Samuel Levantine. "A woman doctor! Who ever heard of such a thing? Why...why... it's not proper."

"And what exactly is improper about it, Doctor?"

"Why, we are working on the human body. Often in delicate areas dealing with even more delicate matters, childbirth and such."

"May I remind you, Doctor, that Dr. Gwyneth Wycome is, herself, a woman? Further, she is a widow. She is familiar with the mysteries of the human body. And she probably has as much birthing experience as anyone in this hospital, and most of that under the most trying of circumstances. And yes, that includes you, Doctor. She has nursed in the most primitive of conditions in our very own frontier west. She has ridden many hundreds of miles on horseback and wagon, and stagecoach, bringing help to suffering settlers. You know all that because I have told you so before. Now, settle down and prepare for the future. Give her a three-month trial. If she can't do the job, then you are free to replace her."

"You leave me no choice, Gladys. But I warn you, I'll not work with her. She can be scheduled with someone else but keep her out of my hair."

Smiling, Gladys Pierpont said, "Ah, Samuel. I promise not to make a fuss when you find yourself backing down. And back down you will. I am confident of that."

NIGHTS, in the routine of the hospital, were mainly times of quiet reassurance and comforting of the patients, overseen by nurses. Only seldom was a doctor in attendance. Actual doctoring matters were left to the daytime shifts. Regardless of that long tradition, Gwyneth was not surprised to be assigned to night duty.

Dr. Samuel Levantine hadn't bothered leaving his small office to greet her, but the other three staff doctors welcomed her, if reluctantly and with unspoken questions. One young doctor, a Dr. William Grant, seemed overly intense, eager even, in his greeting, reaching for her hand with an enthusiastic handshake and a grand smile.

Gwyneth, at age eighteen, had been naive and vulnerable when she first walked into a Civil War surgical tent as a volunteer nurse-helper. That naivety had lasted less than one week, smashed into nothingness by a very handsome doctor with roaming hands. A single slap on the man's face in front of the tent full of suffering and dying soldiers, as well as other medical staff, put an end to the grabbiness.

At eighteen, Gwyneth had been mature in body and mind, knowing that men were interested in her, and why. That she would not be considered beautiful by the standards of the day bothered her not at all. She wasn't unattractive, and that sufficed for the life she had planned for herself. After her marriage, her mother-in-law had called her wholesome. Trent had referred to her, in their private times, as lovely or tempting. She understood the game and simply smiled in response.

Her marriage to Trent, the young cowboy who had smiled and talked his way into her heart while she was helping the small-town doctor mend his broken arm, was not done out of naivety. Theirs had been a good marriage, saddened only by the reality that together, she and Trent were not able to produce a child of their own. But their ranching venture had been successful so that when Trent didn't survive his last ride on a rank, half-broke horse, Gwyneth was left lonely, but financially secure. It was the cattle money that had seen her through her medical college years. Much of that money still gathered interest in a big downtown bank.

Through marriage, years of hard work and thousands of hours in the saddle to establish and build the ranch, widowhood, frontier nursing, and two years in a college with men, Gwyneth had no problem sorting out the impulses and intents of the men she met. There was no need of a slap to cool Dr. Grant's ardor. A very brief, simple, dexterous, fingers-only handshake blew out the light in his eyes. Temporarily, at least. The rest of the staff was welcoming, if a bit hesitant.

# Chapter Three

On Gwyneth's first night shift, Mrs. Gladys Pierpont, herself, walked through the hallways and wards of the small hospital with Gwyneth in tow. She felt strange in the white coat she had purchased for herself. Silently, she thought, *I'm looking forward to getting used to it.*

"We do the best we can, Doctor. There is a constant need for more funding. Fundraising is almost all I do. We try to assign the money we receive to the most needful areas, which, of course, are patient care and all that can mean. We have begun a separate fundraising effort so we can have the building prepared for when electric lighting becomes available. The people in charge of the system predict that will be within two years. You can see by the unwelcome noise and mess in the hallways that we have men here during the day installing piping for when we get running water and indoor plumbing. Always looking to the sanitation problem, we deemed indoor plumbing and running water to be of prime importance. We are very much looking forward to the end of the installation process, and to when it will all be available for use. The staff don't think I know what the whispering in the lunchroom is about, but they have a small bet going around about who will be the first to use the facilities. Just harmless fun."

As they walked through the wards, Gwyneth was concerned that some children with clearly communicable diseases were bedded down beside those with other illnesses or injuries. She made no comments until they arrived at the maternity ward. There were three women in residence, two who had already given birth and one who still waited her time. Gwyneth smiled and spoke to the one woman who was awake.

"Did you have a boy or a girl?"

"It's a boy. I've only seen him once, for a few minutes, but he looked healthy enough."

"And how are you feeling?"

"I feel all right mostly. A bit weak and I hurt some. I'm still discharging. I don't know how long that can go on."

Gwyneth excused herself for a moment while she walked to the table near the door and brought back the lamp. She settled that on the woman's bedside table and said, "Let's take a look."

Before pulling back the cover, she turned to Mrs. Pierpont. "Where can I find water to wash with?"

Mrs. Pierpont, clearly troubled, answered, "Just there in the hallway. But what are you planning to do?"

"Why, I'm going to do what you hired me for. I'm going to attend to this patient."

Inviting no response, Gwyneth located the washstand and scrubbed the best she could in the cool water. She then returned and folded back the bedcovers, exposing a blood-soaked cloth that had been strategically placed for the purpose. In shock, she spoke without looking back up. "Mrs. Pierpont, please hurry and find a nurse. Bring her here quickly. Tell her to have a good wash."

Mrs. Pierpont, a single lady with no maternity experience, stood in shock. Staring down at the patient, she couldn't help but see something she had never before seen or imagined. As Gwyneth pulled away the filthy cotton wad, the matron nearly fainted. Risking her first job on her first night of duty, Gwyneth sharply said, "Now. Please. There is no time to waste here."

Gwyneth left the patient long enough to fetch the container of water and a wash pan. With nowhere else to put it, she set it on the floor beside where she was working. Her first gentle swipe with a wet cloth came away in distressing condition. Gwyneth dropped it on the floor and picked up another clean, folded cotton pad. The second wipe exposed the problem. She turned to the nurse who had just arrived and asked, "Do you know where the supplies are kept? This lady needs sutures."

Mrs. Pierpont gasped aloud. "Wha...what are you doing?"

"As I said just a moment ago, I'm doing what you hired me for."

"Perhaps you should wait..."

"What? Wait for one of the men, perhaps the one who should have seen to this long ago? This woman can't wait."

The nurse arrived back with several metal cases containing medical instruments, needles, and suturing thread. Gwyneth said, "If your hands are clean, find me a large, curved needle, and thread it with linen suturing material. Cut off about three feet of thread and soak it in alcohol, needle and all, then pass me the needle. Hold the thread up so it doesn't come in contact with anything. Then go and place a lightly folded flannel sheet into the oven of the stove in the lunchroom. Place a couple more in the warming oven so they'll be ready for use.

"And, Mrs. Pierpont, please find me some more cotton padding."

With hardly a whimper, the patient endured the treatment. Gwyneth again patted the area with a neatly folded cloth and watched for a moment. The bleeding was down to a light seeping. She smiled up at the woman. "You're a brave, patient woman. But now we must change this bedding. Can you stand if I help you?"

When the bed was empty, the nurse energetically drew the sheets into a wad, folding them and the pillow slip into a bundle, and dropped them on the floor. She rushed to the storage closet and came back with a clean sheet for the mattress cover. She then scooted to the lunchroom and brought back the pleasantly warm flannel. She was clearly a practiced hand at bed making. She flipped one sheet over the mattress and looked at Mrs. Pierpont, who had hardly moved since the episode had started. "This would go more quickly if you wanted to tuck that side in."

Delicately, slowly recovering from all she had seen and heard, the matron bent to the task. In no time at all, the young mom was back in bed, tucked under the heated sheet, with two warm blankets warmly swaddling her.

Gwyneth looked at the girl who had helped. "I'm Dr. Wycome. I don't know your name yet, but you appear to be a good nurse. We'll have a chat another time. Thanks for helping. Now, if you could find this lady something to eat and a hot cup of tea, we can let her get some sleep. And your main task this night is to keep an eye on her. Call me if anything amiss turns up."

Gwyneth scrubbed her hands again, then spoke to Mrs. Pierpont. "Should we continue our introductory tour?"

"Young lady, I expect you will do just fine on your own. God help the other doctors. And don't forget to make a note of that treatment in the patient's log. Good night."

"Good night, Mrs. Pierpont, and thanks for the assistance."

# Chapter Four

Dr. Samuel Levantine was in the habit of starting his days early. He made it his first duty each morning to check the patient logs. He stood nearly paralyzed in indignant wonder and anger when he read Gwyneth's report. He stormed out of the office carrying the medical chart, looking for her. He found her sitting on a bench, tying the laces of her street shoes.

"Dr. Wycome. What is the meaning of this?" He was shaking the chart almost in her face.

"Just doing my job, sir."

"Who gave you the right..."

"You did, sir. When you hired me. The woman was bleeding terribly and had been for several hours. She needed immediate attention. She's fine now. I just checked her a few moments ago."

"You should have waited for a more experienced man. Why you might have done irreparable harm to the patient. And where do you think you're going now? Running away, are you?

"I'm going home to sleep, sir. I've been here nearly twelve hours. Unless there's an emergency I don't know about, my shift is ended, and I need sleep. As for doing irreparable harm, that was a near thing, but it wasn't my doing. Without immediate treatment, we may well have had a corpse on our hands this morning."

The forcefulness of her words was enough to make the chief doctor back off. "I'll look into this more."

"Yes, that's a good idea. Good night, sir. Or perhaps good morning. I'll be back at six."

~

THE INCIDENT and the time slipped away. She was being treated with a little more respect as her patient care was noted and silently appreciated.

Gwyneth brought some wrath down on her head the day she rearranged the children's ward. With determination, she called in a couple of nurses, and together they moved several beds. Teasing the children that they were going for a ride, there was much laughter in the ward, something that was seldom heard. This brought another visit from Dr. Samuel Levantine.

"Dr. Wycome, you will frustrate me. It's as if you joined our staff with that particular goal in mind. What have you done now that so upset the other doctors, especially Dr. Grant? William is not usually one to get his dander up, but I just had a most unpleasant few moments trying to explain that I didn't know why his patient was no longer where the good doctor had bedded him. Please justify your actions in a way that even I can understand."

"Certainly. Moving the beds around so that the children with communicable diseases were held to one end of the room is the logical thing to do. So was adding the scrubbing and disinfecting station. It is imperative that staff wash thoroughly between patients. I commandeered the help of a couple of nurses, but no blame rests on them. They were simply following my instructions. We hung a white curtain between each bed, isolating them from other patients, and another curtain isolating those few beds from the larger portion of the room."

After Gwyneth had clarified that the beds she had moved all held boys and girls with communicable diseases, he nodded his head. "We had them all separated at first. To the point of having separate wards. But the hospital has become busier with time. Almost monthly, we're seeing growth, threatening to exceed the space offered in our premises. Perhaps we have become a bit too casual with the time pressure we work under. Good work, Doctor. I'll get a memo out to the staff. But if I may suggest, it is possible that the methods you saw in the war tents or on the frontier are a bit precipitous for us city folks. We lean more toward discussion and group decisions. Life or death is seldom a matter of seconds or minutes with the work we normally do. We usually have time to sort it out with some consultation. I'm afraid you somewhat frighten the other doctors, although I must say, the nurses adore you."

"Thank you, sir. May I take that to mean my probation time is up?"

"I suppose you might at that."

# Chapter Five

The weeks became months. Gwyneth didn't particularly enjoy Chicago, but she was trying to gain the best the city had to offer. She had made a friend, another woman at the boarding house. Together they attended plays, dined in restaurants they felt they could afford, and walked endless miles, often along the lakefront. They had tried swimming in the lake once, but the water was far too cold for their enjoyment. Once, they rented passage on a cruise boat for an afternoon on the lake. After church on Sundays, the routine was to return to the boarding house and rest up toward the taxing demands of the week to come.

Gwyneth had no man in her life, nor did she wish for one. Her work was her passion. And with that passion, the desire to one day open her own office and clinic remained strong. She knew she would soon move on from the hospital, but she believed there was still more for her to learn before she stepped out into her own practice.

Most of the maternity work had been passed along to Gwyneth. She enjoyed working with the mothers, and after the births, with the babies. Several times, she had to explain to the patients that no, she was not a mother herself. The thought saddened her, but she tried not to let that show.

Dr. Levantine called to Gwyneth as she was rushing to the maternity ward. A Mrs. Wright was sensing that her time was approaching.

"Dr. Wycome, I want you to take Dr. Theodore Nelson here and introduce him to our work. He is new to us. He is under your gentle ministrations until I decide differently."

Wondering if there was a bit of sarcasm in the *gentle ministrations* comment, Gwyneth said, "Come along, Dr. Nelson. We are in a bit of a rush this morning. A young lady is about to bring her future heir and heartache into the world. What experience do you have on the topic, Doctor?"

"Well, actually none. If we were to wish to get right to the point."

Although he couldn't deny his curiosity, privately, he had been hoping to keep it that way, but he dare not admit to that. It was his ardent hope to be assigned to the children's ward, where he would be perfectly comfortable.

"Well then, what practical understanding do you have on the subject, Doctor?"

"Again, when you ask it right out like that, Doctor, very little. None at all, I might just as well say, except that is, what we received in doctor's college. But that was book learning only, with some unease with the topic involved, and even at that, it did not delve deeply into the mysteries of populating future generations."

Gwyneth stopped walking so abruptly that Dr. Nelson was a complete step ahead of her before he managed to stop.

"Are you telling me, Dr. Nelson, that you have never assisted in a birthing experience, or even studied the matter?"

"That would be an accurate synopsis of the situation." His voice was hesitant, and his hands were shaking.

"Are you a married man, Doctor?"

"Oh, my no. I have just come from college. Grandmother

should have immediately withdrawn both my allowance and my tuition if she thought I had entered into matrimony."

"So continuing with our assumptions, would it be true that the sight and functions of the female anatomy is somewhat of a mystery to you?"

"Well, one is not born with that knowledge, is one, Dr. Wycome?"

"No. No, they are not. But I'm wondering what kind of a medical college would allow graduation without covering the topic. After all, women make up fully half of the population. There is a very good chance that you may run into one sometime during your career."

"I can assure you, Doctor, that I attended a very proper college. Very proper indeed."

Seeing no purpose in prolonging the examination, Gwyneth said, "Come along, Doctor. We will attend to your continuing education."

Gwyneth greeted the patient with a chipper. "Good morning, Mrs. Wright. How are you feeling now? The nurse tells me your contractions are steady and predictable. I expect we'll make acquaintance with your little one very soon now."

It seemed that most doctors asked questions without waiting for the answer, as if they already understood the situation without the assistance of the patient. Gwyneth had fallen into that habit.

Gently, she folded the bed sheet back and reached to push the patient's nightdress aside. As she did that, she glanced at Dr. Nelson. She exhaled a frustrated breath. "Dr. Nelson, you are going to be of little help in this procedure with your eyes closed."

In spite of the contraction the patient was enduring at the moment she giggled at Gwyneth's words. She glanced at Dr. Nelson, saw his discomfort and distress, and giggled again. It took all of Dr. Theodore Nelson's dignity and determination to not retreat to the hallway and then to, well, he wasn't quite sure where he would go. With a slight shuffling of his feet and a gulping swallow of built-up saliva, he said, "Ready, Doctor."

The next hour was everything Dr. Nelson feared and dreaded. Including his first time cleansing a newborn and wrapping her in a warmed sheet, although there was a slight smile on his lips, and he gently, almost lovingly, laid the little one at her mother's breast. Gwyneth dismissed him at the conclusion of the procedure, suggesting a hot cup of tea may be just the thing, given the circumstances.

DR. WILLIAM GRANT was unable to hide his attraction to the only female doctor he had ever known. They were leaving the institution together at the end of their shifts one day, and he thought he would see if time had mellowed Gwyneth. "Dr. Wycome, it is a beautiful afternoon, promising a pleasant evening. It would be my great pleasure to treat you to dinner and then, perhaps, a walk along the lakeshore. Would you honor me in that?"

"No, Doctor. Please don't label me as rude, but I have no interest at all in keeping male company. Yours or anyone else's. I'm hoping you will accept that as a fact and we'll not mention it again."

"I will do as you wish, but surely you must hold thoughts of, at least companionship, if not marriage."

"You are forgetting, sir, that I am a widow. I have had a marriage. A very good marriage that ended all too abruptly. I am now perfectly content in my position."

"Yes, I know you're a widow, and I can't imagine the hurts of losing a mate. Would I be prying too much to inquire as to what happened, to bring about your husband's death?"

"He was thrown from a horse. The result was a broken neck. And don't misunderstand. Trent was a very good rider. But on the frontier, where we had our cattle ranch, we were always short of riding stock. Men rode animals that were barely broke, only weeks or short months from their native wilderness. Don't look at the Sunday afternoon riders you see here, around the city, with their little English saddles and their shiny boots, and imagine you understand frontier riding. There is no comparison. Our horses were not pets to be pampered. Trent's death was just a thing that happened. It was no one's fault."

"And do I take it that you ride also?"

"Dr. Grant, I have ridden thousands of miles, as well as having driven wagon teams. I can sit a wild horse as good as most cowboys. Now, I must leave you here. My boarding house is just down this next street."

"All right, Gwyneth. Good night then. If you ever change—"

"I won't. Good night."

# Chapter Six

Gwyneth's time at Lakeside Women's and Children's Hospital was coming to an end. She sensed it even if no one else did. She had worked there a full year, and then some, doing every task that needed doing, and most of them multiple times, gaining the respect of the doctors, nurses, and the hospital board. The most difficult times had been when the best of care was insufficient to save a patient. While there were few deaths numerically, each was indelibly printed on Gwyneth's memory. Added to those were the two times she had lost patients in the frontier of Colorado, once when a cowboy succumbed to a hopelessly dreadful horn gouging, and the other when the mother survived but the child, born with the umbilical cord snagged around its neck, resulting in asphyxia. The little boy arrived in the world blue from lack of oxygen. None of Gwyneth's efforts could entice the little fellow to take his first breath.

The only serious conflict, at Lakeside Women's and Children's, after the minor incidents of the first few days, came when two men half-dragged and half-carried a young man, bleeding from a wound sustained in a street fight, up the stairs to the back door of the hospital. Gwyneth heard the frantic banging on the door and ran to find out what was happening. First, she was startled by the troubled and fearful eyes of the two men who were holding their friend. Then her eyes fell to the wounded man. All three were black.

"Ma'am. You got to help. Isaiah here been hurt bad. He be bleeding something terrible. Please, ma'am."

Gwyneth was torn. This was, after all, a women's and children's hospital. And in the months she had worked there, they had never admitted a man, or a black patient of either gender. That situation, dealing with the races, was so common that few ever gave it serious thought.

Fresh blood flowed over the man's shirt, screaming out *this man has only minutes to live, perhaps only seconds*. Protocol suddenly seemed unimportant. Gwyneth's every belief, her every instinct, was to preserve life. That instinct pushed every restriction against treating men, against treating blacks, aside as if they had never existed. If there was ever a chance to save the life of the wounded man, it was now. She made a decision, knowing it may cost her the position she had enjoyed since graduating doctor's college.

"Bring him in. Just wait at the door while I get a stretcher."

She hurried to the children's ward, looking for Annette Grady. Nurse Grady had been known to have a bit of a rebellious spirit. She was the one nurse who would join Gwyneth in breaking a few unwritten rules, and perhaps a couple of written ones as well. And grin at the doing of it.

"Annette, come quickly and bring that stretcher along with you. Bring it to the back door hallway."

Settling the wheeled stretcher in the hallway close to the back door, where the light of the fading evening sun could fall on it, Nurse Grady looked up from the rolling miniature bed and gasped when she saw the three black men. She gasped again when she saw the blood running down the one man's shirt and pants, from a wound somewhere above his belt line. They wouldn't know where until they stripped the filthy shirt off.

With eyes wide, she looked at Gwyneth. "Dr. Wycome, are you sure?"

"What I'm sure of is that this man will be dead in a few minutes if we don't do something. Now scrub your hands and bring the water pot and a basin here. Don't forget the disinfectant. If there's another nurse available, send her along. Quickly now."

To the men, she said, "Lift your friend onto the stretcher. Be quick, but as gentle as you can. Strip his shirt off."

While they were doing as Gwyneth had said, she was at a scrubbing station, thoroughly working over her hands with strong soap and disinfectant. She then ran to the storage cabinet where the few available surgical instruments were kept. Grabbing what she thought she would need, she was soon back with the patient.

Nurse Grady ran down the corridor with the water container in her arms, splashing a portion of the water on herself and the floor along the way. Nurse Bonnie Chisum was following her with an armful of cotton pads and a roll of bandage material.

Gwyneth lifted the young man's eyelids. Gaining no response, she decided to proceed immediately. The patient was clearly unconscious, a fact which she planned to take advantage of. To arrange an anesthetic for a major surgery, which was rarely performed at Women's and Children's, would take too long. The patient had no time to spare in his young life.

The small round hole told her a bullet had entered his left side above the bottom rib, exiting out the back. What path it had followed and what damage it had done, she wouldn't know until she opened him up. The size of the entry wound suggested the shooter had used a .38, or something similar. Gwyneth took it all in with only a brief glance. Speaking to the nurses, she said, "I'm going to be making an incision here before this man bleeds to death. I'd like to have your assistance, but if that's more than you can handle, it would be best if you left now. You men should go outside and wait."

Gwyneth again checked the young man's response to her touch on his eyes. He remained unconscious. Gwyneth hoped he would stay that way. As a nurse, she had assisted while many a young soldier suffered through major surgery while still awake or half awake, as the rudimentary anesthetics available, and the crush of waiting patients created an untenable situation. She prayed nothing like that would be repeated at Lakeside Women's and Children's Hospital that night.

When both nurses held their ground, Gwyneth said, "You girls tip him onto his right side. I'll roll a couple of pillows under him to hold him in that position.

"Now, Bonnie, you take some of those pads and wipe as much blood off as you can. Then you give his entire center region a good, but quick wash. Slather on the disinfectant. We'll attend to the back wound later. There's very little blood there. Annette, you stand close, ready to do as I say."

With the young man's body cleansed as much as their facilities allowed, Gwyneth picked up a scalpel. "Are you all right, Annette?"

"I'm guessing we'll both know momentarily."

"Don't fall on the patient if it comes to that. Or on me."

Both nurses had assisted during minor surgeries, but never for a major internal invasion. In preparation for the unknown, Nurse Grady grabbed the stretcher and worked her feet into a more solid feeling on the shiny linoleum. She was still preparing her mind when Gwyneth made the incision. She wobbled just a bit as the skin opened. As if reassuring herself and Gwyneth, both, she said, "I'll be all right." That her voice was a bit squeaky and barely above a whisper went unmentioned.

Nurse Chisum stood like a statue, as if this was old hat to her.

Gwyneth had gained the habit of whispering aloud as she worked. She had started the habit back at Bessie Creek when she was delivering babies for frontier women. It was a way of assuring the young mothers, especially the ones delivering their first offspring, that this procedure had been done many, many times before and that she was going to be all right. So, with the wounded man, she whispered her way through the cutting away of a bit of ragged flesh. Whispered as she opened the incision a bit more, explaining her actions, and whispered even more loudly as she assessed the real damage, once she had mopped away most of the gathered blood. A bit of pressure on the internal wound slowed the bleeding considerably. Her whispers turned to audible talk as she said, "Bonnie, find Dr. Levantine. Bring him here on the run. And Annette, you go to the storage cabinet and bring an assortment of clamps. Now, if you please."

Fighting her way through a memory loaded with medical facts and theories, she tried to recall all she had ever learned about the spleen. It was quite recently that patients were living productive lives after the removal of this blood-cleansing organ. And few doctors had any firsthand experience with the necessary surgery. But with need being the mother of invention, as she had heard somewhere, Gwyneth was intent on venturing out. There was no repairing the wound. The bullet had done too much damage for that. It was do the surgery or stand by and allow the young man to die.

She raised her voice. "You men outside. Come to the door."

When the door opened, she quickly said, "Don't come any further. I just need to inform you that your friend is in very serious condition. The bullet struck a rib and turned to pass through the spleen. It has the appearance of being fired from a small-caliber weapon. A .32 perhaps. We can do nothing about the wound. But the good news is that he might live with the loss of the spleen. I'm going to remove it and pray for the best result. I want you to know that if he dies, we will have tried everything possible. Now you run just as fast as ever you have run. Run to Chicago General and have them send an ambulance on the quick. Tell them Dr. Levantine has requested it. Go now!"

With a great scurrying, and echoes of shoe leather landing on the linoleum flooring, and the flapping of doctors' coats, Dr. Samuel Levantine, followed by Dr. William Grant and two senior nurses, thundered down the hallway.

The first, totally predictable words from Dr. Levantine were, "What in tarnation are you doing? This is a women's hospital. Women and children."

Clearly, the good doctor had worked up further queries on the run from his office, but Gwyneth gave him no opening to voice them. Somewhat lacking in expected respect, she said, "There is no time for squabbling. You can fire me later. Right now, we have a life to save. Now get yourselves scrubbed up, all of you, nurses again too."

"What are you proposing to do, supposing I don't call a halt right now?"

Without looking up from her work, Gwyneth answered, "I am proposing to save a life, Dr. Levantine. And I'm going to need help doing it. This man has suffered a gunshot wound. The bullet glanced off the bottom rib, ricocheted into his spleen, doing severe damage, and exited out his back. I am going to remove the organ. I will be needing all the assistance you can provide, either physically or by voiced advice.

"I'll need more hands than just mine to clamp off the blood flow. Please scrub. And sterilize those clamps. Now. And Annette, prepare a variety of needles and suture thread. Soak them in alcohol until I call for them."

With a few select comments, the least of which was, "This is most unusual," Dr. Levantine submitted, doing as he was bid, pushing his coat sleeves over his elbows and scrubbing thoroughly. Dr. Grant did the same. Then, with unusual modesty, Dr. Levantine said, "Dr. Grant, you are much younger than I and will have a steadier hand. I will stand by to assist, but you will take point in this matter. Now, everyone, do your best."

In less than half an hour, Gwyneth knotted the last internal stitch. She closed the wound with a few strips of tape. She had been gritting her teeth so long and so hard, they were hurting. Perspiration was pouring off her brow and she appeared to be exhausted, although that was not really the case. She was simply relaxing after having been tensed up with extreme concentration and effort the entire time. Leaning against the hallway wall, focusing on the young man whose eyes had just begun to flutter, she said, "Annette, hurry now. Take a clean bed sheet and place it in the stove oven in the lunchroom. Let it warm for a few minutes and rush it back here. Bonnie, if you would prepare the double of a warm blanket to wrap around this boy after Annette brings the sheet back, I would appreciate it. He's going to be in considerable pain, but there's nothing I know to do about that. Keeping him warm might help a bit.

"Dr. Levantine and Dr. Grant. You are both much stronger than me or the nurses. It would be a great help if you could lift the patient just enough to take a few wraps of cotton around his middle that would hold the tape in place and help to keep the wound clean."

Waiting, and hoping to hear the rattle of an approaching ambulance, everyone began to relax.

For the first time, Gwyneth allowed her eyes to look in the direction of the two doctors who were standing together at the foot of the patient's stretcher. Dr. Levantine was the first to speak.

"What you did was altogether wrong, Dr. Wycome. But it was also altogether marvelous. With our very basic facilities, I would have never approached such a challenge. We are not, nor do we plan to be, primarily, or even largely, a surgical hospital, especially for internal surgeries. There are others filling that role. Perhaps the push for progressing and expanding our services will become the difference between us older folks and the younger generation who will be taking over our roles. Congratulations, Doctor. Even if the patient doesn't regain full bodily function, it was still a marvelous effort. But now I'm hoping Women's and Children's doesn't become a magnet for needy street people. Our mandate here is quite enough to keep us busy."

After a few silent seconds, as if the thought just came to his mind, he said, "I have no idea how I am going to account for this when administration comes to discuss the expenses involved."

No one had anything to add to that thought.

Leaving the supervision of the patient with the two senior nurses, as nurses Annette and Bonnie removed their blood-spattered aprons and began their own thorough scrubbing routines, Dr. Grant peeled off his white coat, which was showing more than just a few blood stains. He would wash the blood from his hands after the nurses completed their turn at the basin. Without asking permission, he stepped to Gwyneth and eased her white coat off her shoulders. It was in worse condition than his own. She complied by turning a quarter turn in the small hallway space to make the simple task easier. As the coat slipped off, there was a startled gasp from the two male doctors and a wide grin from nurse Bonnie.

Dr. Levantine said, "My word, Doctor. Is that what I think it is, belted around your waist? Why in the world? Oh my, this is most extraordinary."

Dr. Grant, coming to Gwyneth's defense, feigning a chivalry he didn't really feel, nor was he confident he could back up with action if needed said, "I expect, Dr. Wycome, that it was expedient for you to carry a sidearm for self-protection on the frontier, but it does look a bit out of place here in the city."

Gwyneth glanced down at the small .38 cal. pistol that she was never without. Her hands were still red with blood. Belted to her left side just in front of her hip bone, and positioned for a right-hand draw, the weapon, snug in its holster, was barely visible.

Bonnie, her hands still dripping wash water, and nearly overcome with an urge to giggle, said, "What a wonderful idea. I'm going to have to get me something like that."

Dr. Levantine looked at her as if he was imagining the entire staff of Women's and Children's rushing out to purchase weapons. His small social world had no room in it for such a thought. With the moment passing and everyone too exhausted to continue the controversy, Doctors Levantine and Grant turned and retreated down the hallway.

Bonnie watched them until they turned a corner and fell out of sight. She then smiled at Gwyneth. "May I hold it?"

"No, you may not. Dr. Grant was correct on this much; there is little law on the frontier. We did our best to care for ourselves. But our weapons were not toys or novelties. No one familiar with weapons would ever allow another person to handle their gun. If and when I ever lift this .38 out of its holster, you better believe it will not be for fun.

"Now, if you've cleaned as well as you can, you'd best return to your ward work. And Bonnie, Annette. You did well. Thank you. I'll see that administration receives a positive report on your work."

THE MORNING after the surgery on the young black man, Gwyneth was called into Dr. Levantine's small office. Wishing to avoid more inquiry or reprimand, Gwyneth went with some trepidation. She was relieved when the discussion centered around training and knowledge, not following petty orders.

"Dr. Wycome, I wish to know where and how you received such knowledge of internal medicine and of the surgery required to successfully remove a spleen. I will interject here that Chicago General reported this morning that the young man is doing well, is conscious, and that they have most of his pain under control. They are singing your praises over there. Well done, young lady. But please don't go looking for or inviting more of such cases. We are still a women's and children's hospital, and such we shall remain.

"But now, back to the question. You appear to know more about internal matters than most young doctors. How does that come to be the case?"

"I was fortunate in the college I chose, Doctor. Or perhaps I should say in the college that chose me. I did have a couple of schools that refused my application. It is a sad reality that most big cities include small populations that are mostly unseen by the public and totally ignored by governments of any level. The early death rate for these poor folks is far above the average. They live in misery and want and largely die alone and unknown. The morgues see that they are buried and that's the end of it.

"My college contracts with the morgue to make their facilities and the unclaimed bodies available for medical training. It is a distinctly miserable and unpalatable part of surgical training, but we somehow lived through the ordeal, although I will admit to a few sleepless nights. We explored everything time would allow. From internal organs to bones and joints, to the brain and the mysteries of the nervous system and blood flows of the spinal column, we covered it all. Along the way, we had before our eyes examples of malnutrition, excessive alcohol consumption, and self-abuse that most of us can't imagine or understand.

"We took turns with the scalpel while the others watched and scribbled notes. I wouldn't wish to repeat the experience, but nor would I wish to be without it. There is no more secret to it than that, along with my habit of subscribing to and reading every medical journal I know about."

"Thank you, Gwyneth. We'll say no more except that your knowledge saved a young man's life yesterday. If Chicago General can control infection and other possible problems, there is a reasonable chance he will have a second opportunity at life."

# *Chapter Seven*

Gwyneth heard from the in-house scuttlebutt that the reason there was nothing more said about the wearing of a weapon was because, between Mrs. Pierpont and Dr. Levantine, they were unable to come up with a response that didn't have a negative side. That feared negative being the loss of their first female doctor. So they said no more, simply acting as if it didn't matter. Or had never taken place.

The truth was, however, that Gwyneth was already planning her next step at the invitation of Chicago General. One week after performing the emergency surgery on young Isaiah, a runner from Chicago General hand-delivered a sealed note to Gwyneth. It was short and precise.

*Dear Dr. Wycome.*

*Dr. Harold Grimshaw, chief of staff at Chicago General, invites you to attend a private and confidential meeting with him and the managing director of the hospital board, at 4:00 PM on May 17, current. Please return your response with the courier of this note.*

Saying nothing to anyone, Gwyneth wrote a short, *Thank you, I look forward to the meeting.*

Gwyneth stared, fully impressed with the large foyer and

surroundings at Chicago General Hospital. After a brief explanation for her visit, an attractive, well-dressed young lady ushered her to the administrative offices and made introductions.

Dr. Grimshaw took immediate control of the meeting. The managing director of the board said not a word the entire time.

"Doctor, I am led to believe that you began with nursing experience in one of those wretched war tents. And that you moved on to assisting a small-town physician in the west. That you were the wife of a frontier cattle rancher who tragically lost his life, but that you stayed on, holding to the ranch while offering nursing assistance to neighbors and other settlers. Several years gaining that experience, along with taking in knowledge of native plants and herbs, and some of the ways of the Indian population, aided by an Indian lady, which led to a solid friendship with her and some others of the Ute Tribe, finally led you to journey back east to attend medical college. Do I have that about right, Dr. Wycome?"

Gwyneth couldn't help but laugh just a bit. "Dr. Grimshaw, it's as if you read my personal diary. But since that could hardly be possible, I must assume you have extraordinary research assistance. There are a few gaps in that history, but they're small and not of great significance."

The meeting briefly turned to the treatment of young Isaiah, with compliments on what was done, along with recommendations on what else might have been done. Gwyneth took the recommendations as a bit of teaching from this experienced and well-respected senior physician and surgeon. Within half an hour, the meeting ended. The primary question placed before Gwyneth was, "What would you hope to gain by making a move to Chicago General, Dr. Wycome, and how would that benefit yourself and Chicago General if such an invitation were to be laid before you?"

Gwyneth had the answer ready before the question was even asked. "I would take advantage of all opportunities available for personal advancement and hands-on knowledge of anatomy and surgical skills. My college training was excellent, but it's never really enough, or quite complete, is it, Doctor?

"Before coming to Chicago for college, as you have so accurately laid out, I had three years picking up rudimentary knowledge of nursing and surgery, as brutal as it was, in the surgical tents on the battlefield. That experience pointed me in the right direction for offering simple nursing assistance out west, where cuts, gorings, and bullet wounds were almost the order of the day. Through those years, with no other medical assistance available, it was necessary to do what seemed logical and workable. And I'll admit to leaning on guesswork when the situation was beyond my knowledge. I often found myself harking back to that small Kansas town where I assisted the only doctor in the area when I lacked knowledge of my own. His knowledge was less than complete, and his training rudimentary, but his willingness to teach, and for me to do things under his direction, were a great encouragement. Even with all of that, it wasn't always enough. There were failures, I am sorry to have to admit.

"I would bring with me all of that history and training for the betterment of the hospital and its patients. I would, in turn, make every attempt to soak in the knowledge of more senior medical personnel. Any advancement in knowledge must eventually go down to the benefit of the patient, and perhaps, somehow, to the overall practice of medicine. Don't you agree, Dr. Grimshaw?"

The meeting ended with the half-expected offer of a position at Chicago General. Gwyneth made the move across town with fond memories of Women's and Children's and an eagerness for what the future held for her.

# Chapter Eight

On her first day in service at Chicago General Hospital, Gwyneth was assigned to assist in a Cesarian birth, something that was very rare at the time, although the medical profession was showing interest. The head of obstetrics, Dr. Grady Klym, had imported the concept after losing three patients through very difficult natural births in a single month a short while before. Believing the deaths of the young mothers and their pre-born babies could have been prevented, he set about learning all he could from the medical journals. Gwyneth, too, was familiar with the term but had never seen it done. With the very weak mother but a living baby, the procedure undertaken that first day was considered a partial success. Dr. Klym grimly told his staff, "The baby is fine. When the mother is healed and up and walking, we'll celebrate. Not before."

Gwyneth was assisting and learning the whole time. Three months had passed before she was led into the room set aside for major surgeries. The doctor in charge of general surgeries, Dr. Peter Castonguay, a young, smiling, robust man said, "Dr. Wycome, today you are in charge. Believe it or not, we have a cattle horn gouging situation. I know, I know. We're in the middle of a big modern city, not some cattle driving range. But this city has a very large stockyard on the edge of town. Apparently, a worker and a large steer had a disagreement. The steer won. Now it's our, and specifically your, duty to put the worker back together. I'll be standing by, but don't let that make you nervous or cause you concern."

Gwyneth smiled and answered, "I can't imagine why having one of the top surgeons in the country looking over my shoulder should make me nervous."

Dr. Castonguay smiled and replied, "I hope to never be seen as an overbearing ogre, Dr. Wycome. You'll do just fine. Perhaps you've seen a goring before, being from the west and all."

"Being from the west is not like a communicable disease, Doctor. Nevertheless, I admit to having dealt with a rather serious goring one time with the patient lying on the kitchen floor with the two riding partners who carried him in from the range holding him down. Having no anesthetic of any sort, with great forbearance, he lay almost still during the procedure. I used a kitchen knife for a scalpel and needle and thread from the wife's sewing bag for sutures. And all the time I was telling them that I was just a nurse, not a doctor or a surgeon. None of that changed the situation in the least."

A nurse who had been listening in asked, "Did he live through it?"

"Lived through it and was back in the saddle in one week. I will add that I had stressed that one week was not enough for healing, but the ranch needed him. The west is made up of strong people. Male and female both."

Dr. Castonguay shook his head. "Someday, Doctor, you should write out your stories. I'm betting it would be good reading."

"Like the time I removed a man's appendix while he lay on his own kitchen table?"

"Yes. Like that. But now, let's attend to the immediate problem."

~

And so, the time moved along. Gwyneth was soaking up knowledge like a sponge. As it had been at Women's and Children's, she knew she would not be making her permanent career at Chicago General. But she was gaining modern, practical expertise like she could never hope to do outside of a large hospital. She still held in her mind the image of a hand-painted wooden sign swaying in the wind, advertising to all who cared to look: *Dr. Gwyneth Wycome, Physician and Surgeon.*

She had yet to decide where that sign would be positioned, east or west, or perhaps down south. Perhaps even Texas. She wrote regularly to Abe and Helen. They wrote back telling of the opportunities Texas had to offer. She had made no commitments. That decision could come later.

Nurse Beatrice Brodrick, commonly known as Bea, was fascinated by Gwyneth's stories, especially the part of riding horseback over the wild western hills and plains. Every chance she got, she brought the subject up again. Finally, one day, when the normal rush and tear of the hospital appeared to have settled to a slow hum, she broached a subject that had been on her mind for weeks. She hesitated, made a false start, but finally managed to say, "Dr. Wycome, I know it would be asking a lot, but I would love to learn to ride a horse. I've gone down to the riding academy several Sunday afternoons after church to watch the goings on. I'm sure there's more to it than what I can see from the sidelines, but I'm also sure I can pick it up with a bit of expert advice. How would you feel about giving me a lesson or two? I would be happy to pay for the rental of the horses."

After some discussion, Gwyneth and Bea met at the stables on the bridle paths leading to Washington Park and Lagoon. Gwyneth had explained about split skirts and had purchased a new one for herself. They arrived in grand style, having rented a cab for transport. Bea was an extraordinarily attractive young lady, single and available to the right suitor. When the two ladies stepped down from the cab, many of the young men in the closely surrounding area turned, staring. Bea was shining in beauty and bristling with enthusiasm. Gwyneth, a few years older, still attractive and looking mature and competent. A man unfamiliar with judging women's ages might see the pair as mother and daughter. It would have been a poor decision for any man to suggest the possibility vocally.

They waited while three other groups were matched to horses and appropriate saddles and then they stepped forward.

"And how can I serve you young ladies this day?"

The speaker was little more than a boy, perhaps being in his late teens in age, but overly confident in his position. He grinned, swinging his eyes from one attractive face to the other.

Gwyneth said, "We'll thank you for bringing out two solid animals. Fit for the trail. Western saddle, if you please."

Bobbing his head, the young man entered the stable and was soon back, slowly leading two animals that were showing considerable age, swaying a bit in their backs, with sagging jaw and lips, and with much graying around the muzzle.

Gwyneth said, "You take these poor animals back and set them out for retirement. They've given you all the service you're going to get from them. I'll walk back with you to see what else you have."

"Only staff allowed in the stable miss."

"Then bring out something fit to ride. And quickly now, the afternoon is running away on us."

An older man stepped forward, saying, "It's all right, Trev, I'll help the ladies."

Grudgingly, the young man turned and led the old horses back into the shade.

"Now, ladies, be patient for just a few moments. I'll be right back. Did I hear you say you prefer western saddles?"

"You heard correctly. "

"Side saddles?"

"Never," was all Gwyneth answered.

There was a streak of the bold in the old man and a bit of a desire to bring down some of the arrogance of the rich out into the open, as misjudging as he was on his two current customers. And that day, there was a goodly crowd waiting to see just what the ladies had planned for the afternoon. After all, it took more than beauty to sit a horse well. And with no man attending them, almost anything could befall the ladies.

"These look better to you?" He was leading a fine-looking fifteen-hand roan gelding along with a very handsome and proud sixteen-hand bay. They were bridled, but the saddles were lying loose on the blankets, their stirrups flapping with the animal's movements. If the senior hostler was hoping to stump the ladies with the saddling task, he was about to be dealt a surprise.

"They look fine. The roan will be just right for my friend's first lesson. If he's not what you present him as, I will be back to deal with you personally." With that, she took the reins of the bay and rubbed him a bit on the neck, whispering words that no one could hear. The hostler led the roan around to where Bea was nervously standing. She took the reins and looked at Gwyneth as if all assistance would come from that direction.

Gwyneth quietly said, "Now watch carefully, Bea. I'll do this slowly." She then adjusted the saddle on the blanket, moving it this way and that until it settled in well. She hung the stirrup on the saddle horn before reaching under the animal's belly to grasp the offside cinch strap, pulling it toward herself. Carrying the leather band up to the ring that hung below the side of the saddle, she dropped the cinch leather over the top of the ring, letting it fall down until it was just snug. Holding the leather in place, she crossed the cinch band until it was snug on the face of the cinch, laying the end beneath the ring and then pulling it upward. She now had a smooth wrap around the cinch leather.

Simply dropping the loose end behind that wrap and tightening each contact point one by one, while pulling it all tight, and the saddle was ready for use. She would lead the animal around a bit and then snug the leather again. Saying, "Watch again," she repeated the procedure on the roan. When she was done, she gave a hard look at the old man. "I know this is your job. But just to show you that I am no novice, I did it this one time. I hope you got a bit of a kick out of testing me."

Gwyneth held the roan's reins and assisted Bea in mounting. Bea tended to be graceful in all she did. Whether she was making a hospital bed, cleaning up a soiled patient, or putting on her coat to go home at the end of shift, she was the picture of grace in movement. She was so now, in her first try at mounting a horse. Gwyneth felt like cheering. Instead, she mounted her own animal, which took a few quick side steps and turned in a circle once. Gwyneth sat the saddle as if she was glued there. There was a small cheer from the crowd and a few laughs.

Stepping the bay close to Bea's side, she said, "You're right-handed, Bea. That means you would be wise to keep your right hand free in case of need. Hold both reins in your left hand. Simply touch the rein against the animal's neck when you want him to turn. And pull back easily when you wish him to stop. I'll ride right beside you. There is nothing to fear."

The ride was a total success. Bea was thrilled with the experience. Laughingly, she said, "Of course, if I had fallen off, who knows, there may have been a handsome young Sir Galahad come to my rescue."

Gwyneth smiled at her words but cautioned, "You might also be hurt and end up in hospital, having to make your own bed and care for yourself. Doing all your own nursing."

They shared a grin, thinking of that possibility.

ON THE THIRD Sunday afternoon riding, a male rider rounded a bend coming toward them. Gwyneth and Bea were chatting about some forgettable topic and paid no attention.

But a strong male voice said, "As I live and breath, I do believe that just may be Dr. Gwyneth Wycome. Who the other beauty is, I don't know, but has anyone ever seen such collective loveliness on this, or any other bridle trail? Greetings, Dr. Wycome."

Gwyneth's head snapped up to look into familiar eyes. She gave a slight tug on the reins to bring her animal to a halt and said, "Why, Dr. Grant. Strange to see you here. I clearly remember you telling me you had never ridden and suggesting that you might gain such knowledge with a bit of time spent in my company as instructor. Which part of that story were you making up, Doctor?"

"Not a bit of it, Gwyneth. My stating that I was unfamiliar with saddle and horse was totally true. And I have been these several months, at some expense, I may add, to advance to where the instructor and guide is prepared to allow me the use of the animal without his constant attendance. But whatever the situation, it is my delight to lay eyes on you again. And who is this vision of loveliness at your side?"

"Dr. William Grant, may I introduce Miss Bea Brodrick. Miss Brodrick and I are honored to be employed at Chicago General. And we have found a commonality in that we both enjoy the outdoors, and the time spent on a good horse and saddle."

Dr. Grant touched his fingers to the brim of his hat. "My pleasure, Miss Brodrick. Or is it Dr. Brodrick?"

"Good afternoon, Dr. Grant. Pleasure to meet you. But no. My medical world falls short at nurse."

Dr. Grant smiled. "The world needs nurses, Miss Brodrick. And I'm sure you are among the best at your profession. I cannot imagine Gwyneth Wycome associating with any but the best. But now I must get this nag back to the comfort of its stall. There will be others waiting for its return. Again, it was very good seeing you both. I will bid you adieu and wish you both well." This time, he lifted his hat, smiled, nudged his horse into movement, and replaced his hat.

When enough distance separated them that Bea had confidence no words would be heard, she asked, "Are you sweet on Dr. Grant?"

"Certainly not."

Gwyneth's quick reply was so sharp and positive that Bea turned to look at her and smile. "Well, he is sure sweet on you. I just thought perhaps... actually, perhaps I'll let that go."

"Good decision."

# Chapter Nine

Gwyneth was delighted to be constantly challenged to learn more, study more, practice more. It was as if the big hospital was competing to see which of their staff could rise the highest, the quickest. She put in long hours at the hospital and filled most of her evenings with study and reading. She had subscribed to important medical journals, reading them from cover to cover at first, but gradually sorting out the important articles from the less vital.

If she was to one day serve in her own private clinic in a town or city, there were many specialties she would be unable to offer. She would skip their study, concentrating on the more practical knowledge for the time being. The big hospitals with their ever-growing budgets, large staffs, and expensive equipment that were constantly needing replacement and upgrading, would always stand in for serious specialty treatments. Every time those thoughts entered her head, she would pause and consider her options.

Small towns were springing up all over the west as mining ventures and agricultural opportunities attracted thousands of emigrants from the big eastern cities and rural areas, as well as a host of world nations. Many of those towns suffered with either a shortage of qualified medical help or no medical services at all.

Through a series of letters, she had made contact with the west she was familiar with, the apothecary shop in Pueblo, the doctor she had nursed under in the trail town where she had met Trent, and Eustice Ward, who was caring for a small but growing church at Bessie Creek. Eustice had assured her that Bessie Creek was becoming better established and was looking more each year as if it might survive, rather than suffer the fate of so many western towns, becoming just another collection of worn and tumbling down buildings, so common where enthusiasm had gone before reality.

Through Eustice also, she had reconnected with Daniel and Night Light. Although neither had written personally, they had passed on their news and good wishes through the preacher.

The city of Pueblo continued to prosper, but according to Samuel Meier, the owner of the apothecary shop, there was a clear need for a well-trained and competent doctor to supplement the services already available. There was as yet no hospital in town, but there was talk of that situation changing soon. It all left her with too many thoughts and choices to deal with quickly. Fortunately, she was still happy at Chicago General for the time being.

In her time in Chicago, both at Women's and Children's as well as Chicago General, Gwyneth had been the epitome of propriety. Her personal modestly and moral correctness had staved off several interested, but doubtful suitors. She was suitably wary of a couple of the bolder types, but others had equaled her correctness, hiding their private thoughts and desires. The situation changed when Dr. Cliff Rickhart discreetly slipped her a note as they were waiting in line for service at the small lunch counter in the staff room. Gwyneth placed the note carefully into the pocket of her white doctor's coat. She was anxious to see what the note contained but would restrain herself until a better time. That better time came near the end of her shift when she was sitting at the bedside of a very ill gentleman. She glanced around the room before slipping the note out. The small envelope was sealed. The note itself was written on monogrammed cardstock. The monogram stated simply,

*From the desk of Dr. Clifford Rickhart.*

It read, in bold, clearly legible black ink, *Miss Wycome. I would take great personal pleasure in your company, in concert with my parents, Mr. and Mrs. S. Y. Rickhart, at the opening of Little Greta, at the Grand Opera House, on Sept 12, current. Your verbal response at an opportune, private time would be acceptable and welcome.*

*Cliff Rickhart*

Gwyneth quickly placed the card back into the envelope and slipped the envelope into her pocket. Cliff Rickhart was a star among Chicago General surgeons, if such a thing could be imagined. He was the go-to person for all difficult or complicated surgical treatments and was secretly gushed over by most of the female staff. To have been noticed by such an eminent medical man was a surprise, to say the least. Yet, should it be a surprise? She had traveled widely. At least widely, as far as her world was defined. She knew she had been accepted by cowboys, settlers, city men and women, as well as some of the best medical people she was ever likely to meet. And yes, she appreciated the acceptance as nurse, wife, rancher, and western settler. And now as a doctor who was gaining in renown as each day passed.

That many men had taken special note of her was too obvious not to see. But Cliff Rickhart. That was another matter altogether. Tall, well put together, already graying mustache. Impeccably polite and considerate of doctors, nurses, and patients alike. Never a hint of a wrongdoing. Traveled in the highest social circles the city had to offer. Born into wealth, but one would never guess that by his manner. Never a sign of impropriety.

But the note in her pocket was evidence enough. Dr. Cliff Rickhart had taken notice of Dr. Gwyneth Wycome. What to do? The theatre? An opera? With his wealthy parents? She had not one single experience in her entire life to prepare her for such a thing. But the date was soon. Just a couple of weeks. Who could she talk with to gain some perspective? No one, that's who. At least among her narrow list of acquaintances. And yet there was Bea. Even if she had no more experience than Gwyneth, she looked and acted as if she did.

At the first opportunity, she scouted the hallways and wards until she found Bea. She sidled up to her side and, using the ruse of looking at the patient, she said, "We need to talk."

"We do indeed. I was going to hunt you down when I finish here."

"How would you feel about going for a feeding of Polish pierogi with maybe a spicy sausage?"

"See you at Bartosz at six thirty."

With no further talk, Gwyneth turned and left.

At the small café, Bartosz, which was buzzing with customers, over half of whom were speaking Polish. A smiling, middle-aged man wearing a once white apron, now graying from its many washings, and a tall chef's hat, watched as Gwyneth made her way among the buggies, wagons, and horses cluttering the yard, parked every which way. Bea had already taken a seat at a small table beside the window. Simplicity was the word for Bartosz, the name of the place as well as for the owner, who was also cook and waiter.

Coffee and water were self-serve. The table napkins and cutlery were available by choice from a counter near the door. The simple menu was chalked on a blackboard nailed to the wall above the small counter where Bartosz would be waiting for his payment, as people got up to leave. Even from the kitchen, he never missed the scraping of a chair leg across the wood-planked floor, a sure sign that someone had finished their meal and was ready to advance into their plans for the remainder of the evening. Laughter and loud talk were normal and acceptable.

As Gwyneth entered, turned and closed the door, Bartosz shouted from the kitchen door, "Welcome, my lovely Doctor. You come for goot food only Bartosz can cook. Your beautiful friend, she is by the window. You go. I come with food right away. You eat. Is goot."

A good many heads turned to watch the doctor make her way to the table. Most of those eyes turned from Gwyneth to rest on Bea for an uncomfortable length of time before returning to their dinners. Gwyneth took her seat, smiled, and said teasingly, "I see you're up to your old tricks again."

"What in the world do you mean by that?"

"Oh, you know, distracting every man in the house, making their wives wonder if they should just go right ahead and kill them now or wait till they're home."

"I'm going to start wearing a hood with the eye slits cut out. Or maybe I'll just stay home."

"You'll do neither one. You're a beautiful young woman, a lady in every respect. How people respond is not your problem. The real mystery is, why you haven't been swept off your feet yet by some handsome man who will love you for life. Now let's change the subject. But only a bit. I received a note."

"Interesting. So did I."

Wondering if the note writers were one and the same and suspecting some kind of a practical joke, Bea said, "I hope they're not both from the same writer."

Gwyneth answered, "There's only one way to find out. You first."

Bea hesitated, wondering if Gwyneth shouldn't go first, but finally said, "Dr. William Grant, the gentleman we met on the bridle path, somehow managed to get a note to me at the hospital. He would have no idea where I live, so I suppose it was his only option. Still, it was a bit of an embarrassment when the head nurse passed it to me. Even though it was in a sealed envelope, my first thought, after wondering who it was from, that is, was how many hands did it pass through before it came to me."

Gwyneth smiled at her friend. "Depending on what the note contained, Bea, and I can only imagine one topic, you could find the message either exciting or troubling. Are you going to tell me the rest or make me guess?"

"I'm only troubled by one possibility, Gwyneth. When we first met Dr. Grant on the bridle path, it was so very obvious that he only had eyes for you. I need to be convinced that when you said you had no interest, you were being truthful and not simply coy."

"Well, let me assure you, I was not being coy. I'm not even sure I would know how to be coy. Whatever he is communicating to you will not involve me in any sense of the word."

Bea reached into her pocket and lifted the envelope onto the table. "Here, read it for yourself."

"No, Bea. That is a private communication. I would be uncomfortable reading someone else's mail. Just tell me the essence of it."

"All right. The essence is that Dr. William Grant wishes me to join him for dinner, after which we would gather with a small group for an evening cruise on the lake."

"What have you told him?"

"Nothing yet. I only received the note the day before yesterday."

"What do you want to do?"

"You understand, Gwyneth, that I have almost no experience at all in socializing with the opposite gender. In the small town where I was raised, I knew everyone, girl or boy. And they all knew me. It's the nature of humans, of a certain age, at least, it seems, to giggle and tease when two people show an interest in one another. Especially those who grew up together. That is an impediment to pairing off, even casually, in a small town. It does happen, of course. There were several intermarriages between local families. But there were no young men that I found to my liking. Since coming to the city, I have shared lunch a few times with , but it was never anything more than that. I'm not sure I would even know how to act sitting at dinner with Dr. Grant."

"My dear friend, I can't imagine you not knowing how to act. Or what to wear or what to say. It all seems to come naturally, almost effortlessly, to you. In fact, that is a part of what I wish to talk about. But the important thing is your answer to William. And if you are asking my opinion, you already know what I am going to say. Tell him yes. It may lead somewhere, and it may not. But in the meantime, you've enjoyed a free dinner and a boat ride."

"It would be a big shift in my life."

"If not now, then when?"

Not answering that question, Bea said, "What's on your mind?"

Just at that time, Bartosz made his noisy way through the crowd with two steaming plates held high above his head, one in each hand.

"And now for the treat for my beautiful doctors. No one but Bartosz for special people. Special food. Bartosz food. No one makes like Bartosz. You eat, you enjoy. You want more, you call Bartosz. Don't forget to thank God for food. You thank God. You pay Bartosz. Is good system." He shouted some unintelligible words in Polish as he retreated to the kitchen. Several diners who understood the language laughed.

Bea ignored the food, while Gwyneth bowed her head slightly and said a short thank you. When she was done, she picked up a fork and knife and cut into a pierogi. Bea, still ignoring the food, laughingly said, "You can't get away with that, Doctor. C'mon, spill it."

"After we eat. These are best hot from the stove."

When the dishes were pushed aside, Gwyneth settled her chin on her hands, elbows on the table. She would never do that in a fine dining room, but at Bartosz, it was not an unusual posture.

"I have received a note too. To cut it short, I am surprised by who the sender is, but I am interested in taking him up on the invitation. So as not to keep you in suspense, I will tell you the note is from Dr. Cliff Rickhart. He wishes me to attend an opera with him and his parents. Dinner to follow. I have decided to take him up on the offer, for the experience, if for no other reason. But I have a problem. Obviously, I have no satisfactory clothing for such an evening. And I'm not altogether sure I will know how to act. You are a natural with clothing. Everything you wear is perfect. So I need your help. And I have decided to trust my instincts when the moment is upon me, to know how to act."

Bea quietly clapped her hands together just once. "That's wonderful. Marvelous. A step into the limelight. An evening of hobnobbing with the wealthy. And who knows what else? All right. It's settled. We're both off duty on Saturday. Ten in the morning at Mademoiselle, the most fashionable ladies' store in town. One half hour there to see what's on offer, then it's over to Gaylene's. We'll allow for an hour there, then it's off to lunch. We'll go over the choices as we eat. The afternoon will be for buying. Shopping in the morning, purchasing in the afternoon. Dress, lingerie, stockings, shoes, gloves, earrings, unless you already have a good pair. Oh, it's going to be fun, and you'll end up being the talk of the opera house and the restaurant after, no matter where they take you. I almost wish I could get William to take me just so I can watch the action. You'll floor them all."

Gwyneth exhaled a big breath. "I guess I asked for it. But there goes most of my savings."

# Chapter Ten

Gwyneth's answer to Dr. Rickhart was received with a small smile and a "We can't talk here. I'll find a reason to ask you into my office."

The week leading up to the date with Cliff Rickhart was unusually busy at the hospital. Several cases of whooping cough and other childhood miseries had the staff running off their feet. Of particular concern were several patients with measles. These children were kept isolated from each other as well as from the rest of the hospital. Few deterrents to communicable diseases existed. It had been discovered that rigorous attention to sanitation and the use of disinfectants, all adding hours of work in the communicable disease wards, were the best safeguards for families and medical staff.

In mid-week, on the surgery wing, Gwyneth had been called upon to assist Dr. Rickhart with a seriously shattered hip and leg. They stood across from one another during the procedure, with Dr. Rickhart in charge and Gwyneth assisting, along with two nurses. Mumbling almost under his breath as he concentrated on his work, he said, "I am impressed, Dr. Wycome. Each of your moves is exactly the right thing. It's almost as if you're one step ahead of me, waiting for me to catch up."

Gwyneth could think of no logical response, so she let it go.

Almost as a reverse duplication of the whispered message between Bea and Gwyneth some time before, as they passed in the hallway, Bea said, "Sam's at six?" Gwyneth simply nodded and kept going. But she spent the rest of the workday wondering about Bea's date with William Grant the evening before.

~

THIS TIME, it was Gwyneth who arrived first and waited to be shown to a table. Sam's, for all the simplicity of the name, was several steps above Bartosz as far as ambiance and dining experience went. There were no shouted greetings from the owner, who was not named Sam, but Katrina. Katrina was a lovely middle-aged lady, a widow. At an opportune moment on an earlier visit, Gwyneth inquired as to how she managed to own a restaurant in an age when most women were kept busy in their homes.

"I lost my husband to a heart attack. With three children just coming into their teen years and very little money left in the sugar bowl, I had to do something. With a loan from my father, I opened a hole-in-the-wall sandwich shop. The downtown crowd seemed to like my sandwiches and the desserts I baked fresh every day. Later, with the loan paid back, I felt free to expand. The dress shop next door closed, and the landlord agreed to knock a wall out. It's come together very well, and I'm my own boss. And on my days off, which are primarily Sundays, I get to love on my grandchildren. It's a good life. It also saved me from the small choice of re-run husbands that sidled up to me along the way."

Gwyneth found the story poignant and thought-provoking. All through her private dinner on that occasion, she couldn't keep her mind off Trent. Or perhaps she didn't wish to keep her mind off her long-gone first love. Her only love.

Bea burst into Sam's, ignored the hostess who was only trying to do her job, and glided onto a chair opposite Gwyneth. Bristling with enthusiasm, she said, "I had a wonderful evening."

"You might just as well tell me as much as you wish known."

"There's certainly nothing to not know. I'm sure we were the most proper couple in the entire city. We had dinner at a modest but nice restaurant on the waterfront, walked a bit after, waiting for the time for the boat cruise, and joined six other people on a lovely sailboat for an hour. The sun disappeared about halfway through the cruise, leaving its red and orange flare shining for miles across the bay. I'd never been on a sailboat before, but I was determined to get the most from the evening in case it never happened again. William then hailed a cab and stayed with me until I was home, including walking me to the door. I didn't know if I should thank him, shake his hand, or just turn to the door and enter. He saved me from my indecision when he said something like, *I had a wonderful evening. I hope you did as well.*

"I assured him that every part of the evening was to my delight, especially the boat ride. He simply smiled and asked if he could see me again. What could I say to that? Of course he can see me again."

Gwyneth was grinning from ear to ear at the telling of the evening's events. "Did you enjoy William's company or just the dinner and boat ride?"

"Don't tease. You know the answer to that question. William is a very nice man and a gentleman to boot. We exchanged a bit of our pasts while leaving much out for another time. Contrary to my thinking that all doctors come from wealth, William is from a modest background. His father is a carpenter. His mother, of course, stayed home to raise five kids. William is in the middle of the pack for age.

"The whole family, including the two older brothers, all

chipped in to pay his way through college. He's still paying them back bit by bit."

Gwyneth wasn't sure her friend could even remember what she ate that evening, she was so wrapped up in the story. The get-together ended with Gwyneth congratulating Bea on her newfound friend, and Bea, in turn, encouraging Gwyneth on her date with Dr. Cliff Rickhart, which was coming up in just a few days.

Gwyneth had one of her rare mid-weekdays off. She rose at her usual five thirty, washed and dressed, and had a small breakfast. She poked through a new medical journal but couldn't raise enough interest to dig into it. She decided the fall day was warm enough to go for a walk. She would then find a quiet spot for a light lunch. That would take her all the way to noon, leaving her an afternoon and evening to fill.

Fighting off a bit of unexplained depression, she put on her coat and wondered about a hat. She had placed her better western wear, folded carefully, into a small steamer trunk. On top of the clothing, she had left room for her off-white Stetson hat, a special gift from Trent, purchased in Dodge on their way west. She had worn it much over the years, caring for it carefully, although it did show more wear than she liked. She would always treasure it, no matter how many other hats she would buy and wear. Thinking of the day ahead of her, she asked herself, *Why not*? She dug out the Stetson, fitted it carefully over the waves in her hair, leaving the long tresses hanging down the back and over her shoulders, and ventured out.

The air was cool and crisp. The leaves were turning to their fall display. A display she never tired of and missed when she was west. She felt somewhat jaunty as she stepped out the door, conscious that she would certainly be noticed wearing the Stetson. She didn't much care. She had always felt good in the hat, and now it reminded her of all the things she had come to love in the west.

The lunch spot was as pleasant as she hoped it would be. But the afternoon still stood empty before her.

As she stepped onto the sidewalk in front of the café, the road was jammed with its usual traffic. Among the carriages, buggies, wagons, and single horses, a two-horse cab rolled noisily past. An idea began brewing in her mind. To fulfill the new thought would require a certain type of carriage. Patiently, she waited and watched. Finally, there it was. Just behind the big freight carrier. A carriage looking somewhat like a stage-coach with the driver high in front, outside, and room for passengers inside. She could see no heads in either of the cab's side windows and decided there were no passengers.

Boldly, she stepped to the curb, waving. The driver made no motion as if he had seen her. Wanting very much to attract his attention, she quickly looked around to see if she dared. Feeling a bit mischievous, she decided she did dare. She puckered her lips just as Trent had taught her and let out a most unladylike, shrieking whistle. Not only did she catch the attention of the driver she wanted, but she also caught the attention of everyone within shouting range. All were looking at her. She lifted her Stetson and waved directly at the man she wanted. Catching her motions, he pulled the cab over to the edge of the road and stopped. He was on the opposite side from where Gwyneth stood, but she wasn't going to let that stop her. Carefully, lifting her skirts free of her feet and the dusty road, she stepped off the curbing and made her way through the traffic. She heard whistles and shouts of appreciation as well as some of anger. She ignored it all.

"Are you for hire, sir?"

"'Tis why I get m'self up come a morn'n, ma'am. What's it fer ya."

"I wish to hire you for the afternoon."

"Tell me where you wish to go and climb inta the cab. Take what seat ya wish and tell me when yer set."

In a delightful and happy frame of mind, she lifted her foot to the sidestep of the carriage, boosted herself onto the high, outside driver's seat, and said to the startled driver, "This is the seat I want. And where I want to go is everywhere. I've been in Chicago going on four years and I've done little but work and study. Now I wish to see the city, from the stockyards to the lakefront." She was forced to speak loudly to be heard over the clatter of hundreds of steel-rimmed wagon wheels on the brick-surfaced road.

From the downtown area, along the waterfront, and through miles of fire-devastated business and residential roads, and then south to the stockyards, the cheerful driver directed his team. Giving in to temptation, Gwyneth asked for the reins. The driver was reluctant to turn his rig over to this outgoing woman with the Stetson hat, but a short history lesson from Gwyneth's past years convinced him to give her an opportunity. After a quarter hour of careful study, watching her actions, the man relaxed and settled back in his seat, content to simply give directions through the city. The afternoon ended with a tired but exhilarated Gwyneth paying the driver a bit over his asking price and thanking him profusely. She staggered just a bit as her feet touched the sidewalk. Although weary, she would remember this as one of her better days in Chicago.

# Chapter Eleven

DURING THE NEXT FEW DAYS, HER TIME AT THE hospital was filled with work. There had been no opportunity to speak with Dr. Rickhart. She heard nothing at all from him until the end of the day, barely hours before their scheduled meeting at the opera house. Finally, a harried Cliff Rickhart tracked Gwyneth down at the busy administration desk. He held a slip of paper out and whispered, "If you would write your address on there, I will have the carriage pick you up."

Gwyneth had been unsure what to expect of the evening, but an impersonal cab ride, with no attendance from her escort for the evening, was not the start she had envisioned. Nevertheless, the doctors, including herself, lived under pressure that most other workers never felt, with little personal time. She was willing to accept that reality. Still, it would be a poor beginning.

She would also be rushed. Even if she got free of the hospital on time, which was not in any way a daily experience, to get home, heat water for a bath, and get dressed, there would be no time to spare.

Finally, the time for the cab's arrival was at hand. She had fussed, pampered herself, studied the result in the mirror, and fought off self-doubts. Was the dress she and Bea had picked out acceptable? Would she fit in with the monied crowd or would she stand out as the western nobody she felt herself to be? What about Will's parents? It seemed unusual to her that their first time alone together with Will should be spent with his parents. But, again, she accepted what was to be. If she had evening-stopping doubts, she should have spoken up earlier. *We're going to have a lovely time*, she told herself over and over.

The clatter of horse hooves and the grinding of wagon wheels on the road, plus the light clanging of the brass bell mounted beside the driver's seat, announced the arrival of her conveyance. She slipped into her wrap, looked one more time in the mirror, and stepped out the door. The waiting cab wasn't the usual spare, street conveyance. What stood in front of her humble cottage was a beautiful, black lacquered landau carriage. The driver, elderly and dignified, complete with a black top hat, sat on a raised seat in front. The folding canvas top was lowered, in celebration of the slightly chilly but otherwise lovely fall evening. As she approached, the driver stepped to the ground, opened the side door of the carriage, and held out his arm in the event the lady would need help stepping in. She didn't.

"Good evening, Mum. Please make yourself comfortable. We shall be at the theatre in no time at all. There are lap warmer blankets if you feel the need, Mum." With that, he rose to his seat and the landau was soon moving.

CLIFF RICKHART, dressed in formal wear and looking handsome, handsome and rich, in fact, waited as the carriage made its way through the traffic, stopping at the curb. The opera hall was bright with gas lamps, glittering as if all the candles in the world had been lit at the same time. Cliff was alone. Gwyneth surmised that his parents would be waiting in the warmth of the hall's foyer.

"Good evening, Gwyneth. You look lovely this evening. A sight for weary eyes."

Gwyneth laid her hand lightly on his folded arm, pretending he was assisting her from the carriage. *It's all a game*, she thought as she stepped to the sidewalk and glanced around her at the many other ladies who were also playing the game.

"Come, Gwyneth. It's a bit warmer inside. Father and Mother are anxious to meet you. And the opera will begin soon."

Once inside, Cliff gently lifted Gwyneth's wrap from her shoulders, folded it over his arm, and took her elbow to guide her to the waiting couple. His mother stared her up and down with a half-hidden, sour look on her lips.

"Father. Mother. I wish to present Dr. Gwyneth Wycome. Gwyneth, Mr. and Mrs. Sylvester Rickhart."

Mrs. Rickhart, somewhat vacantly, said, "How do you do, Doctor."

Cliff's father smiled and said, "It's good to meet you, Gwyneth. And I'm happy you chose to join us this evening. Cliff has told us that you're quite new to the city. Have you been to the opera before?"

"No, I can't say there were many opportunities in my earlier years, and since coming to the city, I have been studying and working."

"And you are the better for it. I don't know that any good thing ever came from an opera, but we come because it's the thing to do. Just who decided that is unknown to me, but there it lies anyway. I find my mind sometimes questioning why our great, destructive fire of a few years ago failed to wend its way down here and put an end to it all."

"And that is quite enough of that, my dear," said Mrs. Rickhart officiously. "Shall we go in?"

Cliff stepped aside long enough to deposit Gwyneth's wrap in the coat room and then followed his parents into the theater. Gwyneth somehow found herself seated between Cliff and his father. She suspected the seating was engineered by Mrs. Rickhart. The next two hours were a study in endurance for Gwyneth. She sat in wonder as one act after another thrust their mysterious, ear-assaulting voices on the poor suffering audience. At one point, following a particularly ridiculous movement from a cast member, she burst into sudden glee. Several of the audience around her turned her way in censure. Cliff's father tipped his head in her direction, grinned, and patted her arm, which was resting on the arm of her seat. She suffered the remainder of the action with stoic self-control.

Finally they were able to file into the foyer. Cliff retrieved her wrap, and they stepped out into the still pleasant evening. The landau driver, knowing from past experience that the senior Rickhart would not be wishing to spend more time at the theatre than necessary, was among the first to bring the carriage around. They all stepped in, and within a few minutes, they were exiting again in front of a well-lit restaurant. Gwyneth was somewhat impressed when the maître-de welcomed them by name before delivering them to their reserved table.

Cliff needlessly helped her with her chair, and seated, she found herself directly across the rectangular table from Mrs. Rickhart. Cliff, perhaps wishing to advance Gwyneth in the eyes of his parents, said, "Dr. Wycome is one of the most talented surgeons we have ever employed at the hospital. We are fortunate to have her. And I am privileged to have her in my company this evening."

Afraid of what would come if Mrs. Rickhart were to begin the conversation, delving into Gwyneth's past, she opened with a query of her own.

"May I ask, sir, are you a physician too, Mr. Rickhart?"

"Oh heavens no. Cutting, poking and probing, as the poor defenseless victims suffer the indignities, not knowing what will be missing if and when he wakes up, is not my vision of a day's work."

Smiling at this man whom she was sure she could come to like, she said, "Well then, may I ask you to describe what you feel to be a more, shall we say, genteel occupation, Mr. Rickhart?"

Coming to his father's defense and hoping to steer the conversation away from his very worldly father's thoughts on work and worth, Cliff said, "Father has several great lakes steamers, plying the waters with cargoes of iron and other ores, grain, timber, livestock, and whatnot. Father is more at home on these inland seas than he would be confined indoors, at any occupation."

Gwyneth smiled at the man. "I feel more at home in the outdoors, too, Mr. Rickhart, but that is not where my occupation leads me."

"And have you spent much time in the outdoors, Dr. Wycome?" Cliff's mother had spoken for the first time since taking their seats. Every action, every look, every inquiry appeared as if the mother was intent on protecting her son. From exactly what, Gwyneth wasn't sure. If the inquiry held the intent of clarifying thoughts of class, it failed.

"Oh, many years. And I loved it."

The statement caught Cliff's father's ears. "You weren't doctoring outdoors, I don't suppose, Gwyneth. Would I be imposing if I were to ask a bit of your history?"

"Not at all. I got my first taste of the medical world at eighteen when I walked away from home, whereupon I accepted rides east and south until I was within hearing of the cannons. I then grabbed a ride with a supply wagon and worked my way to the war's front, where I volunteered for nursing duties. There were never enough doctors or nurses, so, even with my total dearth of experience, I was put directly to work.

"The conditions the doctors worked under and the dreadful wounds suffered by the soldiers took more than just a bit of getting used to. I wept many times as I carried away an amputated arm or leg or helped tote a dead soldier away to make room for another patient on the operating tables. It was simply beyond belief. Sanitation and hygiene, even the simple washing of hands, were almost unheard of. But it was also a great learning experience, and it set my life goals for me.

"After the war, I nursed for a competent doctor in a little Kansas trail town. We dealt mostly with broken bones and horn gougings. And more gunshot wounds than I care to remember.

"I made my way further west after that, to the frontier of rural Colorado, where, together with trusted friends, we established a cattle ranch. The ranch did well right from the start, although it was a long way to market. I offered nursing assistance to neighbors on the ranches and to a small town that was endeavoring to come to life close by. Most of the nursing was quite similar to what work I did at Women's and Children's Hospital here in Chicago. Mostly birthings, broken bones, and gunshot wounds.

"Finally, I sold off both ranch and cattle and came to Chicago to attend medical school. And that's almost a decade of my life broken down into about two minutes of time."

Mr. Rickhart shook his head in wonder. "All that by a girl hardly old enough to be out of school. Amazing. And wonderful."

To that point, Mrs. Rickhart had listened without interruption. Now she said, "If your ranch, as you called it, was so good, why did you sell it?"

"Well, first, Mrs. Rickhart, I had never given up my dream of going to medical school. And when my husband died in a riding accident, I saw my opportunity and followed through."

At the mention of a husband, she could feel the silence descending around the table, or at least around Mrs. Rickhart's chair, like the pall of doom. Cliff already knew most of her history but had obviously not shared it with his parents.

"Husband? Dr. Wycome? You have been married? Oh my."

Gwyneth took strong offense at Mrs. Rickhart's words. "Why yes, Mrs. Rickhart. Why would that surprise you? Many people get married. I believe I might assume you to be among them. My husband was a good man, an excellent rider, and a very knowledgeable cattleman. And a pioneer to the western lands. The type of man who is giving his all and sometimes spilling his blood to build our great land. I remain very proud of him and thankful for the years we had together."

Failing to appreciate his wife's concern that their son's date for the evening was a widow, and not some innocent society girl, Sylvester said, "I would like to have known him. He sounds like a man I could get along with."

Disgusted, Mrs. Rickhart said, "Wave for the server, Sylvester. It is time we ordered."

Gwyneth was trying to read the various messages from the Rickart family, the most mysterious of which was the silence of Cliff. She had never thought of herself as damaged in any way through her marriage, but clearly, Cliff's mother did. Perhaps he did as well. Perhaps he had invited her along out of some misplaced pity for her lack of a social life. Or perhaps it just wouldn't do to arrive alone at the theater and be out of place among all the happy couples, with the ladies glimmering in their expensive gowns. Or perhaps she was being unfair to the man. Nevertheless, she was slowly seeing more and more through the shallowness of the class conscious.

When the server came for their orders, all three of the Rickharts ordered a fish plate. Gwyneth smiled at the server and said, "I believe I would enjoy that roast of beef."

Mrs. Rickhart said, "The specialty of the house is the fish."

"And that's wonderful for those who enjoy fish. Unfortunately, my pallet has never been able to adapt itself to the denizens of the deep. I'd leave them all down there if it was up to me."

She turned back to the server. "I'll have the beef if you don't mind."

She knew she was prodding the older woman, but she was beyond caring. The silly woman was simply playing follow the leader with the other society pretenders. As far as Cliff was concerned, she was beyond caring. The date, if that was what it was, had really ended minutes ago.

"I have eaten rattlesnake stew, cougar steaks broiled on the end of a pointed stick over an open fire, and about every type of wild bird, shot down on the wing and baked in the coals of a dying campfire. Mostly, we lived on wild game, venison and such. To have beef on our table, we would have had to kill one of our own animals, and there's no profit in that. I enjoyed them all, but the one time I ate fish, I found myself longing for a bowl of cabbage soup, seeing it as a grand improvement."

Sylvester Rickhart burst into joyous laughter, making a comment comparing the western menu from that on his boats.

If Mrs. Rickhart had clamped her lips any tighter, she may have needed surgery to pry them apart.

Sylvester grinned wordlessly at Gwyneth, as if they were co-conspirators in some humorous plot. The dinner ground to a welcome end, her wrap was again retrieved, and they made their way to the landau. Cliff ushered Gwyneth onto the rear, forward-looking seat while his parents sat facing them. The patient driver, who, at his age, probably was wishing he was home in bed, flicked the whip in a feather-light touch on the rumps of the faithful team. Cliff had instructed that they should be returned to where Gwyneth had been picked up. Clearly, there was to be no private time without Mother there to supervise and direct. Protect? That remained as a possibility.

The streets of downtown Chicago were dimly lit with gas lights held above the road on tall poles. The lamplighter had been through the area earlier, lighting the lamps one by one. But the space between the lamps remained almost totally in darkness.

The landau wasn't more than three city blocks away from the restaurant when, looking ahead and to the side, for the lack of attention-holding conversation, Gwyneth saw suspicious movement in the shadows. She sat up in alarm, reaching for her

.32 cal. pistol that was well hidden in the folds of her gown. At least three shadowy figures were approaching the landau on her side. There may be more on the other side, but she couldn't see that way. Wondering, she sat up straighter and leaned over the side of the carriage.

In suspicion and preparation, she slipped her wrap off her shoulders, letting it fall to the seat. Sylvester picked up on her actions and came alert. As the shadowy movements were clearly showing unwelcome intent toward the carriage and its riders, she leaped to her feet and stepped once onto the front seat beside Sylvester and then, with an athletic leap, was over the folded canvas top and onto the seat beside the driver. She heard a female voice utter, "My word," but paid no attention.

One man, a big brute of a fellow with a flat, small-brimmed hat covering most of her view of his face, was just reaching for the bridle strap on the offside horse. He missed, but started running along beside the animal, still intent on his goal. There could only be one explanation for his actions, and that was to pull the team to a halt. The gang's intent became clear enough that even Mrs. Rickhart couldn't miss it as a grinning face rose over the side of the carriage right beside her. Gwyneth turned quickly to see what was taking place behind her.

Sylvester Rickhart was on his feet, showing defense. And, surprising Gwyneth totally, Mrs. Rickhart was also standing now, hoisting one of the umbrellas that were kept in a slot along the inside of the carriage, held against sudden need on a rainy day. Things were happening very quickly, and Gwyneth couldn't take everything in, but she saw Mrs. Rickhart twist her arms back as far as her evening gown would allow and jab forward, hard, with the still rolled umbrella, directly into the face that had grinned at her just seconds before. With a show of splattering blood and a scream, the face, and the man, disappeared, dropping to the brick pavement. Will was struggling with another intruder while his father was dealing with yet another who was trying to gain entrance on his side.

Sylvester had a pistol gripped in his hand but had yet to discharge it.

She looked back to the team. The big oaf had finally caught up to the team and grabbed the bridle. The offside horse was slowing while trying to drag the attacker along with its still free teammate. Knowing that if the carriage were dragged to a halt they would be in serious trouble, Gwyneth lifted her .32 and aimed at the thug's running feet. Her first shot whanged off the bricks, but her second shot penetrated the leather of the man's boot. His scream of pain accompanied his release of the bridle.

The elderly driver was slumped against the back of his seat as if trying to disappear from sight. Gwyneth grabbed the reins from his hands, leaned far forward to provide her more slack in the leathers. With a loud, "Hiyah, hiyah, get up there, you nags," she laid the leather on their backs. There was no feather lightness such as the driver had used. The sudden move shook off the fellow who was holding to a tenuous grip on the nearside animal's bridle and the team was freed to run as they probably hadn't run in years. Holding the reins in one hand, Gwyneth tucked her weapon back into the little pocket she had sewn into the new gown and out of sight.

Like an apparition out of the gloomy night, as if he had been hanging onto the carriage and standing on the step, while the horses ran full out, a man's head and shoulders appeared on Gwyneth's right. With hardly a thought except for survival, she lifted her dress clear of her leg and kicked the man as hard as she could, connecting under his chin. Silently, he slipped back into the mysteries of the night. There was a slight thump and a bit of a rise in the rear portion of the carriage as he hit the road, but she had no intention of stopping to see what they had run over. She continued to urge the horses to a full, somewhat dangerous gallop on the dark streets. She had heard another shot from the carriage seating area earlier but had no opportunity to inquire who had the gun, friend or foe?

Still standing and yelling at the team, she felt a touch on her arm and glanced down to see Cliff kneeling on the seat behind her. "It's over," he shouted, past all the other noise surrounding them. "You can bring them to a walk."

Meaning to pass the reins back to the driver, she looked down at him. Clearly, he would be doing no more driving this night. The terror he felt showed in the eyes that looked back up at her, and his posture was slack to the extreme. She gently sat down beside him and said, "How would it be if you simply take your rest and give me directions. I'm totally lost. I'll hold the team."

"Right at the next intersection," was the response. The ride back to her cottage was taken in quietness. If it wasn't for the slight swaying of the carriage and rattle of hoof and wheel on the bricks, one might have been convinced they had stopped moving. Arriving at the cottage, everyone but the driver stepped down to the road. Sylvester was the first to speak while Cliff was holding Gwyneth's arm as she descended from the driver's seat. Before taking the last step, she smiled at the driver. "That was kind of fun, wasn't it? A bit of excitement to close out the evening."

"If you say so, miss." The voice that said the words held no assurance of the truth of the statement.

Sylvester grinned at Gwyneth. "I agree with you, young lady. It was kind of fun. After the hooligans were brought under control, that is. You can handle a team. You proved that in spades. I don't believe that team has ever been put to the test like that before. And even this old carriage held together. It certainly helped when someone shot that fellow beside the offside horse. Must have been someone on the street trying to assist us."

"Must have been something like that," answered Gwyneth, feeling a bit of an emotional letdown as the excess adrenaline slowly drained from her system. "It does show what can happen when everyone is working together and fighting back, friend or stranger. And if I'm not being too bold, Mrs. Rickhart, I must say, you swing a mean umbrella."

"Yes, quite."

Sylvester laughed and said, "Don't let Mother and all this society nonsense fool you. We first met all those years ago when she signed on as cook on one of my boats. Mother can take care of herself. She takes care of me and Cliff also, sometimes to our detriment in my humble opinion."

Gwyneth wondered if he was making an excuse for his son. Sylvester spoke, sounding more like a sea captain than he had before. She could easily see how his words would be heeded in another context.

"Gwyneth, I apologize for the unruly thugs that make such a nuisance of themselves on some of our street. Violence is not unknown, but gun violence is taken very seriously by our constabulary, and our courts. It is fortunate that none of us were carrying a weapon this evening, although I will admit the shots from our mysterious benefactor aided us in our escape. Still, the less said, the better. As far as I am concerned, it didn't happen."

Gwyneth, after spending years in a land where law was made by the folks who had settled there, had no problem with the concept of doing what had to be done and moving on. "What didn't happen? I don't remember anything untoward after enjoying that delicious beef."

THE PATHS of Gwyneth and Cliff Rickhart did not cross for the next two days at the hospital. When they did meet, it was because Cliff wanted to have Gwyneth come to the surgical recovery room. A nurse hunted Gwyneth down and passed the message along. Entering the small, four-bed room, Gwyneth was surprised to see a young black man lying half asleep under a sheet and a warm blanket. Cliff waved her over. "I believe you just may know this young man, Dr. Wycome."

She stepped over to the bed and looked down at the patient.

"Gunshot wound. More mysterious than serious. Won't talk about it. Says someone on the street shot him. Near the theater district."

He was young, black, and suffering. His pain showed on his face. Dr. Rickhart watched as Gwyneth took in the patient's features, searching her memory. She'd had very little contact with any black man and only the one birth with a black lady. But slowly the dim light of memory brightened. Shocked and needing positive identification before she said anything, she lifted the blanket and then the sheet. She pushed the hospital gown aside and looked at his bare torso. There lay a row of stitches down his left side, from near the center of his rib cage, approaching his hip. Isaiah. He could be no other. His eyes opened at the disturbance, but he showed no recognition. She wouldn't have expected him to. He had been completely unconscious during his surgery two years ago, had probably never seen her face. She stared at him, finally saying, "Isaiah, I'm extremely disappointed in you." She paused for a response.

"I know you?"

"You don't really know me, but I certainly know you. Do you remember getting those stitches?"

All he could seem to get out were short sentences or even just single words.

"You?"

"Yes. Me. You were within perhaps three minutes of bleeding to death. I broke every rule in the book doing that surgery. But when you survived, I had high hopes for you. Certainly, something better than running with a gang, attacking peaceful and innocent folks in carriages. I'm ashamed for you. God healed you to give you a chance to be more than this. Get well. Get out of this hospital. And do something with your life. You were given a second chance two years ago. Show some gratitude to your Creator, if not to your doctors. And don't show back up here."

With that, she flopped the blanket back down and turned away. A nurse, with a question in her eyes, watched until Gwyneth was out of the door before reaching for the bedding to straighten it.

Gwyneth had left the room hurriedly, disappointment running through her mind, almost through her entire system if that was possible. Cliff Rickhart caught up to her and bid her to hold up a minute. She stopped, but the look she gave him said she had moved on from the wounded Isaiah. There was nothing of the looks she had cast his way in earlier times. Dr. Rickhart read the situation accurately for once.

"Soon. We'll talk soon."

But they never did. It became as if the evening at the opera had been some kind of a dream, not reality.

# Chapter Twelve

THERE WAS LITTLE SOCIALIZING AT CHICAGO General Hospital. There were always link-ups enough with the younger staff, but that was a private matter, nothing to do with the institution itself. And what happened beyond the doors of the institution was of no concern to anyone. But let a male staff member enter into the nurse's quarters and the rule enforcement would be firm indeed. The one exception to socializing was the Christmas get-together. Even that event was not particularly fancy and certainly not formal. There was no effort to dress in tux and gown. There was no sit-down banquet. There was simply a sandwich and snack table, serve yourself, and a dessert offering, the most popular part of the available food. Champagne was available in very limited quantities.

Guests came and went as their schedule, or their interests allowed. As they could break free, staff on duty were welcome in their white coats or nurses' uniforms.

The single exception to the simplicity was the late evening dance. A small musical ensemble would arrive at around ten and the dance would go until around midnight. It was the one time in the year when everyone on staff magically found themselves at the same social level. Doctors would dance with nurses or cleaners or cooks, and the few female doctors would dance with fellow doctors or maintenance workers, all without reference to the other three hundred sixty-four days of the year.

Gwyneth had her back to the dance floor, visiting with a small group of nurses. With the shortage of tables and chairs, they were all standing. Gwyneth was sipping on her single small flute of champagne. When she heard Cliff Rickhart's unmistakable voice at her shoulder, she turned slowly, wondering what to expect. "Good evening, Cliff."

"Good evening, Gwyneth. The ensemble is playing a selection of slower waltzes. Although I have never mastered the waltz, I've come closer there than with any of the other dances. Would you honor me?"

She set her champagne flute down on a close-by table and moved gracefully onto the floor, with Cliff's hand under her arm, as if to guide her. As she turned toward him, offering her other hand, they fell into the rhythm of the music and took several steps before Cliff said, "Gwyneth. I am a social coward. As comfortable as I am in the operating theater, I am equally uncomfortable in a social setting. I've known since our ill-fated evening at that dreadful opera that I owe you both thanks and an apology. The thanks would be for your accommodating me for one evening. The apology, of course, for my poor planning and poorer execution of the event. I can't think of one single thing that couldn't have been done better on my end. Please say you forgive me."

The dance was virtually forgotten. The two doctors were merely shuffling through the motions.

"I don't remember it totally as you do, Cliff. It's true I'd as soon break an arm as attend another opera, but the meal and the ride home were fun and exhilarating. I'm afraid I fell well below your mother's expectations. Her disapproval of me and my ways were quite obvious right from the start. I'm afraid I let you down somewhat on that account. I really liked your father though."

"And he liked you, as well. And he was thoroughly impressed at how well you took charge of the situation on the landau. You proved your worth as a driver, handling whip and reins as if born to the talent. But the delight of his evening was when you found a weapon somewhere in the folds of your dress and knew just what to do with it. He couldn't stop talking about that for days after. I must say, it surprised me some. Do you often carry a pistol?"

"Always."

"Are you carrying it now?"

"Now and always, as I've said."

"Well, please don't shoot anyone at the hospital. But back to where I was. Mother? Well, she's just Mother. I had planned a totally different evening for just you and I, but I gave in under pressure, and the rest will hover in your memory forever, I'm afraid.

"Actually, I have a history of giving in to Mother. As an only child, I'm afraid she has had an extraordinary amount of influence on my life. My father being away so much didn't help. I am no longer really young, and I am just now beginning to learn how to stand on my own two feet. To that end, this dance, we'll call it, will be my thanks, my apology, and my farewell."

"Farewell, Cliff? What do you mean by that?"

"I have timed my departure date to include this evening's event in the hopes of talking with you. I leave for New York in the morning. I have accepted a position at a New York teaching hospital. It was the only way I could think of getting away. To try to learn how to be an adult in all areas of my life. You have been a delight to me, Gwyneth. I had a small part in bringing you onto our staff, one of the better decisions I have ever made. And now it's my time to move on. Mother has kicked up quite a fuss, but for once, I stood up to her. So thank you again for being who you are and for gracing one evening of my life. I had rather hoped, well, never mind. We were together for one evening at least. I shall always remember that. As to what happened on the ride home—"

But Gwyneth interrupted him. "Why, Cliff, nothing happened but for a pleasant carriage ride on a lovely evening. Nothing I remember anyway. And I distinctly remember your father saying the same thing. Nothing happened."

"Thank you. Just one further thing I must apologize for. Mother, when she thought back through the evening, was mortified that she had spoken so out of turn. I suggested she write you a note, but I don't believe she ever did. I refer to that uncomfortable matter of you being a widow. You need to know that I was aware of that fact and never gave it a second thought. On reflection, Mother came to the same feeling. If you can forgive that one further bit of awkwardness from the evening that never happened, both Mother and I will put that away, taking it as a lesson to mind our tongues and think carefully about our words."

Gwyneth smiled up at Cliff and responded, "It never happened."

"And now, Dr. Rickhart, I have news for you too. I asked that the office keep it from you so I could tell you myself. I, too, am leaving Chicago General. I leave right after New Year. I find I have a hankering for the west again. And my goal has always been to hang out my own shingle. I need to thank you for accepting me as a doctor, equal with the male doctors. And for showing me a better way to do my work on several occasions. I leave here with far more knowledge than I brought to the job. Thank you. I wish you well in New York. And now I must leave you. I have an early shift in the morning. Good night, Doctor, and God bless."

She turned and made her way to the coat room and then to the exit, giving Dr. Clifford Rickhart no time for further inquiry or comment.

# PART TWO

# *West Again*

# Chapter Thirteen

Dr. Gwyneth Wycome boarded the westbound train at the Chicago Union Depot. She held a one-way ticket in her hand, which included meals and a private stateroom. The cost of the private space was exorbitant to Gwyneth's normal thinking, but after the years studying and working in Chicago, all the while saving her wages, she decided to throw caution to the wind and spend some savings for her own comfort and enjoyment. She was fond of reminding herself that she still held tight to most of the money put away after the sale of the ranch and cattle, all those years ago. She would have enough, and more, to open her clinic.

When she would ever return east was unknown. She had packed all her personal effects, thinking of the move as permanent. The luggage identified as hers in the baggage car, was several times what she carried on her eastern trip after her years in western Colorado. As her plan was to open her own office in Pueblo, she had shopped generously for medical supplies before leaving the big city. In addition, she had two trunks packed with clothing, all purchased with an eye to her career as a country doctor. Settled on top of the clothing was a professionally painted, wooden sign advertising *Dr. G. Wycome, physician and surgeon.*

Her excitement ran deep, although there was a lingering sadness due to her leaving the hospital where she had learned so much, and where she had gained several friends, notably Bea Brodrick, the nurse who had become a friend and confidant. But the decision had been made, and she wasn't looking back. Purposely, she chose a passenger car seat that faced the front of the train. Even if only symbolic, she intended to look forward. The past was dealt with and gone. No more looking back.

During her time in Chicago, Gwyneth's mother, her only truly close tie to the east, had died. Her siblings were scattered to their own places, and gradually they grew apart. She had no real reason to ever return to the east.

An air of excitement imposed itself on the travelers as the steam whistle pierced the air, blasting a last warning for latecomers to climb aboard for the west. The giant, black painted engine shuddered as the engineer gradually directed steam to the pistons that turned the six-foot-tall drive wheels. As the train made its first moves, the rhythmic clank, clank, clank signaled that the following cars were drawing tight into the couplings, announcing their departure.

Even the most seasoned travelers laid down their books, leaned forward and toward the window, getting one last glance of the passing landscape.

Downtown Chicago, which seemed so large to the walker or the passenger riding a horse cab, seemed to pass from sight in mere seconds, and not long after, the train was rattling through the rural areas before the view was reduced to farmlands and small towns. Gwyneth enjoyed every moment of it, knowing they would eventually enter into the western plains. With inner excitement, she anticipated what was to come.

Although raised in the east and recently having renewed her eastern roots in school and work, she had become western in every part of her. She often thought about Trent, her long-deceased husband, wondering what her life would be like if he hadn't died falling from a gelding that had never given up his wildness. It was possible she would still be a ranch wife, and that would be all right too. A family was unlikely. The years of marriage had left her barren. Her medical training was no help in her desire for understanding. Medical science had a long way to go to fully understand the reproduction process.

Like most young couples, she and Trent had longed for a son or daughter. Finally, seeing no real choice, they settled for loving each other, seldom talking about children. The subject was just too hurtful. Their close proximity to Abe and Helen Wycome, Trent's parents, who were longing for grandchildren, added an extra situation that required delicate handling. Abe and Helen had returned to Texas, so that pressure would not be renewed by Gwyneth's return west.

Gwyneth had no intention of running all those thoughts through her mind again. But even with those good intentions, the thoughts often came unbidden. In the busyness of hospital work, she had managed to subdue them, for the most part anyway. She would have to discipline herself in the idleness of train travel. She would remember the happy things and focus on the future.

Gwyneth had dressed for travel in a split riding skirt that Bea, her wardrobe advising friend, had told her was quite lovely. She had been tempted to don her white Stetson but thought better of it, thinking it might be out of place on the train. Looking around the car, she saw several similar hats, but they were all worn by men. She rested in the wisdom of her first decision.

There were several empty seats in the car. She found herself sitting alone where there was space for someone beside her and for two more on the facing bench. She never consciously avoided company but was content with the situation. There was nothing stopping her from spreading out, placing her tanned leather bag with the shoulder-length carrying straps, on the seat beside her. She retrieved a book, opened it to the bookmark, and held it on her lap. Intending to read, she instead found herself engrossed in the passing countryside.

Gwyneth had no sooner opened the book and settled in to read when a man dressed in city clothing, including a dark gray Homburg hat, took the seat opposite her. He greeted her with a lift of his hat and a wide smile. "Good morning, miss. These train journeys can become quite tedious, don't you think?" Not waiting for an answer, he continued, "It is nearing lunchtime. May I escort you to the dining room? Dining alone is so provincial, do you not agree?"

Gwyneth, holding the book as if she would prefer not to be disturbed, which was true, glanced at the intruder and turned her eyes back to the page, ignoring the man and the invitation. The silence between them grew until the man placed his hat back on his head, saying, "Yes, well, perhaps another time."

As he rose to leave, he took one last look at Gwyneth to see if there was any response he might find encouraging. There wasn't.

But it was indeed nearing lunchtime, and Gwyneth had, due to her own last-minute fussing, eaten nothing but her last bakery-bought muffin during the cab ride to the station. It was hardly sufficient even at the time. She waited long enough for the self-assured man who had intruded into her space to have found another seat, or perhaps another victim for his advances.

As if an alarm or a notice of some sort had been spread abroad, people from the several passenger cars were wending their way toward the dining car. Only then did she fold her book, sling her satchel over her shoulder, and join the migrating passengers. Each table in the dining car was set for four diners. She purposely chose one where a young mother with two children, ages about ten and twelve, had taken seats.

"Is this seat taken?"

"No. You would be most welcome, but I'm afraid my children are somewhat excited by the idea of being on a train. I hope a bit of fidgeting won't upset you."

"It won't upset me at all. I find myself doing a bit of fidgeting myself. I crossed all of this land on horseback and wagon. By comparison, the train is a pure delight and well worthy of excitement."

The young boy, seated beside his mother and across from Gwyneth, looked at her with awe. "You rode all this way on a wagon?"

"Well, a wagon and sometimes on horseback while someone else drove the wagon."

"Gosh. I'd sure like to do that."

His sister, seated by Gwyneth and much more mature, in her own eyes at least, looked with disdain at her brother. "Oh, Ruben. You're such a child."

"Am not. Anyway, you're mostly a child yourself."

"Stop it, you kids."

Gwyneth smiled and said, "I believe you are all just fine exactly as you are. Perhaps it would be better if we introduced ourselves. My name is Gwyneth Wycome. And I'm traveling west to Pueblo, Colorado."

The mother spoke, saying, "I'm very pleased to meet you, Gwyneth. May I call you Gwyneth?"

"Of course."

"And my name is Maria Handcock. My son is Ruben, as you have just heard. My very mature daughter is Trina. Ruben is ten and Trina is twelve. We are traveling to Cheyenne to meet Lars, my husband and the children's father."

The table waiter arrived just as Ruben said, "My father is a policeman."

The conversation stopped while they each placed an order for lunch. As the waiter stepped away, Trina, in a disgusted voice, said, "You're not supposed to tell everyone that, dummy."

"Am not a dummy."

"All right children. There's no harm done. And you're not

quite correct, Trina. Your father is a US Deputy Marshal, and it's no secret."

"But that man at the station seemed to be following us. I'm thinking it was because he knew Father, or was running from the law, like that other time back in Saint Louis."

"It's still not for us to worry. At least not for you children. You leave it all to your father and me. And I'm sure Gwyneth has other things to think about."

"On the contrary, Maria, I have lived in the west where we had no law except our own, and that's never really satisfactory. I greatly admire men like your Lars. Men who will stand up for what is right, making the world a better place for all of us."

Maria let that conversation dwindle to a halt, asking instead, "Are you meeting your husband, Gwyneth?"

"No. I'm afraid I'm a widow. My husband was tossed from an unruly horse. It didn't end well. No, I am alone."

Trina, listening carefully to the conversation while her brother's eyes and mind were fastened on the passing countryside, asked, "What will you do when you get to where you're going?"

"That's a good question, Trina. Actually, I'm a doctor. For the past few years, I have been studying and working in a hospital. But I have a longing to open my own office back out west. I've learned to love the west, and I've always wanted my own practice. So I'm going to do it."

Past the expressions of awe from the kids and a word of sympathy as well as congratulations from Maria came the voice of a woman a few tables away.

"I've told you already, leave me alone. If I had a gun, I'd shoot you dead."

"Sorry to misunderstand, ma'am. I thought perhaps—"

"On the contrary, you didn't think at all. Not with your mind anyway. Now get away from me."

Every eye in the dining room was turned toward the noise. Gwyneth was not surprised to see the man with the Homburg hat easing away from the woman, with a strange, twisted look on his face as if he was sorry to have been found out. Still, he couldn't control his impulse to stop at Gwyneth's table and again doff the hat.

"I'm pleased to see you found your way to the dining car. Perhaps for dinner, you will allow me to escort you. It would be my delight to do so."

Several eyes had watched the man since he had been so forcefully turned away by his first victim. Now they were watching and listening to every word, but the man with the Homburg appeared to be unaware of his surroundings. He was clearly oblivious of the cowboy who rose from his seat a few tables away, too. Maria and her children sat in fear while Gwyneth said nothing. She simply reached to her waist, pushed aside a few folds of cloth, and dug into the pocket sewn there. The next moment, she produced her .32 cal. pistol, laying it, with no words, on the table, with the barrel clearly pointed toward the man.

The fellow's eyes grew in alarm while he sputtered a few unintelligible words. He backed away, right into the waiting hands of the cowboy. He trembled in fear as the Stetson-hatted rider grinned at Gwyneth and said, "You rest easy there, ladies, I'll take out the trash."

With one hand firmly gripping the man's collar, the rescuer pushed him toward the exit door. They passed through into the tent-like covering protecting the walkway between cars. The door closed, and nothing more was heard. No more than, perhaps, one full minute had passed before the cowboy returned. As he passed Gwyneth's table, he quietly said, "He won't bother you again, miss. Although I would be willing to bet, by the looks of that weaponry you displayed, that you didn't really need my help. I admire that in a lady." With that he took his seat as if nothing had happened.

The few diners who could see Gwyneth's weapon looked first at the gun and then at Gwyneth before smiling. Three men, all seated within sight of Gwyneth's table, reached into hidden holsters and produced their own weapons, laying them out as Gwyneth had done. Clearly, there were folks on the train quite willing to take situations under control when need arose.

Gwyneth put the gun away just as their lunches arrived. Nothing more was said except when Ruben asked, "Is that a real gun, miss?"

"Indeed, it is, Ruben. Let's hope I don't have to use it."

With the lunch break behind her, Gwyneth thanked Maria Handcock for allowing her to share their table. She rose and returned to her private compartment. She opened the small trunk carrying her clothing and a few books, and her gun belt. She wrapped the belt around her waist and slipped the .32 into the holster. She had, years earlier, before Chicago, chosen to wear the rig where it was easily seen, with the weapon on her left, the handle pointing right for a cross draw. With that done, she returned to the passenger car to continue her reading. For the remainder of the trip, she gathered a good many studied glances but no unwelcome interruptions.

# Chapter Fourteen

THERE WERE NUMEROUS STOPS ALONG THE LONG route from Chicago to Cheyenne where many people stepped to the station platforms to stretch their legs and breath in the refreshing grasslands air. Thinking it through, and watching the faces and attitudes of the travelers, Gwyneth came to the conclusion that the trip was either a grand adventure or a slowly moving, tedious grind. It was a bit of both for her. Anxious to get to her destination, she could easily fall into the tedious grind camp. But recalling the days and weeks of her first trip west, paced to the speed of the reluctantly moving cattle herd, the train, even with all its stops, was pure luxury.

Finally, the train pulled into Cheyenne itself. True to the exchange of information, whether fact or rumored fiction, about the nature of Cheynne weather the passengers had shared among each other during the last couple of hours of the trip, the wind was howling up a blow of snow and the crowded single street near the station was wall to wall with folks anxious to greet a loved one from among the alighting passengers. Horses, wagons and a couple of stagecoaches were crowded around the station. The air was cold, the ground covered with snow. It was January in Cheyenne, which sat at an elevation of over six thousand feet.

Ruben looked out the window, which was half covered in frost. "Mom. There's snow everywhere, and folks are wrapped up as if they were going to the North Pole."

Gwyneth, who had developed the habit of joining the Handcock family for meals, laughed and said, "Well, Ruben, it's a long way from the north pole, but Cheyenne, and most of Wyoming, for that matter, has gained a reputation as winter country. Heavy snow and heavy winds are common. You'll want to bundle up in your warmest clothing. But the summers are nice, even if the wind continues to blow. And the scenery is quite spectacular. Toward the mountains, at least."

THE FRIENDLY BOND between the small family and Gwyneth had grown over the days on the train. Maria Handcock said after they had stepped onto the station platform, "Come meet Lars. He's bound to be here somewhere in this crowd."

They eased their way through the crowd, hoping to get inside the station. Suddenly Ruben shook loose of his mother's hand. Shouting "Dad. Dad." He burst through the crowd, rushing right into the waiting arms of a tall, well-built man sporting a huge mustache and grinning from ear to ear. The ten-year-old boy was not light, but his father picked him up as if he weighed nothing at all, giving him a big hug and then setting him down. Trina, not as outgoing as her brother, eased up to her father with a hug around his waist. Her hug was returned with a gentle grip on each side of her head and a kiss on her forehead. Lars then pushed her away to arm's length. "Let me get a look at you. Why, you're bigger and more grown up and beautiful than ever. It's so good to see you all and have you home. Did you look after your mother on the trip?"

Ignoring the question, Trina responded, "It's good to be home."

Lars turned from his daughter to his wife with a big smile and again, with outstretched arms. The conventions of the times said that couples should restrain themselves in public. Maria settled for a moment leaning against Lar's chest while he whispered something in her ear that no one else could hear. When they pulled apart, Maria said, "Lars, I'd like you to meet a lady who befriended us on the train. This is Gwyneth Wycome. Actually, Dr. Gwyneth Wycome. She's heading down to Pueblo to open a medical practice."

Lars stretched out his hand, which Gwyneth gripped lightly for only a moment. It's good to meet you, Dr. Wycome. May I be bold enough to say I wish you were setting up practice here in Cheyenne?"

"Thank you, Mr. Handcock. But I pretty well have my mind set. We lived down that way some years ago, so it's almost like going home."

"You say *we*, does that imply a family waiting for you down south?"

"No family, I'm afraid. Just me."

"Gwyneth lost her husband in a horse wreck while working on their ranch."

"I'm sorry to hear that, Doctor. I hope you do well in your practice."

Lars pointed out the most likely hotel, saying, "They're the best in town, but, depending on the mood of the manager at the moment, they can be sticky about accommodating single ladies. If he gives you trouble, refer him to me."

THERE WAS no problem getting a room, but when Gwyneth stepped onto the boardwalk later in the evening, after enjoying a light dinner in the dining room, her eyes fell on those of the

Homburg-hatted man from the train. He held eye contact for an uncomfortable length of time but finally mouthed words that Gwyneth chose to ignore before turning away.

Gwyneth stayed the night before catching the morning train south. The much smaller train, with no dining car and only one passenger car leading a string of empty cattle cars, rattled through the short grass country, entering Denver late that evening. There was a small selection of sandwiches on the train, but by the time they pulled into the station, Gwyneth was ready for dinner and a night in a good hotel.

Of the many cabs hoping to pick up a fare, one seemed to stand out. Gwyneth looked at the clean and polished carriage, thinking the driver had put some effort into his occupation. He, himself, was clean and well dressed, a welcome change from the somewhat slovenly appearance of so many of the drivers. Glancing past the gathering of cabs of every description, Gwyneth waved her Stetson at the driver, catching his eye almost immediately. His light wave said he had noticed. He urged his horse through the jumble of conveyances, receiving a few shouts of anger for his trouble.

Gwyneth had arranged for overnight storage for her trunks and a transfer to the morning train to Pueblo. She stood at the edge of the platform with only her black leather medical bag, which she took with her most times, and a small overnight bag. The driver jumped to the platform and settled the bags on the front seat. He then assisted a very tired Gwyneth onto the back seat.

"I'm hoping to find room in a good hotel, and dinner. Do you have a recommendation?"

"You jest take yer seat there, young lady. Don't ye worry none. Ol' Blaze knows every accommodation in this y'ear town. I take folks to them all, sav'n the best fer ladies and gents such as yerself."

Horse traffic was slow and dense, but Blaze, in good time, settled his rig to a stop at the canopied and lighted entrance of the Winsor Hotel. He leaped to the ground and said, "The very best fer ya, ma'am. Good rooms, fine service, and only the very elite of clientele. No riff raff fer ya ta worry about here, ma'am. And a dining room ye'll write home about, it's that fine."

Gwyneth thanked the man and paid with a generous gratuity. With a promise to pick her up at seven thirty in the morning, Blaze tipped his hat and hurried back to the station, hoping for another fare-paying passenger.

# Chapter Fifteen

GWYNETH STOOD ON THE MAIN STREET OF PUEBLO, Colorado, momentarily relishing the thoughts and remembrances of times gone by. At her feet lay her overnight bag and the black leather satchel that would tell most knowledgeable watchers what her profession was. There was just something about the medical bag that made it stand out. Most folks—men and ladies both—would say that there was something about Gwyneth herself that caused her to stand out in a crowd, as well. Tall but not too tall. Her wavy hair falling over her shoulders and down her back, setting off her white Stetson in dramatic fashion. Fit and strong, well-dressed, her clothing filled out just right. Not quite beautiful, but attractive in a mature way.

Perhaps the most striking attraction was her studied look of competence, as if this was a person to be listened to and trusted. Overall, it was an image that would scare off a lot of men, if attracting a man was one of her goals, but would attract and almost mesmerize others.

The hotel she and Trent had stayed in years ago was just across the street. The building was beginning to look a little tired, but she remembered the interior as being quite pleasant, as were the staff. She had no idea how long it would take her to find a satisfactory house to turn into her home, as well as a clinic to offer her doctoring services from. She may need to stay in the hotel for some time. After the extravagance of the railway state room, her conscience was nagging at her just a bit. A newer or upgraded hotel was sure to cost more. Perhaps she should keep the living expenses under control until she had developed an income. The old hotel would do just fine.

She waited for traffic to clear and then crossed over to the hotel entrance. The big front door was still as heavy as she remembered. She had to set her medical bag on the wooden entry floor in order to free her right hand to grip the long, curved, brass handle. She was just wrapping her fingers around the brass when an arm reached in front of her.

A quick sideways glance showed a well-dressed man pushing middle age. She recognized him immediately. He grinned a bit, saying, "Please allow me. I've been telling Mason, the hotel manager, that they must ease off on the door closer mechanisms. It's about all I can do myself to gain entry."

Gwyneth pulled her hand away and bent to pick up her bag, all the while remembering, and yet biting her tongue. With the door now open, she quietly said, "Thank you," and stepped ahead of the gentlemen. At the counter, she inquired about a stay of at least one week, perhaps longer. "I'm going to be looking for a house to purchase, and I have no idea how long that will take."

The clerk smiled a welcome and turned the register toward her. "If you will jot down your name, miss, I'll pick you out a good room and work out the best rate I can."

Gwyneth signed *Dr. Gwyneth Wycome* and turned the register back to the clerk. He glanced at it and said, "Doctor. Why ain't that just the best. Do you plan to set up practice here in town, Miss Wycome?"

"Yes, as a matter of fact, I do. But I need to find suitable accommodation first."

He passed her a key and said, "Just you wait here a moment, Doctor."

With that, he scuttled across the lobby and entered the dining room. He returned momentarily with the same man who had opened the door for her. "Dr. Wycome. You might like to meet Mr. Gregory Sampson. Mr. Sampson has the bank just down the street. Deals a lot in land and such. If there's a house for sale, Mr. Sampson knows about it. Mr. Sampson, this is Dr. Wycome. New to town and looking for a house for herself, with room for a doctor's office."

Gregory Sampson didn't offer to shake hands. Instead, he invited Gwyneth to join him for lunch.

"Dr. Wycome, I'm very pleased to meet you. We had what may be called an accidental meeting at the door, but to formalize the introduction and to discuss your needs, I'd like to invite you to join my wife and myself for lunch."

It was only the fact that Mrs. Sampson would be in attendance that allowed her to accept the invite.

"Dr. Wycome, let me present my wife, Sarah-Lee. Sarah, Dr. Wycome has just arrived in town and will be looking for a home for herself, with enough space for a medical clinic."

Somewhat suspiciously, Sarah-Lee responded, "It's good to meet you, Doctor. We can certainly use another doctor in town. The population appears to be expanding almost daily. What attracted you to our community, Doctor?"

Gwyneth picked up on the coolness immediately. Inviting her to their private lunch table without inquiring of his wife first might not have been the wisest thing the banker could have done.

"It's good to meet you, as well. I passed through here several years ago on my way further west. My attraction to Pueblo probably can't be logically explained. Perhaps a bit of nostalgia. But mostly to gain an opportunity to serve not just the town but some of the area around. My first trip through the area was for another purpose altogether. But now that I've gone back east to study medicine, receiving my physician and surgeon's degree, and having practiced in two big Chicago hospitals, I feel competent to open my own clinic. And why not do it in the country I came to love in another lifetime?"

"Why not indeed," was the banker's response.

The server arrived just in time to interrupt the conversation. When they were alone again, Sarah-Lee said, "Perhaps the Benton house would suit the doctor."

The banker leaned back in his chair and replied, "My dear. You are a marvel. Why certainly, the Bentons' new home is just completed, and they're anxious to sell and move. Brilliant. I'll send a messenger over this afternoon to see when it would be convenient for me to escort the good doctor over for a look."

"You needn't bother, Gregory. I'm sure your afternoon at the bank will be much too busy. Miss Wycome may enjoy a walk after lunch. She and I could walk over. It's not far, after all."

Gwyneth lifted her eyes from her study of the printed cloth table topper and looked at Sarah-Lee. Afraid the banker's wife might have caught the relieved look on her face, Gwyneth attempted to smile. She didn't do a very good job at it. But she finally said, "I'd love a walk, Mrs. Sampson. Are you sure you have the time?"

"My dear Doctor. I have nothing but time. Absolutely nothing at all. I reluctantly attend what is jokingly named the Pueblo Improvement Society, just once in each month. So far, we have improved nothing at all, unless we admit that our gossip pattern has become perfected, you might say. As an alternative to the gossip sessions, I would so much enjoy getting out of town from time to time, but those times have become further and further apart lately."

"I enjoy the open country, as well, something there is very little of in Chicago. Perhaps we could rent a buggy one day and go for a ride. You could show me some of the country around."

"Consider that a plan with a date to be agreed upon later, Dr. Wycome. But if I could suggest a bit of a change, I would far sooner ride the horse than have him pulling the buggy. If you don't ride, you could consider it a learning experience. The livery not far from where we live has a good selection of trustworthy horses for rent."

Gwyneth laughed a bit and smilingly said, "I rode horseback from Eastern Kansas, through most of Colorado and into the valley west of here, where we established our ranch. The valley had no name that I ever heard. After arriving there, I rode almost daily, making my nursing rounds or herding cattle on the ranch. I think I'll remember which end of the horse is the front."

"Wonderful. And I'd someday love to hear your story."

Sarah-Lee could see the disapproval on her husband's face. Fortunately, the waiter arrived with their meals and nothing more was said about the Benton house or riding, until they were sitting back with coffee cups in front of them. At that point, Gregory Sampson said, "Ladies, I must return to work. I hope you like the Benton house, Dr. Wycome. And if there is any way I, or the bank, can assist in the purchase, if it comes to that, you have but to call around to the office. If you should find a need for a mortgage or a start-up loan, I'm sure the bank could serve you well. Farewell for now. I'll see you at home later Sarah."

Sarah chose to nod, with a bit of a faraway look on her face.

Gwyneth listened to the banker, watching his eyes carefully for any sign of recognition. She had just given him ample information that might have opened the eyes of a more astute man. But he appeared to remain ignorant of the truth that they had met before, a most unwelcome and trying meeting. Not wishing for a confrontation, but still holding a feeling of disgust at the man's actions when she was closing out the ranch account, she decided to simply allow the matter to be lost in history. But there would be no Wycome Medical Clinic account in the man's bank.

# Chapter Sixteen

Leaving the hotel dining room, Mrs. Sampson said, "Please call me Sarah. Most everyone does. Rev. Grover, the pastor over at our church, is about the only one who sticks to the more formal Mrs. Sampson, even though I have assured him it is not necessary. But he's a very proper fellow. Fine man with a family to be proud of, but cautious. He won't meet with a woman by himself. He insists that either his wife accompany him or the lady's husband, or another significant friend be present. Quaint, but perhaps sometimes called for. I saw that type of caution in your eyes at lunch, too, Gwyneth. May I call you Gwyneth?"

"Certainly. It's usually best for patients or fellow doctors to use the title, *Doctor*, but that's only to set the situation apart from a less formal visit."

"Well, to continue what I started, Gwyneth, I surmise that you are cautious about being alone with a man you aren't familiar with. You may be wiser than you know. As far as I've ever known though, Gregory is trustworthy, at least I certainly hope so. He is alone with women in the bank every day. Nothing suspicious has ever come to my ears. I don't believe he would ever do anything to break your trust, either as a bank client or simply as a woman.

"But by that same logic, I don't like to be alone in the company of another man either. You're going to have far more men than women patients, I'm thinking, what with the constant trail of accidents on local farms and ranches, plus the occasional injury at the mill. But that's all the while assuming they will attend a woman doctor. Some won't, but that number should dwindle over time, and as you gain a reputation."

The walk to the Mason home was actually much further than Sarah Sampson had let on, but the two ladies were both good walkers, so the time passed easily, with pleasant conversation and a girl-like giggle or two.

As they topped a small rise in the road, with the outline of a series of higher rises as background, a beautiful home, set apart from its nearer neighbor, came into view.

"Ah, here we are, the Mason home. In my opinion, one of Pueblo's finest."

Gwyneth stopped and studied the white, cedar-sided home before her. Alternately surrounded by adobe structures, along with some brick and many other Victorian-styled, wood-sided homes, situated among the semi-desert tree and cactus-shrouded sloping ground near the river on the western edge of town, it was clearly a standout, with a peculiar turn of architecture that she could not quite define. Two stories, with a red tile roof. Two dormers, one on each side of the second-floor front, facing the street. Between the dormers was a delightful bay window. Only to herself, she said, *Oh, I hope there's a reading bench in that* . The second-floor windows overlooked much of the downtown area, due to the rise the builders had chosen to place the structure on.

The main floor of the home, facing the street, was fronted by a wide veranda whose roof was tiled, matching the main roof. Directly below the upper bay window was a similarly shaped structural component, except it was turned backward, leading into the home, forming a wide doorway, with a narrow, vertical window on each side of the brass-hinged and latched oak door. Behind the large, glassed windows on each side of the main floor, Gwyneth could see sheer curtains tufted back at their centers to expose the bit of furniture visible from the street, in spite of the shading from the veranda roof. Together with the well-groomed front yard and the comfortable wicker furniture displayed on the veranda, the whole of it was striking and attractive. Gwyneth's mind was racing ahead, wondering what the fenced rear yard was holding secret. Without even seeing the interior, she knew this was to be her home.

Within one week, she had paid over the purchase cost, checked out of the hotel, and moved her few possessions into the now vacated Benton home. During the busy first week of ownership, she had managed to purchase a bed locally and place an order for the remainder of the furniture she wanted, including the needs for the clinic, all to be shipped down from Denver.

She managed to skin a knuckle while hanging the sign she had carried all the way from Chicago. But with the job completed, she stepped down from the ladder and took several backward steps on the veranda. The thought behind the sign, as well as the sign itself, filled her with joy and a sense of accomplishment. *It's done. My own clinic. I did it, Trent. Oh, how I wish you were here to see it all.*

# Chapter Seventeen

True to Sarah Sampson's prediction, Gwyneth's first patient was a worker from the steel mill. A wide-eyed man, exhibiting fear or something similar, drove a two-up wagon at a reckless speed, barely making the corners, and scattering people and animals alike in every direction. Another man and a nurse rode the wagon bed, busying themselves with the worker, wrapped in blankets, lying on a bed of wood shavings and straw. Both were holding hard to the wagon's side with one hand while trying to comfort the suffering fellow with their other hand.

As they pulled to a shouting, clattering stop in front of Gwyneth's new clinic, a young mother, out for a morning stroll, screamed, pulling her errant son away. The boy loved horses, but this was clearly not the time, and these horses, stamping and frothing around the bridle bits, after their long run, just as clearly were not the horses to approach. The nurse stayed with her patient. The driver held the team steady while the second man leaped to the ground, running up the walk, clearing the front stairs in two bounds. He grabbed the rope hanging from the bell clapper and jangled out a noise that might have awakened the dead.

Gwyneth opened the door within seconds. The man had enough remaining courtesy to grab his soft hat and crunch it in his big fist. "Look'n for the doctor, ma'am."

"You've found her. What's happening?"

"Never before seen no lady doctor, ma'am. But I'm guessing old Noah, he won't much care, just so long as you can help him."

"Is your friend in the wagon?"

"Yes, ma'am."

"Well, best you bring him around to the clinic."

"Ol' Noah, ma'am, he cain't no way walk. Maybe-so you'll come take a look before we try to stretcher him anywhere. So as not to hurt him more than he already is, is what I'm mean'n to say."

Gwyneth stepped past the man and hurried down the walkway. Looking first to the nurse, trying to see past her fear-filled eyes, she asked, "What have you got under those blankets, miss?"

"A worker from the mill. His one leg is awful bad broken. Burned too. A small steel mold fell over on him, causing the break and scalding a simply awful path down his leg."

The teamster, on this, his first time driving to the Wycome Medical Clinic, had ignored the side driveway. At Gwyneth's insistence he backed the team enough to make the turn from the road and eased onto the drive and toward the back of the house. There, the summer kitchen that had so delighted Gwyneth when she first saw it, had been cleaned out and turned into the clinic, complete with a wood-burning stove for heating the water necessary for the cleanliness Gwyneth demanded of the clinic, and for heating the room during the winter months. On the counter stood a small hand pump, ready to provide water from the cistern for clinic use as well as doing household laundry.

A second, smaller attached room that had been used as the summer lunchroom for the family had been turned into a living space for convalescent patients. The original doors to the backyard were wide and easily accessible. The two men from the wagon eased the stretcher off the wagon and into the clinic. Under Gwyneth's directions, they gently lifted the wounded man's body enough so the mill nurse could pull the stretcher away, leaving the patient lying on the raised, wheeled stretcher Gwyneth had purchased. Barely awake, proven only by his slightly open eyes, the only expression of pain or discomfort the man showed was a clenching of his teeth and the firm wincing of his eyes. Racing through Gwyneth's thoughts was how much more pain this man was going to suffer before his treatment was completed. She thought again of the horrors of the Civil War medical tents but quickly brought her mind back to the present.

Gwyneth gently but firmly belted the patient to the narrow, high bed. She wished it had included sides to prevent patients from rolling off, but to have that refinement, she would have to order a hospital bed from an eastern supply house. Belting a patient to the bed was somewhat unorthodox, but it removed the fear of an accident that would further exacerbate his condition.

The two men removed the stretcher and allowed as how they'd wait outside until the nurse could join them for the trek back to the mill.

After lifting the covering sheet and fingering the burned and torn canvas coveralls and then the denim jeans aside, for her first close look at the situation, Gwyneth listened for the patient's heartbeat and checked his pulse. She turned to her cabinets to draw the required medical tools and equipment. The nurse hung back long enough to say, "This is a lovely clinic you have here. Hopefully you will do well in Pueblo. I might just as well tell you. We went to the doctor who usually handles problems from the mill, but he was away, attending to some matter on a ranch or whatever. A passing stranger directed us here. None of us had ever heard of you setting up in practice, but I'm ever so happy that you're available."

"Do you not normally use the hospital?"

"The hospital is very new and not well-equipped or staffed yet."

Without taking her eyes off the patient but listening to the nurse all the while, Gwyneth simply replied with a distracted, "Hmm."

Thinking her job was completed but hesitating before pushing the door open, the nurse continued, "That's a nasty job you have ahead of you this afternoon. The patient's name is Noah. Noah Gainford. He's just a boy really. Barely out of his teens and new to the mill job. Came in from a ranch a couple of weeks ago, looking for work. I'm thinking he'll be sorry he didn't stay on the ranch. The mill may try to blame him for the accident, but don't you believe them. Other men have complained about the way the casting is done in the small parts area. There have been other accidents. The managers will say that the mill is very new, and all the procedures have yet to be worked out, but they're doing all they can given the circumstances. But that's a bit of a stretch in my opinion."

Gwyneth lifted her head to study the face of the young nurse and smiled a bit. "You sound as if the patient might be more to you than just a mill worker."

"It's not personal, Doctor. It's more that I hate to see these young men spending their days, their nights too, for that matter, in that mill. By my judgment, they'd be better off in the fresh air on the ranch. Just you do what you can to make him well again and never you mind me."

"You can depend on me doing the best I can, but there will be no avoiding the seriousness of this young man's injuries. I'm sure too that you have already noticed that I have only two hands. This job will require, perhaps, one or two additional hands. Like yours. Please stay. You'll be a great help to both me and Noah."

The girl hesitated, as if weighing the options, but finally she turned to the door and ran out to the wagon. Just what message she sent back to the mill bosses would remain unknown, but she was soon back asking Gwyneth how she could help.

"There's a bit of fire yet in the stove. I made coffee earlier. Stoke the stove up and put a couple of pots of water on to heat. Then dip warm water from the side reservoir and give your hands a good scrubbing, right up to your elbows. And tell me your name."

"Sky Whitely, I'm known by. There's more to it, but that will do for now."

"Well, Sky, that's a pretty name, but right now, it's a steady hand and strict obedience to what I say that is needed. Before we start, are you going to collapse if I have to cut flesh or if you see blood?"

"I don't think so. I'm farm-raised. Fall butchering involved the entire family and sometimes a neighbor or two. I've seen a lot of that side of life before coming to the city. Also, although I never did service in the surgery area, I saw more blood and such than I ever figured on during my two years at the hospital in Denver. I'll do my best for both you and Noah."

Gwyneth prepared what was needed to put the patient under with ether. Before administering it, she shook him awake. When his eyes opened, she said, "Noah. I'm Dr. Wycome. I'm going to do my very best for you, but you need to understand the situation. You have a bit of burn on your upper leg. That should be easily put to rights. But below your knee, and down to where your boot protected you, the burning is worse. And your lower leg is very badly broken. I've only felt from the surface, and I won't know until I've poked and prodded a bit more, but I fear the bones are crushed. I'll do what can be done to allow them to grow together again, but if the damage is irreparable, I may have to remove the lower leg. Do you understand that? I'll only amputate if there is no other choice."

Sky came close and touched the man's cheek. "And I'll be

here working with the doctor, Noah. Together we'll see that you're well cared for."

Noah cast his pain-filled eyes from one face to the other and then stopped at Gwyneth. His voice was barely audible. Gwyneth bent down with her ear close to his mouth. "Do it."

Gwyneth straightened up, gave his shoulder a tight squeeze, and reached for the ether.

"Your job for now, Sky, is to stand at Noah's head and watch. Listen for his breathing. And glance at his eyes from time to time. We don't want to use any more ether than necessary, but we also don't want him waking up. Stand at arm's length at least. You're no help to either me or Noah lying on the floor fast asleep from inhaling the ether. If I need your assistance with the leg, I'll let you know."

Noah's boots had been removed at the mill. Now, Gwyneth reached for her scissors and began carefully cutting away, first the heavy canvas coveralls all mill workers wore, and then the lighter denim pants beneath. And then the white, cotton drawers. Some shattered remnants of cloth were pressed into the broken skin in one spot. She would have to pick them out piece by piece. Sky blushed a bit and turned her head when Gwyneth cut and removed the last portion of the underwear, exposing Noah to the waist. She discreetly laid a towel over him.

His burns started near the top of his groin, so even with the towel strategically placed, there would be a loss of modesty as Gwyneth worked. Noah didn't have to know that. And the nurse would have to get used to it, as all medical workers had to.

Unasked, Sky said, "During two years in the Denver hospital, I've about seen and done it all, Doctor. But somehow, I still shy away, more from the humility forced onto the patient than from my own feelings. But I'll do my job. Don't you be worried about that."

Gwyneth then said, "Sky, you soak one of those clean cloths and rub a bit of soap on it. I'll stand by Noah while you give his leg a thorough washing. Be very careful and gentle around the burn."

With all the preparatory work completed, Gwyneth once again scrubbed her own hands and felt along the length of the leg, squeezing every couple of inches. In one spot, she could hear the scraping of broken bones as she manipulated the flesh.

"Sky, we're going to attempt a fix that doesn't involve surgery. If you can get a grip at his waist, I'm going to see if I can work these bones back into position. There's just the one place where the skin is broken and that's not impacting the bones. The flesh is simply broken from the weight of the item that fell on him, I'm guessing. I can clean that out and bandage it for cleanliness."

She felt along the length of the leg again, pushing sideways very gently where she could feel the separation of bones. A long, stressful half hour had passed before Gwyneth felt assured that the bones were in their proper places, or at least as close as they would ever be, and that no bone splinters were in a position to cause a problem during healing. The concern that couldn't be set aside for days ahead was the blood supply to the lower leg. She would have to watch the foot and ankle area for signs of obstruction of the arteries.

Sky, ever curious and eager to learn, asked, "Do you think it's in its proper place, Doctor?"

"We'll watch for loss of blood circulation for the next few days. If the blood is getting to his foot, I think we're all right."

After once again feeling the leg and thinking it all through, Gwyneth said, "Sky, I believe we are finished here, and I also believe your friend may keep his leg and even walk again with proper follow-up care and gentle exercise. He'll almost certainly have a limp. And he'll lack strength. But that's better than having just a single leg. He'll need around-the-clock care for a short while. We'll talk to the hospital about that. Or perhaps we can work something out here in the clinic. When the time is right, he can be taken back out to the ranch for his long-term recovery. Perhaps you would want to give thought to all of that, Sky. See if there may be a place for you in it. Of course, you would have to leave the mill and come work for me before I could assign you to Noah's care. At least you might wish to think on it."

Sky seemed to have no ready response, so Gwyneth continued with, "Now I want you to lay your hands on his leg, holding it very steady, in case he tries to move. I'm going to prepare a splint. Or rather, a plaster back slab, like half of a cast. That will support the leg while still giving access to the burns, which will need constant attention until they scab over."

The job of tending to the care of the burned skin was every bit as delicate as the work on the bone, but it went much more quickly. The molten iron had only been splashed on the leg for a flash of time, running down and off as quickly as gravity could draw it. Still, the burn was significant, and some skin and the flesh below had been burned away completely. She may consider a skin graft when she was sure the time was right. Otherwise, the wound would have to heal and fill the gap with new growth or scar tissue on its own. The chief danger would come from infection. She had ointments for the burned area, but there was little available, even in modern hospitals, to combat infection.

Completed, Gwyneth studied the result. Whether to herself or to Sky was not clear, but she repeated her private thoughts aloud, "I'm hoping the flesh lost to the molten iron will be replaced by new growth, or perhaps just scar tissue. We'll not know for several weeks."

The doctor went to her storage cabinet again and drew out a matching pair of wooden splints. Very tenderly, she massaged the entire leg with an emollient ointment, avoiding the burned area, before bandaging the splints tightly to the lower leg, leaving the front portion open, giving access to the burned areas. Again, she stretched, this time with her hands above her head. She smiled at Sky, saying, "You keep an eye on the patient while I make a cup of tea. We'll let him wake up now. Do you drink tea? We'll take a cup and then there's some cleaning up to do."

"Is there more to be done with the patient, Doctor?"

"There is. But it's more mechanical than medical. We have to move him off this stretcher and onto the bed in the other room. And somehow manage it without undoing all the work we've just completed. Then we must figure out a way to cover him without the blanket touching the wounds. Perhaps we can roll up a blanket for each side to raise the cover higher than the leg. He may also be sick when he wakes from the ether. The good news is that we can leave him right where he is until another patient shows up needing the stretcher.

"But first, that cup of tea I've been promising myself. Under other circumstances, I'd prefer coffee, but for relaxation and recovery, a cup of tea wins the bet."

# Chapter Eighteen

Thanks to the local Pueblo newspaper, which had somehow heard about Noah and his positive and welcome recovery from the mill accident, the Wycome Medical Clinic was receiving more notoriety than Gwyneth could ever have purchased with large advertising expenditures. Patients were going out of their way to find her clinic. House calls were making further demands on her time. With the aid of a knowledgeable horseman, she purchased a riding animal that was also familiar with working in harness. She added a solid lady's saddle along with the required harness and a slightly used buggy. She was prepared for her house runs or for leisure riding in the evenings.

The two-stall shed at the back of the property, which also offered an open space large enough for hay storage and a place to keep her buggy out of the weather, was perfect for her needs. Expecting to be too busy to care properly for the animal, she would seek the help of someone, perhaps a neighbor boy.

Following the initial newspaper write-up, an eager young lady with a notepad and well-sharpened pencil arrived, asking for an interview, to be printed up in a smaller but competing paper. Gwyneth happened to be sitting on her veranda sipping a cup of tea while she enjoyed the settling feeling that always came over her as she watched the sun sink behind the Sangre de Cristo Range. On this evening, she was visiting with Sarah Sampson, who had become a friend in the weeks since her banker husband had introduced them. The two women paused their conversation as they watched the young lady approach.

"Dr. Wycome? I don't mean to encroach unnecessarily on your private time. I'll leave if you say to. I've come in the evening because I've heard how busy you are during the daytime working hours. I'm with the Riverside News Group. You may have seen our paper. We specialize in matters of interest to the residents of this area of town. I'd like to ask you a few questions if you could spare a bit of time."

Chuckling inwardly, appreciating the girl's nervousness and comparing it to her own when she first stepped into that medical tent years ago, she answered, "I'll give you until this teacup is empty."

Understanding the metaphor and knowing this could be her one and only chance, the reporter settled into a half-seated position on the veranda railing and said, "Thank you. Please sip slowly."

Sarah Sampson, enjoying the freshness of the girl, laughed out loud. "You'd better talk fast. The doctor can put away a cup of tea in no time at all."

"Thank you. Anyway, I'm Brenda Crampton. As you could guess, I'm new to this, but I believe I understand what the readers would want to know, Dr. Wycome."

Gwyneth appreciated the girl's modesty and decided the imposition wasn't disturbing anything important.

Brenda wasn't quite professional in her work, but she was far from amateurish. Her questions were direct and short, inviting short answers, dealing with Gwyneth's background, history, and training. The final, and possibly contentious, question asked was, "You're very new to town, Doctor. In fact, it is being said that the young man with the burned and broken leg from the mill accident was your very first patient, brought here directly from the mill. Do you have an explanation for that?"

"The explanation seems fairly simple. And their decision wasn't to come directly here. Another well-known doctor was tried, but he was out of town on some medical emergency. The doctor's assistant mentioned that there was a new clinic out this way, and a passerby provided the directions. Simple.

"The story I heard from the nurse accompanying the wagon that brought young Noah here is that after the patient was first delivered to the other doctor, they thought of the hospital, which would be normal. But they felt the hospital, being new, wouldn't be prepared to deal with an injury of that severity, and that in any case, they were backed up with people waiting for medical help, some of them in dire straits. In the end, they decided to come here. It was a good decision for everyone involved, I'd dare to say."

"Thank you, Doctor, I'm sure our staff writer will be able to get the correct drift from my scribbles. I appreciate you allowing me into your life for these few minutes. Goodnight. And goodnight to you as well, Mrs. Sampson."

Surprised by the use of her name, Sarah said, "I'm surprised you know who I am, young lady. Do you live in the area? Perhaps I should know you through your parents?"

"No, I was raised in Denver, or at least nearby. But it's my job to know the important folks in the district. Good night again."

Leaving no room for more inquiries about herself, the reporter was down the steps and out of the yard with no time lost. Elevating the banker's wife to a person of importance, deserved or not, and Sarah's appreciation of that fact was not missed by Gwyneth. *It sometimes takes so little*, she thought.

# Chapter Nineteen

A CONSTANTLY PRESSING MATTER THAT ALL SMALL-town doctors, and sometimes even city doctors, faced was how to make a living. It had become expected at the time that a doctor would travel at their own time and expense, to some remote ranch or farm to aid in the delivery of a baby and drive away hours later with a single dollar in their pocket, or perhaps a freshly killed chicken, ready for the pot. And even that small bit of income was dependent upon the farmer having the dollar, or the chicken, to pay. Many did not. Her file of unpaid fees was becoming worrisome. She was able to cover her expenses without touching her banked capital, but it was an additional worry that the capital account was not growing. When the payment from the mill for Noah's care failed to arrive, she found the name of the assistant mill manager and sent him a note.

*Mr. Clayton Bonifare,*
*Assistant Manager, Western States Iron Mill*
*Pueblo, Colorado.*
*Dear Mr. Bonifare*

*Re: patient Noah Gainford*

*I am enclosing a duplicate of the invoice for medical treatment rendered to Mr. Noah Gainford, an employee of Western States Iron Mill.*

*This medical treatment was performed one month ago, successfully, I am pleased to report, but I have yet to receive payment. I am happy to remain at the service of the mill, although I would prefer that no further injuries will make my services necessary.*

*I would much appreciate it if you would arrange for payment in the very near future.*

*Thank you*

*Dr. Gwyneth Wycome*

TWO DAYS LATER, a buggy pulled to a stop outside the clinic door. It was a much fancier unit than the one Gwyneth had purchased. The showpiece, gloss-black harness, with its brass studs and chrome-plated buckles, would turn the eye and capture the attention as it was surely meant to do. The harnessed animal almost screamed aloud, quality and breeding, as it stood at alert. The well-dressed man stepping out of the conveyance lifted a cast-iron weight from the floor of the buggy. The weight was attached to the end of a long leather strap. The other end was fitted to the bit ring on the horse. The purpose, of course, was to prevent the horse from wandering while the driver was away.

Gwyneth was in the process of washing up after delivering another newborn. Sky, who was now in the clinic's full-time service, was removing the sheets and other cloths used in the birthing, dropping them into a tub of water to soak before washing. The young mother had been moved onto the bed in the long-term care room. That room hadn't been in use since Noah—her first patient in Pueblo, a full month before—had been in residence for several days before being sent to the hospital for recovery care. He was now at home on the ranch. Since then, the long-term care room had only been periodically used, seldom for one day or more.

It was Sky who heard the buggy crunch to a stop. Looking up, she whispered, "Doctor, you have a visitor. A very young and handsome visitor. I'm finished here. I'll tend to the mother and child while you see what the fellow wants. I expect whatever he wanted when he set out on his journey will change when he lays eyes on you."

Gwyneth swatted the young nurse on the backside with the towel. "Get yourself away. And mind your tongue."

"Yes, ma'am. Whatever you say, ma'am."

They were both smiling as Gwyneth went to answer the knock on the door. She said nothing as she looked at the man through the screened door. She hardly had time though, as the visitor inquired, "Dr. Wycome?"

Gwyneth pushed the door partway open before answering, "That would be me. What can I do for you, Sir?"

With his Stetson, not commonly worn in town, held in his hand and a big smile on his face, he said, "Just a few moments of your time, Doctor. I am not ill. I have not come for medical advice. Rather, I have come to discuss a communication received recently. Do you have time for that now, or should I make an appointment and come back?"

Sky was certainly correct in the image the man bore. Tall but not at all gangly, as so many tall men tended to be. Conversely, he had the broad shoulders and slimness of a rider. The well-tanned, handsome, clean-shaven face again said, *ranch*, or at least *rider*. His smile was such that it was first to attract attention, but underneath, Gwyneth detected a seriousness. Just how quickly that change could be made was a question.

"Clayton Bonifare, Doctor. I'm here on behalf of the mill. Would this be a convenient time to discuss your billing?"

"We have just now completed our work. So yes, I could spare a few minutes. But this is a medical clinic. For sanitary reasons, we don't welcome visitors. But if you would walk to the front of the house, I'll come through and we can talk on the veranda for a few minutes."

"Thank you, Doctor."

Easing into two white-painted wicker chairs, the two sat looking at each other for a long thirty seconds before Gwyneth spoke. And then the words the mill manager heard were far from what he expected.

"Mr. Bonifare, I like your choice in headgear. I often wear one very similar, myself. If you are going to insist on keeping yours on, I will be forced to get mine. Just to level the playing field, you understand."

She found herself wondering if this handsome, imposing man used the horse, the buggy, his expensive clothing, and the hat, along with his somewhat crooked smile, to intimidate. If so, he would leave disappointed. It wasn't about to work on her. She had seen many a handsome man flaunting what they thought of as their best self. She was well ahead on that game. But what she could do, was leave the next move to her visitor. If the medical invoice was to be negotiation by intimidation, let the game begin. She steadied herself and let her eyes bore directly into his, never flinching. Not speaking. In a test of forcefulness, she would bet her ammunition against his anytime. As she expected, the mini contest was no challenge.

Lifting his hat off and laying it on the floor beside him, brim upward, he said, "Doctor, the mill is not in the habit of paying for the medical services for our employees. Now, the news of the employee's recovery and the good work you did has reached my ears. I, and the other mill management team, are grateful to you and happy for the injured man, but—"

Gwyneth butted in with, "The injured man has a name, Mr. Bonifare. Noah Gainford. He is not a number on a payroll sheet, nor is he some easily expendable, miscellaneous stranger. He is a rancher's son whose life was changed permanently because of a mistake made in your mill. Let's think of him that way. Now, Mr. Bonifare, please proceed."

The mill manager shuffled his feet and squirmed a bit on the padded bottom of the chair, looking for a more comfortable position, or perhaps just a few seconds to gather his thoughts.

"It isn't customary, Doctor—"

"Perhaps the custom needs changing."

"It's not possible, Doctor. It would mean endless claims on the company."

"Perhaps you need to aim for fewer injuries, leading to fewer claims. But in the meantime, these workers need at least your protection, if not more. Your wages are modest, and the mill is very busy. I'm sure the company can afford a medical bill now and then."

Clayton Bonifare thought he would try a different approach. Perhaps a more personal approach. It was a mistake.

"Dr. Wycome, no matter what you or I think, the company has no plans to change working policy. The invoiced amount is not overly large, I'm sure any rancher with even modest success could cover the cost for his loved son. But bringing the matter to the personal, I fully understand that your clinic has expenses that must be covered. If it is just a matter of money until you get established in town, I could cover the tab myself..."

Clayton Bonifare paused as Gwyneth started speaking, but he was tiring of the interruptions.

"Mr. Bonifare, you insult me and my clinic. We are doing as well as we expected to do for a new enterprise. My expenses are covered. And as far as that goes, I'd be surprised if I don't have more personal money in the bank than you do.

"Let me tell you what I see facing me in the other chair. A thirty-five-ish, handsome man intent on making a mark on the community. But I also see a rancher's son who did well in a one-room schoolhouse and was encouraged by his teacher to seek further education. Your parents scratched and scrambled to dig up the tuition and ended up each year selling off a few calves to cover your costs. I know the story all too well. It is common in the ranching country. I have also ranched, starting from nothing. But when I went to medical school, I had ample funding and more. I still have most of it. I would not accept your personal money in any circumstances. Please don't demean either me or yourself with such an offer ever again. But I still want my invoice paid, and I intend to have it. From the mill. Are we clear, Clayton Bonifare?"

"Clear, Doctor. And setting all the rest aside, I would love to hear your story. But that would mean escorting you to a lazy dinner some evening, where we are in no rush. Please think on that."

With that, and leaving no time for a response, he rose, carefully placed his hat on the way he liked it, and eased down the stairs. Without looking back, he was gone. She sat long enough to hear the gelding clip-clop out the back way and down the alley.

NOTHING WAS HEARD from the mill or from Clayton Bonifare for the next week.

In the meantime, the clinic was becoming very demanding of Gwyneth's time, with several calls each day, most for minor ailments but also for periodic surgeries or serious illnesses. Gwyneth was often deep in study of the latest medical journals as well as her older college textbooks, reassuring herself on the most recent medical discoveries and medicines. As most evenings turned into night, Gwyneth was sitting in her wicker chair, her book on her lap, yawning and fighting off sleep.

The clinic was busy enough that it was tempting to concentrate on the needs of Pueblo and push her original plan into the background. But in all her life, that had never been her style. Several times in the past, she had been forced to remind Trent what their original goal had been when they headed west. In their marriage as well as in ranching matters, Trent was the dreamer, she was the feet firmly planted on the ground. Trent never stopped planning. That was his nature. His problem, as it was with his parents, was that he may slip into the temptation to turn his planning in a new direction every once in a while. Gwyneth held the reins loosely when possible but would pull back on the bit when necessary, always being careful to apply enough pressure to get Trent's attention without yanking on the bit, so to speak.

Now, she reminded herself that to follow through on her original plan, she would either have to limit her attendance at the clinic or somehow find another doctor, or at least an additional competent nurse to work alongside her and Sky in the clinic. She promised herself that she could discipline her mind well enough that she could attend to the current demands while keeping the bigger goal at arm's length, but not lost totally.

Having decided that, she closed her journal and climbed the stairs to bed.

# Chapter Twenty

Gwyneth, with the help of Sarah Sampson, had found a young man named Spike, a name he chose not to explain, who was prepared to care for Gwyneth's horse, as well as run some errands for the clinic from time to time. In the weeks since Clayton Bonifare had visited in response to the medical costs incurred on behalf of Noah Gainford, there had been two more injured men brought in from the mill. Their injuries did not compare to those that Noah would suffer through for most of his life, and there were no molten iron burns, but their treatments all took time and medical supplies, which were difficult to replace. Gwyneth had the bills ready, neatly written and placed in a sealed envelope, for the next time Spike made himself available.

"Spike, take these to the mill. You will see the name Clayton Bonifare, assistant mill manager, on the envelope. Be sure to leave the envelope with Mr. Bonifare and with no one else."

She had been tempted to have Spike mention that she was still waiting for a response to the first billing and that she was expecting payment forthwith. But knowing the sometimes-unwise enthusiasm of the young man, and fearing what all he might say, she opted for temporary silence on the subject of the previous bill.

Adding to the several mysteries surrounding Spike, he had somehow become the proud owner of a bicycle, one of the few to be seen in Pueblo. To the handlebars of the bicycle, he had attached an old, cast-off saddle bag. He carefully placed Gwyneth's envelope inside, buckled the straps, and swung aboard. Mystified by the bicycle and its workings, Gwyneth and nurse Sky Whitely watched as Spike peddled down the driveway, swung onto the road, and disappeared.

"I think I'll stick to my horse," commented Gwyneth. Sky just nodded and returned to her patient.

AT THE MILL, Spike had a bit of trouble getting the attention of Mr. Bonifare, whose time and presence were carefully protected by a middle-aged woman stationed at the strategic doorway while displaying staunch determination and an officious attitude. But since Spike was no respecter of persons, his stubbornness outlived that of the guardian. But rather than being let into the office, Mr. Bonifare was fetched and led to the delivery boy.

"Envelope for you, sir, and for no one else. I was told that most emphatic, sir. Thank you, sir."

Spike turned to leave but was called back. Having seen the return name on the envelope, Clayton said, "Wait just a moment, please. I'll send a note back with you."

SPIKE RODE his bicycle to the rear door of the clinic, leaned the handlebars against the window and knocked lightly. "Answer back to you from the mill, Doctor."

"Thank you, Spike. Now I have a second small chore I

would appreciate you handling. Go to the train station and get me a schedule for the train west, specifically, to Bessie Creek. Schedules there and return, along with the fares. And Spike, please don't lean your bicycle against the glass. The last thing we need is a broken window."

Again, she watched the mysterious conveyance as Spike disappeared into the distance. As if to demonstrate his mastery of the two-wheeled implement, Spike removed his hands from the curved pipe handlebars that allowed him to control the direction of travel, leaned back on the seat, and held his hands out to each side, as if to purposely draw attention to this magical feat.

*I'll have that young man as a patient sooner or later. Broken bones are the least he could expect.*

Re-entering the clinic, Gwyneth went first to the recovery room to check on Sky's patient, a very young girl who had just delivered her first child the day before. The patient was sleeping. Sky was seated in the rocking chair Gwyneth had purchased for the comfort of the recovering patients, cuddling the baby. Her eyes were closed while a dreamy look had overtaken her face. Looking at the diligent young nurse, privately, Gwyneth thought, *I truly hope life returns your dreams, young lady.*

Gwyneth was beyond being shocked at the early age of many marriages on the western frontier, and the resiliency of the girls barely out of childhood themselves who became mothers. Within one week, this girl would be back on the ranch or farm, still recovering, feeding her baby, and doing all the necessary chores that kept a country home moving forward. If she was very fortunate, she may have a sister or friend who could attend her for a while to carry some of the load. But many were alone, with the closest neighbor miles away, while simply trying to make a life with her often not much older husband.

That neither really understood much about the facts of ranch life was simply accepted as the way it was. They would learn as all others did, by occasionally listening to a parent, but otherwise plowing through the challenges of each day, and correcting their mistakes as opportunity allowed. That so many survived to raise great families and build profitable ranches was a tribute to their resiliency and to their faith in God.

Thinking on these things wasn't good therapy for Gwyneth. Her ruminating unfailingly led her to reminisce on her own marriage, as good and successful as it had been, failing in only one major matter: her inability to deliver a child. Both she and Trent had assured each other of their lasting love and that they were both content with what was to be. Neither were being totally honest on the subject. Now, years later, she found herself struggling against a moment or two of depression after those thoughts flitted through her mind. Stern personal discipline was required for her to shove the thoughts aside and apply herself to the medical needs of others.

Some small sound from outside caused Sky to open her eyes. She looked up at the doctor and smiled. "I wasn't asleep. It's kind of like an awake dream. Kind of like planning and hoping, I guess."

Ignoring the temptation to enter into that thought with Sky, Gwyneth simply asked, "Everything all right here?"

"Couldn't be better."

With that assurance, Gwyneth returned to the main room and to the small writing desk she had tucked into one corner. She eased into the ladderback chair and opened the envelope from Clayton Bonifare. There were two separated pages inside. The first her fingers grasped and retrieved was a formal letter from the mill.

*Western States Iron Mill*

*Pueblo, Colorado.*

*Attn: Dr. G. M. Wycome*

*Wycome Medical Clinic*

*Dear Dr. Wycome*

*Re: Billing for medical expenses.*

*While the Western States Iron Mill recognises no negligence or direct responsibly for the unfortunate injury to one of the mill workers, one Noah Gainford, who, I am led to understand, received excellent treatment at your medical clinic, it has been decided to honor your bill for services in this single incident. Enclosed, please find a company check to cover your costs.*

*It would not be considered in the company's interest to accept cost or blame for all incidents occurring within company property, however, it is also not within company interest to enter into a lengthy dispute. Please consider this payment as a single incident. In future, the company will consider it as policy to cover realistic costs for injuries reasonably considered as preventable accidents.*

*Please note, the company recognises no liability where the injury is clearly a result of carelessness on the part of the injured individual.*

*Yours truly*
*C. J. Benton*
*Manager,* Western States Iron Mill
*Pueblo, Colorado*
*PS: My wife and I hope you are enjoying the house.*

GWYNETH LAID the letter on the desk with some feeling of satisfaction. Only time would tell if the company would follow through on this nascent commitment to employee safety and care.

When she removed the second letter, a check fell out with it. She studied the amount, comparing it favorably, and from memory, with the billed costs. Smiling, she nodded, thinking, *one step at a time, men, one step at a time.*

The note from the company had been hacked out on one of the new writing machines. Although there was no doubt that the machines, sometimes referred to as *typewriters*, held promise, increasing correspondence production in offices and clearing away the scribbles that represent so many writers, there was still a long way to go before that ideal was reached. The next note, a personal missive from Clayton Bonifare, was handwritten in a beautiful scroll. For a rancher's son, the man showed a fine hand with a pen. The dated note was marked *personal and private.*

*My dear Dr. Wycome*

*I wish to invite, and escort you, to an evening of fine dining. There is a restaurant in the downtown area, strangely named Southern Belle, that offers the best menu in town. It would be my pleasure to arrive at your home at six PM, Wednesday next. Barring a medical emergency that would demand your time and expertise, we could expect to be seated at the Belle, as folks are calling it, by 6:30 PM. I believe I could promise to return you safely to your home by 9:00 that evening. If this arrangement meets with your approval, I will look forward to a more than satisfactory dinner, pleasant conversation with a most charming and lovely lady, and come from the evening wiser and better for having heard something of your travels and growth into the medical profession. Please respond with a note marked private, directed to me personally.*

*Assuming your positive response, I look forward to an evening together.*

*Best wishes*

*Clayton*

SHE LAID the invitation down and then picked it up again. Her last experience with a dinner date turned out to include the man and his parents attending an opera showcasing music she hated. That the experience didn't create any long-lasting ill will had more to do with the frantic but also somewhat humorous incidents surrounding the carriage ride home, and her professional respect for Dr. Cliff Rickhart, plus the fact that, at the time, the two would still have to work together. She most certainly had no desire for another such evening.

Gwyneth stepped to the doorway of the recovery room to advice Sky that she would be taking a cup of coffee on the veranda if she was needed. Seated comfortably on the wicker chair, she leaned back and lifted her feet to the small stool. She closed her eyes and unerringly lifted the cup, with a whisp of steam rising from it to her mouth. The usual midday drink in the clinic was tea. But during her ranching years, she had gone without the English favorite for many months at a time, while she had learned to love the strong, somewhat bitter taste of coffee made over an open fire. The cowboys would have no part of tea drinking, so she found it easier to bend to their demands than make a fuss over such a simple matter.

She savored the first mouthful, swishing it through her teeth and wondering what anyone who saw might think of her actions. Hoping for clarity of thought, she concentrated on the letter she held in her hand. Her strong mind had memorized the few words it contained without really meaning to.

She admitted to herself that she was often lonely. The evenings were long and the nights longer. Even with the long, hard hours of work on the ranch, she and Trent had found an abundance of time to simply enjoy one another. It was not unusual for the two of them to watch the sun disappear behind the hills with neither of them speaking for an hour or more. There was an understanding and an intimacy between them that couldn't be duplicated with anyone but a spouse. Was she ready for a serious friendship that could easily turn into courting and then marriage? She didn't really think so, but with the right circumstances, she may surprise herself.

Was Clayton Bonifare the one who could turn her head in the direction of matrimony? She wasn't even sure she would know how to make the judgment. She could say yes to the invitation and begin the *finding-out* process. Or she could refuse the offer and spend the next while wondering at her wisdom, or the lack of such.

Always having been one who could concentrate on a single matter, pushing all else aside for the moment, she had forgotten the coffee. Her finger slacked off on the cup handle and the mug slipped sideways, splashing hot coffee onto her dress and quickly soaking through to her upper leg. She jumped from the pain of the slightly scalded flesh while a bit of a yelp escaped her lips. Her startled jump further moved the mug, with the result that even more coffee found its target. Coming back to her senses, she sat bolt upright, brushing the liquid off her skirt onto the floor of the veranda. She changed her dress every day, so there was no real loss that way, but, like the cowboys she had been so familiar with would have said, the small incident was a waste of perfectly good coffee. With a smile and remembering her original purpose was to enjoy a cup of coffee, she made a quick trip into the kitchen, topped up the cup from the still steaming pot and returned to her wicker chair.

With the refreshed and refilled cup resting on the flat arm of the wicker chair, she asked herself, *All right, now where was I?* The result of her interrupted thinking was that she returned to the corner desk in the clinic and wrote out a note.

*My dear Mr. Bonifare*

*I am in receipt of your invitation to dinner. Although admitting some hesitancy, I find your invitation acceptable. If it should come that I am tied up in medical matters, I will try to send the courier with that information in time to save you an unnecessary trip to my house.*

*Trusting that our goals for the evening are compatible, I look forward to the occasion.*

*Gwyneth Wycome*

SHE HAD JUST FINISHED LICKING the glue strip to seal the envelope when Spike rolled into the yard. He rapped twice on the screen door while also almost shouting, "Doctor, you to home?"

Always surprised at the young man's energy and unpredictable use of the English language, Gwyneth was smiling just a bit when she pushed the door open. "You have something for me, Spike?"

"Indeed, I have, Doctor. Here are both the schedules and the rates of fares for almost anywhere you might want to go. Just like you was hon'n to have. Is there anything else I can do for you before I call 'er'er quits for this here day?"

"Yes, Spike. I have no idea how difficult peddling that contraption is, but if you can manage one more ride, I'd have you deliver this envelope back to the mill. It is to be put directly into Mr. Clayton Bonifare's hand. I doubt there will be anything more coming from the mill, so when the envelope is delivered, I will ask no more of you today. Thanks for doing all of this."

# Chapter Twenty-One

THE DINNER DATE WITH CLAYTON BONIFARE STARTED out in fine style. Clayton arrived promptly on time. His gloss-black buggy shone like the new moon. The horse, with its brass-studded harness, seemed to prance in delight of his own magnificence. Clayton himself was decked out in a broadcloth, three-piece suit and tie. He wore his Stetson, as usual, with, perhaps, a more than usual jaunty angle. His riding boots came near to outpacing the remainder of his appearance with a brushed gloss of their own. His appearance screamed *wealthy rancher*, far more than *mill manager*.

His light rap on the front door wasn't answered for a few moments, but finally Gwyneth appeared. Her dress for the evening matched, or perhaps even outshone, that of her escort.

Split riding skirts had become the norm on the ranches and the small towns, but in the big cities were seldom seen. But with the help and advice of Bea Brodrick, her special friend, back in Chicago, Gwyneth had purchased a complete wardrobe. Bea insisted, *"You're a beautiful and mature, up-and-coming doctor. You'll be the talk of the town wherever you go. You must look the part. You'll notice too that showing yourself to be the capable and knowing person I know you to be will weed out many of the least honorable of men. Those types can't cope with female beauty and competence. That's a combination all too unfamiliar in this world. Now let's get you decked out like you deserve to be."*

As Gwyneth had luxuriated in her bath at the end of the working day, she planned it all, attempting to remember Bea's advice. First, the light mauve split skirt—never yet worn, with its soft folds cinched at the waist by the tanned leather belt, with the brass filigree buckle catching flecks of the restaurant's lighting. She would pair it with the white blouse, delicately laced at the front, its bodice cut gracefully low, with the standing collar, and sleeves that narrowed into embroidered lace at the cuffs. Over it all, she would wear her sage green jacket, a well-tailored touch which could be taken off at the restaurant or left in place, as she wished at the time.

As had become her standard practice, she had worked a small pocket into the split skirt to hold and hide her .32.

Her seldom-worn riding boots and her off-white Stetson would complete the ensemble. Of course, given the vagaries of the weather, she would cover it all with her lightweight black cape.

Before she responded to the rap on the door, she hesitated. Perhaps it was a bit of vanity. More likely, it was wondering. Was she ready for an evening with a handsome man? She knew she was dressed for Chicago. Was she also dressed for Pueblo?

Leaving Clayton waiting at the door for just a moment, Gwyneth stepped before the mirror built into the oak coat rack near the front entry. A quick glance told her she needed one more thing to set the tone off perfectly. To bring a contrast to her white blouse and her white Stetson. But what she needed couldn't be bought. Her mind flashed back to her riding, ranching days, and the pleasant tan her skin took on with the many hours in the sun. She hadn't spent significant time in the sun in over five years. Her tan was long gone, her skin as white as any skin was likely to be. She adopted an *oh well* look and stepped away from the mirror, reaching for the brass knob.

When she appeared in the doorway, with one hand still on the latch, Clayton had taken a quick look and then a single step back, staring in awe.

"Young lady, you are absolutely glowing this evening. Stunning. What a welcome sight for this mortal man."

Gwyneth smiled but didn't respond. She still held a couple of doubts about the evening, but it was too late to voice them now. "I am ready if you are."

"Indeed, I am ready, charming Doctor. Or perhaps we should set aside our vocations for this evening. It will be just the two of us, ordinary folks looking forward to a fine evening together. And I will do my best to hide the fact that I am overwhelmed. This way, my dear."

With that, he offered his elbow, which she hesitantly took, and they eased down the stairs and out to the waiting buggy. As Clayton had predicted, the drive to the restaurant took a little under half an hour. By the time Clayton had stepped down and passed the reins to the waiting horse handler, the concierge had helped Gwyneth to the ground. Then, together they followed the concierge through the big front door and to their reserved table. Their location was a bit isolated along the inner wall, just a few feet from the slowly burning fireplace.

The last act for the concierge was to receive Gwyneth's cape and Clayton's hat, taking them to the coat room. Gwyneth saw no reason to remove her hat. Most of the women in the room were wearing hats of some sort.

Clayton then stepped forward to assist his guest to her chair. Gwyneth, on the one hand, relished all the fussing, but on the other hand, she was grinning inside, thinking how foolish and unnecessary it all was for a self-assured woman who had ridden half-broke horses, chased cattle over much of the country, assisted in Civil War medical tents, and was now a surgeon herself. In truth, she needed no help. But she wasn't about to refuse it. She hadn't been doted on for several years. She would savor the moment. Finally, through with the formalities of the grand entry and the seating, Gwyneth was free to look around the room. She couldn't help noticing that a good many eyes were turned their way. She pretended not to notice. But Clayton didn't even pretend.

"I suppose politeness prevents you from standing and taking a bow, but if you were to do that, you'd receive a standing ovation."

"I'm afraid I may have misjudged. I'm fascinated by the grand dresses these ladies are wearing. And it's a good guess that none of them arrived wearing a Stetson. I hope I haven't embarrassed you."

"Embarrassed? Why, my dear Gwyneth. Every lady in the room is envying you. Each and every one is wishing they had the freedom to wear clothing of their personal choice and had the natural glamourr not to just make it look so outstanding, but to do it all with such grace. And the men? Well, yes, the men. Not just a few of them will be answering for their interest when they're alone with their wives at home."

The waiter arrived, setting a lit, globe-topped candlestick on the table and offering wine. Gwyneth turned down the wine, asking instead for a glass of water. Somewhat surprised, Clayton followed suit. They picked up their menus and for the next few moments sat in silence, allowing the offerings to tempt their palates. Clayton broke the silence with, "Do you see anything of interest?"

"It's all of interest, except the fish, but I suppose I should really restrict myself to a single choice."

"Or perhaps two at the very most," answered Clayton, with a smile.

Laying the menu back onto the table as the waiter approached, Gwyneth said, "We had a cook one time on the ranch who was a master at doing beef ribs. Both sweet and tangy at the same time. Crisp on the outside while retaining a juicy interior. Even talking about them, I can taste them. But I won't order them here. To really enjoy ribs, you need to be sitting around a campfire at the end of a workday with a clean cloth ready to wipe your face and fingers continually. There is nothing delicate in enjoying a feed of ribs. When it comes to Victorian manners, everything is set aside. Ribs are eaten as finger food, chewing the meat delicacy right off the bone. And throwing the cleaned off bones into the fire, where the flames would burn up the last of the fat and gristle, causing the most wonderful aroma to rise and waft over the campsite. No, a restaurant, no matter how wonderful, cannot do justice to a feeding of beef ribs.

"It helps if the sun has hidden itself behind the hills and most of the day's light has eased into eternity, at least to the point where the dimness will hide the lack of delicacy. I don't think that's the order of the day here."

She smiled up at the waiter, "I'll stick with the roast beef and a small baked potato. That's a never-go-wrong meal."

The waiter nodded and smiled. Whispering, he said, "Your description of ribs should be printed on our menu. Perhaps management could build a campfire in the side yard."

Gwyneth simply returned his smile.

Clayton listened while still scanning the choices. Finally saying, "And I believe I would enjoy that mustard-glazed pork tenderloin."

With the waiter gone it was time to break the conversation trend and broach a more meaningful subject. Clayton was fearful of jumping right into personal matters, so he simply asked, "Where are you from originally, Gwyneth?"

The Southern Belle took great pride in their food preparation, leaving lots of time for casual conversation while the chef worked his slow magic. To stave off the diner's initial cravings, the waiter brought a small loaf of warm sourdough bread along with a dish of hand-churned butter. As they talked, the bread slowly disappeared. Gwyneth told about her family, losing her father, and the resultant poverty. She talked briefly about her determination to serve in the war effort. Clayton shuddered as she talked about sights and sounds that she had finally, sadly, gotten used to. After the telling of her story brought the tale to placing herself with the doctor in the small Kansas trail town, she managed to turn the conversation to Clayton.

"Your turn, Clayton."

"Yes. I suppose it is. Well, to deal first with your spontaneous speculation about my past, at our first meeting, I will say that you were only partly correct."

Gwyneth jumped in with, "That was cruel of me. I was annoyed at your offering me money, but that doesn't excuse my bad manners. Not really it doesn't. Please forgive me."

"Nothing to forgive, I assure you. I was actually enthralled by your forcefulness. And I took no offense at anything you said. But to elaborate. I am not ranch-raised, although I spent my summers on a ranch starting when I was ten years old until I went to college. I put up a lot of hay, mucked a lot of horse stalls, and rode a lot of miles on the range after I was a bit older. No, I am a product of a Denver upbringing. My father was a businessman before he was hired by the railway to take on the position as area superintendent. He wanted me to attend college. I did and enjoyed it. The college is just up north a few miles in Colorado Springs. So my family is quite close, handy for get-togethers at Christmas and such.

"In the event that you are counting times and dates, I will answer your unasked question and say that when my folks arrived in Colorado, Auraria, the original name of the settlement, had just adopted the name Denver. That was in 1859. I was just growing into long pants and was eager to face the world. My father saw to it that I got my chance on that ranch I mentioned. Now, don't mistake what we know as ranches today with that first pioneer start I worked on.

"A man named Webley came to the conclusion that miners would be wanting to eat meat, and what better opportunity could there be than providing beef for that purpose. He drove a small herd of scrubs up from New Mexico, losing over half along the way to Indians and rough country. But he somehow stuck it out and established himself. It's too bad men like Webley never get their names in the history books. And all the while that was going on, the entire west was exploding with growth, including Colorado, and Denver specifically.

"I have no idea how many were hammering rock to extract the hard-won gold, but it was certainly in the thousands. And more thousands in the settlements working with hammer and saw to put together the first crude buildings. And now, so few years later, we live in an established west such as the true pioneers could not have imagined, although many of them are still alive to enjoy their retirements in the many towns of the west.

"My father began a mining supply store, and did well, considering the times and the scarcity of ready cash, but when the railroad came calling with more money than he was making in the store, he sold out and went to work. He's still at it."

Clayton and Gwyneth were both intelligent, informed, and curious people. Their conversation was probing and yet not overly personal. When the food arrived, the talk slowed but did not come to a complete halt. By the end of the meal, after dessert and coffee, they had probed and pushed, finding common ground on some subjects and less on others. Somehow, whether by design or not, Gwyneth had not mentioned her marriage. She referred to *I* and *we* in such a way as to leave the interpretation open to being understood as friends and hired cowboys. Clayton was most interested in her relationship with Daniel and Night Light.

"Are you telling me, Gwyneth, that you found the Indian girl's knowledge of native herbs and roots to be effective in the treatment of medical issues?"

"Most certainly. Night Light didn't have the knowledge her elders would possess, but she knew more than I will ever know. There's still a lot of room for modern medicine, of course, but I would never shy away from using native knowledge if opportunity and circumstances allowed. As an example, the impact Night Light's sweat tent had on a baby's pneumonia was nothing short of astounding."

"Perhaps you should write a pamphlet on the subject. Others with similar experience could add to the store of knowledge, and before you know it, you would have a book for publishing."

"Possibly. But I'm to the point where I have no more hours to work, let alone write a book. I'm thinking of trying to find another nurse and, hopefully, another doctor. I've written to a contact in Chicago, a friend and a well-qualified nurse, hoping she'll come and join me."

Clayton hesitated about his next comment, fearful that it would change the tenor of the evening, but finally said, "I hope you succeed beyond your fondest wishes. There is no doubt that you, yourself, and your knowledge are the drawing cards, but your name really got out to the public with that article in the Pioneer News, following on the heels of the Riverside News Group piece."

"What article was that, and what is the Pioneer News?"

"You didn't see it?"

"No. Tell me about it."

"There are several community papers in Pueblo, as I'm sure you already know. The Pioneer News, with just a small press with limited ability to print in volume. They concentrate their coverage and distribution in the area around the mill. They take special interest in matters regarding the mill. They wrote up the story of the young man with the broken leg, Noah I believe his name is. They wrote about the near magic of your treatment and then made a big splash about how the mill was refusing to cover the costs. They find themselves altogether too interested in all things mill, in my opinion."

"Let me assure you, Clayton, I had nothing at all to do with that. I have never heard of them before and most certainly have not spoken to them, or anyone else, about my private business.

If Mr. Benton paid me just to get the paper off his back, I am most disappointed, to the degree that I'm not sure I will accept any further referrals from the mill. And as for this newspaper knowing about the difficulty in collecting my account, I have no idea about that. Are you sure you don't have a leak within your organization?"

While Clayton thought about his next words, he appeared to be studying the tabletop, wringing his hands and shaking his head just a bit, as if he was talking to himself. Finally looked directly into Gwyneth's eyes. "I am so sorry I brought that up. It's all the truth, but my timing could use some work. Please don't put a wall between yourself and the mill, or between yourself and me. There are two things happening that I believe you will approve of. The first is that Mr. Benton is very impressed with your work. He received a letter a few days ago from Noah's parents singing your praises and thanking the company for covering the costs. I have to assume he was of the opinion that payment would naturally come from the company."

Gwyneth, also feeling that the evening was ending on an awkward note but having no idea how to revert to the former conversations, said, "If he assumed that, it would not be from anything I ever said. We didn't talk about payment. In any case, Noah was in no condition to even consider the matter when he was transferred home."

"Well, we have a series of assumptions, it would appear. But no matter the course of events and the bumps in the road, it is all for the better. The company's board have taken the position that medical costs will be covered where the mill is clearly at fault. So that's a step toward good business, if not compassion."

It was Gwyneth's turn to be silent, only she studied her escort as she held her silence. Finally, she said, "I believe I would like to go home now."

~

THE BUGGY RIDE toward Gwyneth's home was silent for the first few minutes. Gwyneth then brought up a totally unrelated topic.

"I haven't seen anything to particularly worry me since my arrival in Pueblo, and perhaps I'm comparing unjustly with Chicago, but I'm not convinced these streets are completely safe. Do you not carry a weapon of any sort? I couldn't see one on you. Your shirt and suit are too snug to conceal anything of any size."

"Bend over just a bit and reach under the seat."

Gwyneth did as directed and felt the butt end of a rifle. She slid her hand along the wood until she came to the action. Straightening up, she at last smiled. Her face was just barely visible in the darkness of the late evening. "I admire the ingenuity. But how long does it take to release it from whatever you have binding it to the seat?"

"It's in a simple clip. Just enough to keep it from falling out. I can have it in my hand in a second or two. We wouldn't want to be totally without protection, would we?"

Gwyneth reached under the cape and into the little pocket and pulled out her .32. "We would never be totally unarmed."

Clayton shrank back just a bit. "Whoa. Where did that come from?"

"I am never without it. You can't tell when some fella might need to have the true path of life explained to him." With that, she laughed just a bit and returned the weapon to its hiding place.

The remaining few minutes were taken in silence. The rig turned onto Gwyneth's Street and Clayton swung into the driveway, calling for the horse to stop. He then turned just a bit to his right and said, "Gwyneth, I have never before enjoyed an evening such as I enjoyed this one. Thank you for making it so. And please forgive me for bringing up a subject that would have been best left for another time."

Gwyneth slid to the side of the seat and made motions to

step down. Clayton hurried to her side and held out his hand. She took it as she had done earlier, and together, they walked to the door. The veranda lantern had been lit. She put the key to the door and opened it just a bit. "Good night, Clayton. I enjoyed the meal and the company. Thanks for thinking of it all. Now I have to check on my patient and her newborn. Good night."

"Good night, Gwyneth. I enjoyed the evening also."

# Chapter Twenty-Two

GWYNETH SPREAD THE RAILWAY SCHEDULE ON HER desk and leaned close to make out the fine print. Jotting times on a slip of paper at her side, she confirmed that she could ride the rails to Bessie Creek in the morning, have time to look the town over, and ride back to Pueblo that same afternoon. Her preference though, was to find the stage still running. She found little point in traveling to Bessie Creek when the only people she knew in the territory were south of the village, in and around what was once her own Mirrored W, now the B4 belonging to Billy Wilmore, and the Cameron Ranch, the B/C.

There had been little need for the stage in earlier times, but somehow the owners justified its continuance. Perhaps there had been enough growth to keep it going. Or perhaps it had been extended into New Mexico. Gwyneth had never been that far south she had no idea whether there could be justification for the longer route. She wished to see what had become of the Mirrored W Ranch and what Billy Wilmore had done with it. But her main purpose was to ride up to the B/C Ranch and have a visit with Ty, Betty, and the Cameron family. With the loss of Cameron himself, there was sure to be major changes on all the ranches and in the families in recent years. Of course, she was curious about Daniel and Night Light too.

It was Thursday afternoon, one of those rare days with no patients to care for. She could take Friday, and perhaps Saturday and Sunday as well, to make a visit. She would ask Sky to sit in for the weekend, even sleep over in the recovery room. Sky was a good nurse. She could deal with simple matters and send more serious cases off to the hospital.

She had heard Spike shouting and laughing with someone in a neighbor's yard not fifteen minutes before. Hoping he was still there, working around the horse and stable, she headed that way. He was there, although she couldn't see him. She followed the loud singing. Spike, a young man of many mysteries, seemed to have memorized every campfire song ever written and a few others she had never heard of. He really wasn't much of a singer, but if he knew that, he didn't let it bother him. She stood quietly at the stable door until something caused the young man to lift his head from the horse and grin into the silence that quickly fell upon them. He laid his hand, still gripping the curry brush, on the rump of the gelding and said, "What kin I do fer ya?"

"You can take this money and ride down to the rail station. Purchase me a ticket to Bessie Creek on the morning train tomorrow. That horse hasn't had enough exercise lately. Perhaps you should saddle him and ride down to the station, rather than taking your bicycle. And ask the teller if he knows anything about the stage from Bessie Creek south. There's no rush. You could take the gelding out for a good run if you wished. But get the ticket first."

In Spike's favor was the fact that he was totally dependable. And he didn't waste time with foolish questions. It was as if a request from Gwyneth was an order not to be questioned or disobeyed.

~

THE RIDE to Bessie Creek the next morning was not long, but every mile of it seemed to bring back a mix of memories for Gwyneth, some positive, some that sent a chill down her spine. That the ranchers, including the Mirrored W, were introduced to the southern access into the valley, meaning they never again had to fight the narrow, boulder-strewn trail along the river, made the valley prosper. And when the rails were pushed through and Bessie Creek struggled up from the unforgiving ground, the struggles of ranching eased even more.

Gwyneth's single unfortunate memory was of the drunken man who used his fists on her and Helen. Abe had turned the tables on the fella, but probably went too far, whipping the man with the double of a rope. It was only Helen grabbing her husband's arm, demanding he stop, that saved the man's life. As a doctor, Gwyneth couldn't help wondering what had become of him, and the dreadful rope scars he was sure to have, as she did with so many patients that had filtered through her life, never to be seen again.

Bessie Creek hadn't really grown, not to speak of anyway, but it seemed to have settled in. Most of the ramshackle, canvas-roofed shacks had been replaced by more sturdy, better buildings along Main Street. And some outlying temporary shelters had given way to sawn lumber houses, small, but still houses.

With no cares troubling her on this first day without responsibilities since she had opened the clinic, she was about to step into the stage office when a man walking toward her stopped in his tracks upon seeing her. Startling everyone around, he hollered, "You. It's you. The nurse that ruined my wife, making stupid mistakes so's we couldn't have more family. I thought you had snuck away in shame, but here you are. Whose life are you set to ruin this day, woman?"

Gwyneth had no idea what to say or do. She finally blurted out, "Who are you, sir? Do I know you?"

At least a dozen people had stopped what they were doing,

focusing themselves on the dispute. Gwyneth saw no one she recognized.

"Know me? You should know me all right. I was right there when you were doing your evil work. Or perhaps you do such as that so often you can't remember all you done."

"Explain yourself, sir. Tell me your name and what this is all about."

"Names Buck Quinlan. Wife is Addy Quinlan."

"And how might I have known you, Mr. Quinlan?"

"Are you so forgetful you can't remember all what you done?"

"Sir, I have treated hundreds of patients, first as a nurse and now as a qualified doctor. No one could remember all the names. But I'll remember the incident if you will only refresh my memory."

Just at that time, a young woman holding the hand of a perhaps six-or seven-year-old boy stepped between Gwyneth and the shouting man.

"Hush now, Buck. You're talking nonsense, as you always have on this subject."

Turning back to Gwyneth, she smiled and said, "It's good to see you again, Doctor. To remind you, the midwife trying to help me bring this fine young man into the world sent for you. Fortunately, someone found you in town. What you did, no midwife could do. Plainly spoken, you saved me and my child. And this is him standing tall and strong, with both our hearts full of gratitude for your work. What upsets Buck so is that we have had no additional children. Somehow, he blames you. Talks about it constantly."

Gwyneth took the woman's hand and reached for her husband's, but he pulled it back. Still, she directed her words to him. "Sir, when I arrived, Addy was alive but barely, and not conscious at all. The midwives were wonderful support, having everything prepared. Rightly, Addy should not have survived. She and the child were under severe distress. And that the child lived to become a young man you can be proud of is an act of God. There was really little I could do, but what was done was clearly adequate. In the process, your Addy suffered terribly. And let me assure you, I did nothing that would have interfered with her fertility. I understand your frustration, but not your anger. Instead of being thankful for what you have, you're angry because you don't have more. And blaming me in the process. I reject your accusation. Now, if you will excuse me, I have things to do."

Gwyneth had learned long since that if she allowed accusations to smolder or grow, there was real danger of upsetting the doctor-patient relationship. But success or failure, she had to stand up for herself. That didn't mean she was perfect or always blameless. It only meant that she was doing her very best in a growing medical world that was constantly changing with discovery after discovery. In such an imperfect world, with the medical arts in their primitive stage of development, there were many successes, but also too many failures. Her limitations as a doctor left her with feelings she never quite managed to rise above.

Gwyneth hadn't noticed, but every eye was on her during the confrontation with Buck. The ladies eyed Gwyneth, beyond the remembrance of Addy Quinlan's difficult pregnancy, because no one in Bessie Creek wore clothing like this visitor wore. The men, because, well, because none of the Bessie Creek women wore clothing like the visitor wore or presented herself with such style.

The stage line agent had come to the door to watch the confrontation on the walk in front of his shop. There was little in the way of entertainment in small towns, and no one was about to miss what came their way. When Gwyneth motioned that she intended to enter the stage office, the man eased back to the counter, where he stood while saying, "Something for you, ma'am?"

"Yes. Does the stage still run south as far as the Wilmore Ranch?"

"Yes, indeed, and further than that, if you should want to go south a ways. Get you away from all that rancor what Ol' Buck was stirring up."

Somewhat sternly, Gwyneth replied, "I'd like a ticket on the stage tomorrow if there is one running. And I'll take it with a minimum of gossip if it's all the same to you."

The agent could feel the intensity of the comment. "Yes, ma'am, sorry, ma'am. Stage leaves from right here. Eight sharp. Ol' Buster ain't got much wait in his nature."

*So Buster is still driving. I wonder if he'll let me sit up top?* The thought passed through her mind as she was leaving the small office.

As she stepped onto the sidewalk, she decided she was hungry. Glancing across the street and letting her eyes follow the full length of the row of small businesses, from left to right, she saw no eating house. She stepped to the edge of the boardwalk to gain a wider view and repeated the study of the businesses to her own left and right. There was no sign visible, but she noticed first, two people entering an establishment a few doors south, and then three more. Thinking there was a good chance the people were attracted to a lunch offering, she stepped that way.

Indeed, there was a sign, announcing simply, *Food*. It was painted on the window glass, easily seen from the street but not from where she had been standing. Knowing this would be the village's single offering for lunch, she turned the knob and stepped inside. A mixture of stove and cigar smoke, and the greasy aroma of seared beef, greeted her. Every head in the place turned to study her. Even the cook, attracted by the sudden hush among the small crowd, turned from his pots and grill to glance out the kitchen door. Seeing a problem, he stepped through the doorway and wound through the group of tables and chairs, all of which were occupied, although two tables set for four held only two each.

With familiarity that is seldom seen in the city but that is common in places as small as Bessie Creek, the cook said, "Toby, Jessie, how about you two squeezing in there so's to make room for the lady?"

With a rattling of chairs on the wooden floor, the man moved to the side closest to his wife, and held out the just vacated chair, saying, "Please, ma'am, would you join my wife and me. We're Toby and Jessie, as you might have heard that cantankerous pan rattler say. We're the only ones here that are at least half civilized. That's why he chose us to welcome you to town and to the only lunch offering available. These others, some of them at best, are only half-human. And that's on their good days." The comment, easily heard in the small room, brought out several howls of protest and a few laughs.

Gwyneth, enjoying the relaxed atmosphere, smiled and responded, "That's very generous of you, sir. Almost human."

Following up on what Toby had said, and liking the fact that this lovely, fashionable lady was so easily fitting in, the guffawing started all over again but soon settled down as folks returned to their lunches or their visiting. Gwyneth set her small overnight bag and her medical bag on the floor at her feet and gracefully sat down.

"My name, Toby, Jessie, is Gwyneth Wycome. Dr. Gwyneth Wycome, actually."

Jessie spoke for the first time. "Doctor. We'll that's a fine thing. Are you planning to set up practice here, Doctor?"

"It's just Gwyneth among friends. And no, not right now. I'm just looking around. Reminiscing, you might say."

"And why would anyone take the trouble to come all the way to Bessie Creek just to look around. It's not as if there's anything to see here. But then, you did say reminiscing. Have you been here before, Gwyneth?"

"Yes, as a matter of fact, I have. Several times."

"That must have been early on. We've been here for all but the first year or so of the town's life."

"Oh, my history goes back to well before there was a town, or a railway, for that matter. My husband and I, along with a collection of friends and family, pioneered one of the early ranches south of here. When my husband was killed, I hung on for a while, still holding the cattle and land, and offering nursing services to ranches, and by then, the earliest settlers in what was to become Bessie Creek. I finally sold out and moved back east to study medicine. Now, with several years of study and hospital experience, I'm back west for a while at least. I have a clinic in Pueblo. But I still know a few folks here, so I thought I'd take a day or two and do some visiting."

"Would I be prying to ask who bought your ranch?"

"Not at all, Toby. I sold my Mirrored W to Billy Wilmore. Is he still ranching south of here?"

"Sure enough. And now that we fit a few pieces together, we've heard of you. Remember what folks had to say about your doctoring more than I remembered your name, but I remember the talk sure enough."

"Oh, I do hope everything you heard wasn't awful. There must have been at least one or two who survived my ministrations, Jessie."

Jessie returned Gwyneth's smile, replying, "I don't remember hearing a single word of complaint. Delivering babies and retrieving lead from folk's bodies seems to be what you're best known for."

"Well, that's a relief. Poor Mr. Quinlan doesn't have such fond memories."

Jessie laid her hand on Gwyneth's wrist and said, "Buck Quinlan needs to learn to be thankful and to keep personal business behind his own door. I've talked with the midwives who attended before you were called. They agreed they had never been confronted with such a problem as what Addy presented, had no idea what to do. Believe me, they speak of you with admiration."

The talk continued during a leisurely lunch with Gwyneth wondering what loyalty was holding the few folks who still called Bessie Creek home. To ask would cast doubt on the village, so she said nothing. It would only be stating the obvious to say that the village was not destined to prosper. There was no real possibility of expansion in the surrounding countryside. The land was unfit for small farms. A kitchen garden couldn't be grown without irrigation. Unless mineral was discovered close by, there would be nothing else to attract a growing population.

The lunch partners parted after Gwyneth asked about Eustice Ward. It turned out the would-be preaching man was still holding services for the few who showed interest each Sunday. Otherwise, he was working on the B4. Just coming to town on Friday nights to minister to folks on Saturdays and Sundays.

GWYNETH WAS unclear about stage services on Sundays. She had neglected to ask the agent, but Buster would outline the options for her. She was riding south on Saturday, hoping to be invited for a one-night stay-over at either the B4 or up the hill at the Cameron place. And if the stage wasn't running, she would try to borrow a horse to get back to the rail line in time for the evening run back to Pueblo. Knowing the good nature of the ranchers, she wasn't particularly worried, either way. Someone would come to her aid.

On Saturday morning, Buster turned from jamming one more leather bag into the boot to see who was approaching. He could hear the light footfalls on the boardwalk, lighter than any man and lighter than most western women, who get used to wearing work shoes or riding boots, no longer noticing the noise of their own passing. That had to be Gwyneth.

Stifling a grin, the stage jehu on the southbound stage said, "Bout to leave without you there, stranger. Got no time fer big city frippery and lollygagging and look'n fer special service and favors. Ain't got no feather pilla fer ya ta set yerself on neither."

"And it's good to see you too, Buster. My, how you've mellowed since I last saw you."

Releasing his held back full-face smile, Buster held out his hands in a two-handed welcome. "Come here an' let me git a look at ya, Gwyneth. My what a sight fer these old eyes ye are."

Gwyneth took both of the offered hands in hers and squeezed, smiling at her old friend. "Buster. There's just no one I hoped more to see on this little excursion of mine than you. You're looking fine, fine. Shouting at horses and men and eating a constant diet of dust seems to have done you well."

"Git yerself up top there, doc. Got ta git this here rig a mov'n. We can have us a visit along the way."

Buster pulled right into the B4 yard, rather than stopping outside the corrals like he usually did. Between Busters shouted orders to the team and the noise the conveyance made, there was no chance of surprise. Two boys rushed out to tote in the freight ordered from town while another younger lad held the team. Buster hollered, "Billy. Gladys. Ya got company." A beautiful young lady came from the stable, glanced around the yard, placed her pitchfork against the stable wall, and walked quickly to the stage. Buster looked up from the lifting down of packages and said, "Sissy, this here is the doctor what delivered yer mother of that brother yer constantly whin'n about."

"Why, Buster, I'll have you know, ladies do not whine, and my name is Summer."

"As yer father would say, 'Right ye are there, Sissy.' Step up here and say hello to Dr. Gwyneth Wycome. Come fer a short visit."

Gwyneth was startled by the beauty of the young lady, marveling that such could be the offspring of the big, gruff, but good-natured Billy.

"Summer. I'm so pleased to meet you again. When we first met, you were just a little tyke correcting your father about your name. Am I to guess that you're still trying?"

"It's all kind of hopeless, but these men would miss the challenge if I let it drop. And it's good to meet you again as well, Doctor. Here's Mother and Father now, freshly called away from whatever excuse Father was using today to avoid physical labor."

The welcomes and handshaking seemed to go on forever by the time the entire family was introduced. There had been one more addition to the family, a girl, since Gwyneth had delivered their son in her clinic before the sale of the Mirrored W. Buster had moved on after telling Gwyneth she had best lay over until Monday, as there was no stage service on Sunday. Eustice Ward, as she had already been warned, had ridden out the evening before to revert to his ministry duties. It seemed she may not see him at all on the trip.

As on most ranches, lunch was a big meal. On the B4, everyone, family and riders alike, ate together in the cookhouse. The house kitchen, with the beautiful stove Trent had ordered for Gwyneth years before, was rarely used.

After a leisurely noon meal, and with the kids returned to their duties, Billy and Gwyneth fell to visiting, while Gladys listened to the talk and nursed her little girl. Daniel and Night Light had been on Gwyneth's mind. The inquiry about them brought the response from Billy: "One of the best riders I've ever hired. Wished he would have stayed. And Mother had come to depend on Night Light for company as well as for native wisdom. They discussed Indian history, as much as Night Light knew, herbs and plants, and how to survive when things got tough in a bad winter. We miss those two. But Night Light got lonesome for family.

"Apparently, they're a wandering bunch, never know quite how or where to find them. But a handful of them half-naked riders rode into the yard big as you please, as if they owned the place, which I guess their grandfathers may have, but they made no trouble, just wanted to see what they called their sister, although Night Light says they were cousins, or second cousins as we would count them, or some such. Anyway, they near ate us out of our ranch and herd, and then in a week, they all packed up and rode away, Daniel and Night Light included. Ain't seen hide nor hair since."

There wasn't much more to talk about, and Gwyneth was anxious to ride up to the B/C for a visit with Betty Cameron and Ty. Building up her courage, she said, "I'm longing to see Betty Cameron. I would be ever so grateful if you would give me the loan of a horse."

With no discussion or questioning, Billy walked to the kitchen door and hollered. "Sissy, I'd like it if you'd saddle a ride for the doctor and then go with her up to the B/C."

Cringing a bit at the volume the man was able to produce, Gwyneth thought, *Wouldn't much matter where Summer was, she'd be able to hear that message if she was down the root cellar with the door closed.*

Within a few minutes, Summer was at the door, beckoning to Gwyneth. "All set when you've heard enough of Dad's foolishness."

"Now, see here, young lady. Don't you be disparag'n the one that loves ye most, outside of yer Ma, ye understand."

"Yes, father. Are you ready, Doctor?"

THE TWO LADIES, one young and eager to learn, one older, but wiser from the events of her life, made a slow ride of it. The chatter ranged from the giddy to the serious. The trail had been widened to accommodate a wagon, so there was no problem riding side by side.

Gwyneth was impressed by some of the wisdom Summer expressed, but also distressed by how little she knew of the world outside the valley. There were great risks for a girl with Summer's beauty and naivety. The two were a volatile mix. Very carefully, Gwyneth ventured into the uncomfortable territory of boys and girls and some of their temptations. "It's confusing when you're young, Summer. The body and emotions are telling you one thing, while your parents, and the teachings of your church, and society, for that matter, are not quite saying another, but it will sound as if they are. What they're really saying is *there's a time and place for everything*.

"What is appropriate inside a loving marriage is not at all appropriate outside that marriage. And yet it feels like the same emotions are involved, and largely, that is correct. So we need self-control and self-respect. And respect from whoever we're with, whether on a simple, fun afternoon in the saddle, with a picnic lunch to share, or a more formal courting situation. You have to take and remain in control. You will soon know if the young man you're with respects you or not. Without that respect and an agreement on values, you will never give an early attraction the opportunity to grow into a lifelong loving relationship, and you could get yourself into a misery that will plague you all the days of your life. You're a beautiful young lady, Summer. If you were in the city, you'd have boys hanging around like ants at a picnic. Out here, or even in Bessie Creek, your opportunities are limited, which could all the more result in giving in to temptation."

From there, the conversation moved on to personal health and caring for oneself, and topics that naturally fed out of that beginning.

Summer was silent, except for her questions, but attentive. As the Cameron Ranch came into view, Summer, blushing a bit, said, "Thank you, Doctor. Mother tries, but really, she doesn't know what to say. I'm thinking she didn't know much of anything when she married, but somehow, she and Dad have managed to hold it together and build on whatever drew them to one another originally. Whatever Mother wanted to tell me somehow wouldn't release itself from her throat. I feared she was going to choke, so we agreed silently that no more would be asked or said."

Looking down the slight slope into the Cameron yard, there seemed to be kids everywhere, and everyone trying to shout and laugh louder than the other. But suddenly there was silence. The silence was brought about when one boy of about eight or nine years saw the two riders. He glued his eyes on the visitors, and one by one, his siblings or cousins, or whoever they were, broke off the yelling and followed his lead in staring. The same boy, without turning to direct his voice to the house, hollered, "Ma. Ma. There's folks a com'n. Sissy fer one. Don't know who tother one is."

Betty Cameron stepped onto the small back stoop, flipped the kitchen cloth over her shoulder, and raised her hand to shade her eyes. Her blank stare turned into a giant smile. "Hello, Summer. Are my eyes lying to me, or is that Gwyneth you've dragged all the way up here?"

Summer waved and hollered back, not nearly as loud as her father was able, "It's me all right, and your eyes are just fine. The doctor has come for a visit."

Betty waited while they rode closer before she stepped off the small porch. Holding out her arms, she said, "My dear, dear friend. I'm wondering what brought you way out here, but then I don't really care. It's just so good to see you. Step down here and let me give you a hug."

Gwyneth stepped down and submitted herself to the hug while Summer lifted a young one onto each horse, telling them, "Ride them to the water trough and care for them."

The animals really needed only minor care after so short a

ride, and the children, as small as they were, could've done little anyway. They kicked their heels on the saddle fenders, having little effect on the horses, but the message got through to the equine brains and they were soon at the stable. Coming from Sissy, whom the kids fell just short of worshiping, the order to care for the geldings set them to work with fork and hay after the watering.

Welcomed into the spotless kitchen, Summer and Gwyneth took seats at the table, smiling as Betty bent into the homemade cradle positioned by the rocking chair where Betty would sit to take advantage of her few quiet minutes to rest and recuperate. In a moment, she presented the baby to Gwyneth, saying, "The latest, and I hope the last."

Mystified, since the last news Gwyneth had known was that following the death of her husband, Betty had remained single. It was true that Gwyneth had wondered about the seeming mass of children in the yard, but she hadn't yet had an opportunity to hear an explanation. She reached for the baby but couldn't disguise the question on her face. Betty picked up on the message immediately. Embarrassed, she said, "Oh, Gwyneth. Of course, you couldn't know. You've been gone for some time. I remarried three years ago. Met Gerald while we were on a shopping trip to town. He was working the counter at the general store. There was no one else in the store and we got to talking.

"Turned out he was a widower with three children. Lost his wife to some mystery disease. Owned a small ranch down New Mexico way but couldn't manage with no woman to hold the home together and mind the kids. Couldn't afford any riders. Sold out and headed here at the invite of an old friend who owns the store. With the children in school, he had been managing. But he needed help to raise a family, and just as clearly, so did I. Ty has grown into a fine, responsible rancher and cattleman and a big help as my eldest son. But... There's always a but, isn't there? Anyway, Gerald is working the ranch along with Ty, and we're happily married. Ty has his eye on Summer's older sister. Where that will go is not yet known. So now you understand the baby and the fifty or so kids you saw in the yard."

Gwyneth laughed, saying, "I didn't hardly think it was fifty, but there's a few young ones out there, for sure."

Holding the floor for another question, Gwyneth asked bout the ranch itself.

"We're doing just fine. Ty's grown into a man to be proud of, something I'm not sure would have happened if his father had still been here. What Ty, and now with Gerald's help, has done, is clear a couple of paths into the higher, but adjoining valleys. He had to have a fella from Bessie Creek, man who worked on the railway roadbed and was familiar with the use of blasting powder, help him move the worst of the blockages. The grass is better here than it is in the valley below and we've enough, and more land to hold all the cattle we'll ever need."

The afternoon of visiting seemed to fly past with question after question aimed, first at Betty and then at Gwyneth, in return, as the two friends caught up on several years of being apart. Betty finally noticed the big, wind-up clock sitting on the top of the stove's warming oven. "Oh my, look at that time. We can still visit, but I have to get to my pots and pans."

Without even having been asked, Gladys Wilmore had assured Gwyneth that there was space enough and more for her to stay over, and that she would have Summer and one of the older boys escort her to Bessie Creek in the morning. Thinking of that and knowing Betty would be busy from dinner preparation time until all the children were bedded down, she stood, saying, "Betty, I've had a wonderful time visiting with you. I'm so happy to have found you well and with a new lease on life. But we must get back to the B4, and you have your chores to tend to. We'll say goodbye, my friend.

"I may or may not decide to open a clinic in Bessie Creek. I wouldn't leave Pueblo to do it, but with the train, I could perhaps be here a couple of days each week. In any case, I'll do my best to get back down this way again. And I'll look into what you told me about the other settlements to the west living without any medical assistance. God bless. Greet Ty for me when he's in for the evening."

Betty called the kids to say goodbye to their visitors. The small ones ran in as a group while a couple of older ones lagged just a bit. Glancing at the children, Gwyneth was able to see that one boy, a lad of perhaps twelve years, had a swollen jaw and a pained expression on his face, the expression was exaggerated by the way the young fellow was holding his lips and jaw to the side. When Betty introduced the lad as Oscar, Gwyneth shook hands with him and asked, "Is that a toothache that's causing you some trouble?"

Oscar simply nodded, looking at his stepmother for advice on what to say. Betty responded, "Poor Oscar has suffered nigh on a week. There's no dentist anywhere around. We may have to take him into Pueblo if it doesn't heal up pretty soon."

Pointing at a sawn tree stump used as a seat on the porch, Gwyneth said, "Sit down here, Oscar." When the boy was seated, Gwyneth kneeled down in front of him. Gently placing her fingers on his bottom lip and pressing just a bit, Oscar opened his mouth. "A bit wider, please, Oscar."

Again, with finger pressure only, Gwyneth signaled that the boy should tip his head upward a bit more and turn to the sun. She probed with her index finger, leaned closer for a better look, sat back on her heels, and said, "Young man, I'm a doctor, not a dentist. But I can tell you that your back tooth, what is called the second molar, one of your baby teeth, is seriously infected. It's going to fall out soon anyway, to be replaced by an adult tooth. I could pull it for you if you wish. There would be some pain, but only for a moment. Then, as soon as it heals up, all the pain would be gone. Would you like me to do that for you?"

Gwyneth had never been a mother, but she had often longed to experience the trust she had observed in children's eyes as they looked at their mothers for comfort or guidance. Betty said, "I didn't intend to impose, Gwyneth. In fact, I somehow didn't connect Oscar's tooth problem with your doctoring. But if Oscar agrees, it's all right with me, and I know his father would agree and thank you for helping."

Without words, Gwyneth looked at the boy. Close to tears, an embarrassment for a quickly growing young man, Oscar nodded. Anticipating Gwyneth's needs, Summer had gone to the still saddled horses and returned with the black bag that Gwyneth hauled with her wherever she went. Gwyneth smiled her thanks. With the opened case resting on the porch beside her, she withdrew a small pair of long-handled pliers, tucking the implement into the wide cuffs of her dress sleeve to hide it from her patient. Again, showing wisdom without being told what to do, Summer stepped behind Oscar, knelt as Gwyneth had done, and placed her hands on Oscar's shoulders, both to steady him and reassure him.

"Open wide and hold open, Oscar. Tip your head back as you did before and hold still. Don't turn your head or pull back. Betty, if you would get a clean cloth and a glass of water, that would be a help. And a pan for Oscar to spit into when he needs to. Now, Oscar, I'm going to ask you not to swallow. If you need to spit something out, let me know by tapping my arm. This isn't going to take long, so I think you'll be fine."

The little ones formed a curious, studious circle around the doctor and patient, sitting cross-legged on the porch. Two of the older boys stood a small distance apart, snickering and elbowing each other as their whispers got louder. "Careful your brains don't come out along with the tooth, Oscar."

"You're going to be uglier than you already are, what with no teeth."

"Don't cry now, Oscar."

An older girl who fit into the blended family somewhere said, "Hush, you fools. Next time it could be you."

Summer whispered something into Oscar's ear and tightened her grip.

Finding the infected tooth was not difficult. The pus-filled abscess was a clear indication, like a sign pointing the way. Gwyneth very carefully took a grip with the pliers and eased the tooth sideways, one way and then the other. Oscar tightened up in every muscle and moaned a bit before settling down again. Two more wiggles with the pliers and a slight pull, and Gwyneth withdrew the instrument with the tooth firmly held in its jaws. "All right, Oscar. You did fine. Now spit into that pan."

A mess of blood and yellow pus came from his mouth. He shuddered a bit and sat back.

"You're doing fine, Oscar. Removing the tooth will allow the pus to drain out and the gum to begin healing. Now take a sip of water. Don't swallow. Spit again into the pan." There was less pus but still a bit of blood.

"All is well, young man. Now you take that cup of water and go alongside the house and give your mouth a good rinsing. Spit the first couple of sips out and then take just a small drink. Do that until there's no more pus or blood showing. You rest a bit this afternoon and don't eat on that side of your mouth for a couple of days. A dentist would do a bit more to clean out the abscess, but I don't have anything with me that would help. It might heal a bit more slowly, but it will heal. I'll leave this tooth right here on the stool for you. It's not very big. The tooth below is growing, pushing this one up, and soon enough, it would have pushed it out if the infection hadn't started. It's hard to believe something so small can cause so much misery."

Gwyneth was surprised when she felt some pain in her hips and legs as she stood to her feet, wondering if that might be the first sign of old age. Hesitating, but finally deciding to move ahead with her thoughts, she said, "Betty, if you don't object, I'd like to send you a selection of toothbrushes. One for each of you. Your family will have far less tooth trouble if you can get them all to brush every day, cleaning them thoroughly. I'll send along a package of toothpaste to use when you're brushing. Perhaps you could ask the general store to stock some. Some brushes too. They don't last forever. They need to be replaced time to time."

As if she had never thought of it before, Betty replied, "I've never had one, and I'd given it no consideration. You send them on down. And tell me what they cost. I'll send back payment. And payment for Oscar's tooth too."

"Think of it as my gift to a friend."

Betty was effusive in her thanks. The ladies hugged and said their goodbyes again while Summer was gathering the horses. Just as Gwyneth and Summer were about to put the horses into motion, Oscar came from the side of the house. With a small, lopsided smile, he lifted one hand in thanks. Gwyneth answered in the traditional cowboy way, touching a couple of fingers to her hat brim, with a slight nod and a returned smile, as if the two, doctor and patient, now had something in common, some connection between the two of them.

# Chapter Twenty-Three

It wasn't long before they were riding into the B4 yard again. They rode into an unusually silent yard, but nonetheless, a yard in turmoil. Still a distance from the buildings, Summer held her arm out, signaling Gwyneth to a halt. Within sight were two of Summer's brothers hunkered down behind the wooden well screening. Silently, the two women studied the sight before them. Summer spoke first. "It looks safe enough. We'll go on in, but let's keep our eyes open for whatever is causing the trouble."

Riding closer, it became clear that the men had armed themselves, while the women were fussing over someone lying on the grass at the side of the barn. Billy and one of his riders were squatted beside the women, their rifles loaded, cocked, and held at the ready. The other men had arranged themselves behind any barrier they could find, their rifles up and ready, like the others, watching, looking for movement or threat. Neither Summer nor Gwyneth had heard any shots.

Summer led Gwyneth behind a shed and along the back of a corral that led to the stable. They dismounted, freed the horses, with saddles and bridles removed, while they, themselves, eased along the stable wall until they could pull the rear door open and enter. Gwyneth entered first, carrying her black bag, while holding her .32 down along her right leg, swaddled in the cloth of her split skirt. Summer hesitated before fully entering the building, with her eyes sweeping the light forest and the hillside behind the buildings. Satisfied that whatever threat might have been there earlier was now gone, she stepped inside and pulled the door closed.

Gwyneth was studying the interior of the dim building. Summer whispered, "See anything amiss?"

"Not a thing. Whatever happened, the problem appears to have settled out. Let's go see what the women are fussing over."

Summer stepped out first, walking cautiously to where her father was holed up, beyond the corner of the smokehouse and past the leading edge of the barn. Although food was far from her mind, the smoky, brine-saturated air from the smokehouse filled her lungs with a flash of memory. How many hams had been rendered wonderfully, beautifully edible after the weeks they spent being slowly permeated with the smoke? *This is a foolish time to be thinking of breakfast*, she told herself. Continuing her slow walk, she was soon squatted beside her father.

"What's going on?"

"We're not sure. There was nothing but the usual ranch noises, no warning at all, when suddenly an arrow flew out of nowhere, it seemed. Caught your brother in the shoulder. He yelled and twisted in surprise before he fell to the ground, so we don't even know which direction the thing came from. Ain't seen nor heard one single thing after that moment. Since Daniel and Night Light packed up and followed their family into the hills, we've seen no Indians here, nor anywhere around. Not quite sure what to do now. We sure don't need Indian trouble."

"I think they're probably gone, Dad."

"And ye could be absolutely correct in thinking that, but I'd hate to be wrong and find out the hard way. You watch out for yourself. I'm for joining those other fellas keeping watch at the foot of the hill." With that, he rose and scooted away as quickly as he was able.

Gwyneth took a chance and walked openly to where the wounded man lay. Kneeling beside Gladys, the problem was easy enough to identify. An arrow with what looked to Gwyneth like hawk feather fletching was protruding from a man's shoulder. The shaft was shorter than she had imagined an arrow would be. The shirt had not yet been cut away. Although the young man was in considerable pain, judging from the position of the arrow, neither his life, nor his long-term health were in any serious peril.

If she was to judge from a quick first look, the arrow penetrated only far enough to come up against a bone. Although she knew little to nothing about Indians or their way with the bow, she was sure a well-driven arrow could do more damage than that, which, along with the length of the shaft, left a question or two unanswered. She bent forward and undid the top few buttons of the shirt and spread it apart.

Satisfied that he wasn't needed on the hillside watch and trying to cover every possible direction with his eyes, Billy ran hunched over and dropped back down beside his wife. The barn protected them on one side, the machine shop on another. The smokehouse a bit further back. An older brother kneeling there was watching the other two sides. Before Billy could ask a question of Gwyneth, Summer, again, gently set Gwyneth's black bag on the ground where she could easily reach it. The young lady was showing all the signs of an attentive and intelligent assistant to the visiting doctor. Gwyneth opened the bag and lifted out a pair of scissors. When she cut the shirt and then the long johns the victim was wearing, Gladys said, "I can see you needed to do that, but it leaves me with one more mending job." She wasn't really complaining, just stating a fact.

Gwyneth responded, "Just that bit. Enough to get past the arrow while you slip the underwear and the shirt off this shoulder and arm. And while you're doing that, someone can get some hot water and a couple of cloths. I'll be right back. I hope. And I really should know the name of the man I'm going to have to do some work on."

"Slade. He's our second-to-oldest."

"And the smartest and wisest and strongest," grinned Slade. "And did I mention best-looking?"

Gwyneth patted him on the shoulder, saying, "I'm sure that's all true, but we still have to get that arrow out, and that could be a bit of a test. You rest easy for a minute or two."

With that, she rose to her feet and walked to the other end of the barn, where the trail started to what was once Daniel and Night Light's tent and later, their cabin. Digging around in her memory for almost forgotten words Night Light had taught her in the Ute language, she steadied herself, collecting her nerves and hollered, in the best Ute she could recall, "Wandering Eyes. Is that you out there? Did you forget that we are friends? You are welcome at our fire. But no more shooting."

She waited a half minute, hoping for a response, remembering that the old man, father of Night Light, was not a man to hurry. Finally, with the sounds of a series of light steps she could barely make out, the brush parted and a much younger man than Wandering Eyes stepped out. He held no bow. This one carried a rifle. Setting his feet solidly and standing tall, as if to impress, or perhaps frighten this woman who spoke his language, but not well, he said, "The father of Likes The Night is no more. I am Walks A Lot. Brother of Likes The Night."

"I remember you, Walks A Lot. When you were here with us before, you did not shoot. Our men did not shoot. Why do you come as an enemy now?"

"No enemy. Young man shoot. Young man not wise."

Gwyneth did not understand the words for not wise, but she let it pass.

"Come have coffee with us. But do not bring your guns."

Walks A Lot turned to the hillside behind him and spoke instructions. Soon, three more men came into sight. They carried their large knives in sheaths hanging from brightly colored cloth belts, but no guns that she could see. Gwyneth, looking at them, was pleased that they now wore long-legged, tanned hide pants, not the breechclouts of their first visit. As they stepped nearer, Gwyneth smiled at Walks A Lot and said, "I am happy to see you again, Walks A Lot. Do you remember some of our English talk?"

Reverting to Daniel's name for his sister, he answered in English, "Night Light teaches in the village."

"Good. Then we will talk in English. There is much to talk about. But first, I must remove the arrow from one of our young men. Come, I will introduce you to our men."

When Gwyneth turned around, most of the Wilmore family, plus a couple of hired riders, were standing in a small semi-circle watching her and the Indians. Everyone, that is, except one tall, hard-eyed, rough-looking, startlingly thin man, a hired rider on the B4. That man held his rifle at the ready, facing the main house and the empty grassland, looking all around as if on guard.

Still a bit fearful of what might come next. Gwyneth said, "Billy, come meet a friend of mine."

Billy approached cautiously but showed no fear. Billy was not in the habit of showing fear. He had never met an adversary that could best him. His purposeful steps were slow but steady. His eyes glued on the four Utes, all the time wondering how many more were skulking in the bush or surrounding them while they were making peace-talk with the four. The happenings of the day had, at first, troubled him, wondering if they were to have an incident that demanded a shooting response. Now he was merely curious, although the latent anger about his son being shot with an arrow would not soon be forgotten. That same arrow, placed in a critical spot on the victim's body, could be as deadly as a 44-40 slug.

Having found in life that the first to speak with a sound of authority and strength held the advantage, Billy drew his walk to a stop, standing beside Gwyneth. Close to the Ute but not too close. "Who shot my son?"

"Young man. Sent home. No more shooting."

Gwyneth, having to get back to her patient, turned and walked slowly toward the group of watchers. As she moved past them, she said, quietly, "I believe there will be no more trouble, but stay alert and don't let them get behind you. And for goodness' sake, don't do anything stupid. We still don't know the reason for this visit, but I sense no threat."

Remembering something she had been wondering about before the Indians showed themselves, she turned back to Walks A Lot, saying, "Show me an arrow. One such as the young boy shot our man with."

The Ute stared at her with questioning eyes. Becoming impatient, she held out her hand, palm up. "I have to cut the arrow out. I need to see what kind of tip is on that arrow."

Understanding the question, Walks A Lot said, "Young man. Learning the hunt. No tip on arrow. Pointed stick."

Those few words answered the question of why the arrow hadn't penetrated further.

The mixture of languages was helped when Walks A Lot retrieved an arrow from his quiver. He held out the vicious implement, showing the chipped stone arrowhead, but saying, "Young boy. No stone."

Gwyneth accepted that as an answer and turned again toward her patient. Before she did what had to be done, she said, "Slade. This is going to hurt. You bite down hard and try not to yell out or show signs of pain. The Indians pride themselves on suffering silently. If you cry out, they will believe it is because you're weak."

Gladys had removed the shirt and spread the long johns out as wide as possible, slipping the underwear off one shoulder without removing them. Lying on the grass beside the injured young man was a pan of hot water and a few clean cloths awaiting their time of need. Lying close by was a bar of soap that, just by its looks, appeared as if it might take off the dirt, plus the top few layers of skin.

"The long johns have to come off and the area thoroughly scrubbed. It will hurt less if you don't bump the arrow."

Gladys complied with Gwyneth's suggestion, wetting a cloth and rubbing soap on it before tackling the several days of sweat and dust. Slade let out a moan only once when Summer, intent on helping, by holding the arrow, mistakenly moved it just a bit sideways. Gladys dried the area and Gwyneth bent to her task.

With her fingers pressing down on the skin around the arrow shaft, Gwyneth hesitated, looked Slade in the eyes, and nodded, indicating that now was the time. With a slow but firm tug on the arrow, she soon had it removed.

Slade gasped again as he expelled held breath. His shoulders and chest muscles relaxed, and he slumped just a bit, but he made no utterance that could be heard beyond where he lay. Gwyneth held the shaft up and, holding it at eye level where it was easily seen by Slade and the others, examined it. Blood and torn flesh, along with shredded bits from the cloth of both shirt and long johns, showed around the vacated wound and clung to the wooden shaft. Although it was an ugly implement when used in hate or anger, it was also beautiful in construct.

Skilled hands had worked the shaft to almost a perfect cylinder. The bird feather fletching was a work of art. Where the tip had been carved to a point, one side was just slightly longer than the other, but it had flown straight enough to hit its target. The point was burned just enough to harden it. All in all, a deadly implement of war or a valuable weapon for hunting. And a teaching tool for a Ute boy growing into manhood, where he could be trusted by the band to be a hunter and a warrior. But now that it lay in her hands, it would never again be used in anger. She passed it to Slade, saying, "A souvenir for you."

With the initial trauma over, Gwyneth said, "Well done, this far at least, Slade. Now I'm going to clean this up a bit, and it's going to hurt some more, but it won't be more than you can handle."

As she set about with tweezers, digging for and removing cloth and bits of skin, she glanced up at Gladys, who had never left her son's side. "Don't ever try pulling out a stone-tipped arrow. You'd pull the shaft from the tip, and then you'd have to dig out the stone. That kind has to be pushed through to the other side or drawn out through a deep cut."

With the cleaning up of the wound completed, the doctor reached again into her black bag and withdrew a small vial. She held the deep blue colored bottle where Slade could see it. "Slade. This is the big one. There's no telling where that arrow has been or what might have been on it that could cause infection. And truthfully, your underwear could stand a changing. Those bits of cloth didn't carry anything you want to have rotting away in your wound. Now this liquid will kill most any kind of germ, and it's going to feel as if it's killing you, but the sting lasts only a few seconds. Now bite down hard again."

Giving Slade just a second to prepare himself, she tipped the bottle only far enough to allow a few drops to drip into the wound and around the entry point. Every muscle in Slade's strong body tensed and tightened. He mashed his teeth and pursed his lips, shaking his head side to side with his eyes squeezed shut. But only a slight, pain-laden sound escaped his lips. Gwyneth twisted the cap back into place and returned the bottle to her black bag. Slade was slowly relaxing, struggling to sit up, as if he intended to get up and run to escape his tormentors.

"We're all done, Slade, and I couldn't have asked for a better patient. Now your mother is going to get some strips of clean cloth, and Summer is going bandage you up. Never mind complaining. I can see your thoughts. Your younger sister has the knack for this sort of thing. You sit quietly and let her fix you up. You have to keep the wound clean, and the bandage will help. You rest a bit and then, when the Indians are gone, you make your way to the creek with a bar of soap. Don't wet the wound, but don't stop scrubbing until you're clean all over."

Slade responded, "Thanks, I guess, Doctor. But I ever see you riding into our yard again, I might go hunt up a saddled horse."

Gladys admonished her son for the comment, but Gwyneth smiled and simply walked back to where the men were talking with Walks A Lot and the other Utes. As she was approaching, Billy moved toward her, saying quietly, "These men have come with a message. There's illness in the village. Daniel sent them with a written note." As he passed the note to Gwyneth, he continued talking. "I still suspect there are more Indians hunkered down in the bush, watching. We're probably under their guns this very minute."

Gwyneth read the message scratched on a page torn from a notebook. *Illness. Family sick. Need help. Most of village sick. Maybe doctor by now at Bessie Creek. Guessing might be typhoid. Not sure. Send anything that could help. Thanks. Daniel.*

Gwyneth studied the Ute standing before her. The last thing they needed was typhoid in the valley, and these men could be carrying it.

"Are any of you men sick?"

"No. Sick stay at village."

"Are you living on the reserve?"

The men shuffled their feet, studying Walks A Lot as their leader. Clearly the question disturbed them. The army had said they were to move to the reserve. The penalty for not doing as they were told could be severe. But Wandering Eyes had always led a small, peaceful band, living almost entirely in the rugged mountains. Admitting that they had defied the army might bring serious trouble, and they didn't know if they could trust this rancher and these others. Gwyneth held up her hand, understanding the situation.

"It is all right. I understand. How far away is your village?"

"One day ride. Sun to sun."

Gwyneth figured he meant sunup to sundown, one day.

"It is late this day. Can we ride at night?"

"We ride."

"Walks A Lot. You men rest here. Don't come into the yard. I will get ready to ride. I will come here to you."

Giving no opportunity for discussion, Gwyneth turned back into the yard. "Billy, I'll be wanting a saddled horse. A good horse. Watered and well-fed. And Gladys, I'll be wanting all the clean cloth you can spare for face masks. Tear up a couple of bedsheets if you have to. I'll send you some new ones from the city. Send along the strongest soap you have. If it's typhoid, there is very little I can do, but it's believed the disease is caught from unsanitary living conditions and spread through sneezing or coughing. The masks might help. And the soap.

"I would eat something too before I ride if there is anything ready. And perhaps a sandwich for along the way."

Summer spoke up. "I'll come with you. I'll change into warmer clothing and be ready when you are."

Gwyneth started to form an argument, but Summer cut her off. "I'm going!"

Billy rarely laid down rules for his nearly grown family. He had taught them independence and as much as he could about how to enjoy and protect that independence. Now, he studied this very determined daughter for a moment before saying. "Daughter, those you go to help are important in this world and in their own families. But you are more important. To me and your mother, and in this world, if I might have the freedom to say so. God has his hand on you for good. You won't be doing that good if we lose you to typhoid. You take care of yourself and listen to Gwyneth."

The rider who had stationed himself as guard earlier stepped forward. "Names Wyatt, ma'am. It will be my honor to ride with you ladies."

Almost immediately, another voice said, "And me too." That was from Billy's eldest son, Charles.

THERE WAS some discussion among the family, but in the end, four riders were fed, dressed warmly, armed, and ready. While Gladys was preparing whatever she could put her hands on to send along, Summer and her older sister dished out half of the beef stew prepared and ready for the evening meal, carrying it in a pot along with four wooden bowls and a big spoon for dishing out the meal. The Ute would eat with their hands as they always did. They walked with this to within ten feet of the waiting Indians. There, they placed it on the ground. While Hanna, the older sister, went for a bucket of fresh water, Summer said, "You men eat, drink."

When all was ready, the two ranchmen were each leading a heavily loaded pack horse. Billy had been in the habit of stockpiling needful items over the past number of years. Ranching in a remote area meant they would fare best if they practiced self-sufficiency. Instructing his older son and daughter to be generous, they had loaded the pack animals with blankets, spare clothing, a large box of precious matches, and whatever else fell to hand.

All four riders had large bedrolls with extra clothing tucked inside behind their saddles. All were well armed. Billy called a last halt with a question for Walks A Lot. "Is there food in the village?"

"Men sick. No hunt."

With little or no thought required. Billy hollered to the last hired rider in the yard. "Seth. Get yourself out to the herd and drive in two young steers. Big. And strong enough for a fast drive."

He then turned back to Walks A Lot. "Walks A Lot. You go now. Move fast. Leave two of your men behind to bring the steers along."

Billy watched as Gwyneth and Walks A Lot talked. Finally,

the Ute leader understood. After a few quick words, two of the Ute dropped back, waiting.

Saying nothing more about food, Billy spoke loudly, as it seemed only he could. "We're not letting y'all out of this yard without we plead with the Lord to ride with you."

With that said, he held his two hands high and prayed a heartfelt prayer for the well-being of the Ute and the safe return for those riding on this mission of mercy.

As the evening drew into night, Billy couldn't get his mind past the idea that the Ute village was without adequate food and were suffering from an unidentified disease. Hopefully, the two steers would solve the one issue, at least temporarily, and Gwyneth could solve the other. Perhaps.

# Chapter Twenty-Four

The folks remaining on the B4 had a restless night. Billy, unable to sleep, finally arose and got dressed. Jamming a handful of roasted beef in his mouth and a couple of biscuits into his coat pocket, as he passed through the kitchen, he left the house, saddled a horse, and rode out to the herd. He told the night rider circling the herd to get on back to the bunk house and get some rest.

Billy didn't come back to the house until the day rider arrived to replace him. During the hours of dark, although his entire financial well-being rode on the animals under his guard, he gave them little thought, allowing his horse, who knew the night herding routine, to circle the bunch at his own speed. But he imagined, step by step, the progress the others were making as they followed Walks A Lot over the rough ground to the south and west. The lives and well-being of people who were important to him, people he loved, were at stake. Indian lives, the visiting doctor's life, his rider's life, and two of his own family.

There was far more unknown than known with typhoid and so many other diseases. So much could happen. There was little even a good doctor could do. When his thinking and worrying came near to getting the best of him, he remembered the prayer he himself had spoken. Did he believe the maker of all things was able, or did he not? Of course, even as able as He was, the Lord sometimes allowed events to come to an unhappy ending. He again prayed, asking that this not be one of those times.

As BONE weary as Gwyneth was, she knew Summer had to be just as weary. And the Indians who had ridden to the ranch were now on the return trip, having the effect of doubling their miles in the saddle. As stoical as they were, they had to be feeling the hours passing in the night. Wyatt, as little as she could see through the dimness of the night, appeared to be unchanged. The hardness of his features seemed to be setting the pattern for the rest of him. She hadn't seen nor heard anything of the two Indians driving the pair of steers. *Wyatt should probably be the one bearing that task. The Indians aren't cowboys. Too late now. Forget it and ride. Don't lose sight of Walks A Lot.*

With the eastern sky showing just the dimmest promise of the day to come, Gwyneth saw the hazy outline of a small grouping of pointed, mixed canvas and hide rooflines. There was listless smoke rising into the windless dawn from a few of the skin-clad teepees. Even as they covered the last half mile into the village, it all seemed to come to life. But the life was sleepy, no, it was more than sleepy. Sleepy would indicate people coming to life following a night of rest. She decided languid might be a better term.

The few people she saw were moving slowly, as in a stupor, or a state of helplessness. Even when a child called out the news, pointing at the arriving riders, there was no real excitement in the village. Gwyneth had seen and been involved in numerous medical situations representing any number of diseases, but she had no experience with a plague, or with a disease so ready to spread from person to person, with no one having the knowledge to stop it, or at least slow it down.

The bitter thought crossed Gwyneth's mind, *Some of these people are going to die. Some have probably already died. Lord, give me understanding I don't now have. Help me to help these people.*

The two men driving the steers had caught up to the larger group just before dawn. The arrival of the beef caused more stir in the village than the return of their riders had. Six adults and several children stepped toward the returning group. They stopped at the edge of the camp and stared, their eyes fixed on the beef. As the realization that the cattle meant their camp famine was about to end, some stood in wonder while others talked loudly and fast, pointing. A few of the children laughed.

The hard-driven beef was just as eager to stop as the riders were. Before entering into camp, Gwyneth, a bit startled, said with urgency, "Walks A Lot. Tell the people to not come closer. Go back to their tents. We will come to them as soon as we're settled."

Walks A Lot, his throat scratchy and sore from tiredness and lack of water, spoke as loudly as he could. Soon, the people were back at their tents, seated, and watching listlessly.

Giving further instructions to Walks A Lot, Gwyneth said, "We will camp in a clean place. Away from the village. We need a place that is free from human waste. If there is water there, that would be good. But it must be clean water. Where do you say that should be?"

Walks A Lot struggled with the words Gwyneth had used for human waste, but he finally made the connection. Fighting down what he perceived as an insult, he took too long to answer. Gwyneth added a few more words. "Waste very bad for sickness."

Walks A Lot took in that information and then, wordlessly, he turned up the low hill behind them. The group followed, except for the men holding the steers. At the base of a low cliff rising above a level area, he waved his hand north to south. "Clean. You camp."

Gwyneth smiled and said, "Thank you. You camp here too. And any others who are not sick. Build your tents not very close together. We will all wear masks. Maybe we not get sick. Kill animal for food in clean place too. Not close. Away from here."

The look on the Indian's face said he would have to think on some of that. He rode away slowly in the direction of the two steers. With much talk and pointing, he showed the men where to take the animals, one for immediate butchering, one for grazing until it was needed.

With all that settled, Gwyneth dismounted and started to unload a packhorse, but Charles and Wyatt were both there, encouraging her to sit and rest. Perhaps even lie down for an hour or two. She and Summer, too. Gwyneth decided she could rest later. More immediately, she wanted to talk with Daniel and Night Light. She walked slowly, feeling the hours in the saddle and the loss of sleep, to the edge of the camp. There she stopped and hollered as loudly as possible, "Daniel. Night Light. Are you sick, or can you come?"

The two stepped from their teepee with Night Light emitting a squeal of surprise and delight when she saw Gwyneth, while Daniel took a second longer look and hollered, "Gwyneth, is that really you?"

"It's me all right. I was visiting at the ranch when your note arrived. Are you well?"

"We are both well now. The disease has been in the village for past three weeks now. We were both sick at first, but we recovered quickly. All right now. Our youngest child is no more, like so many others."

"We need to talk, Daniel. But first, you and Night Light, and your children must have a thorough wash and burn your clothing. We brought other clothes to share. I will lay them on the grass here. What do you use for water? I don't see a creek or stream."

"There's a good stream not far away. But the best is there's a hot water seep just up the hill. There are many hot water streams in this area. Everyone uses that for bathing."

"I didn't know about the spring, but that's good. We don't wish to waste time now that we're here. Go clean yourselves up. Soap and hot water."

IN THE THIRTY minutes it took for Daniel and Night Light to bathe themselves and the three remaining children, Gwyneth and Summer did rest. Summer denied her brother's accusation, insisting, "I did not fall asleep, I was only resting."

Gwyneth could easily see that sibling teasing wasn't a new thing in the Wilmore home.

With Daniel and his family all masked, they came closer to Gwyneth and the others. All those who had come from the B4 were also masked.

Gwyneth smiled beneath the mask, saying, "How I would love to give you a hug, Night Light, but it will have to be another time. But come, I have something for you."

The two women went to where the horses had been unloaded. There, on the ground, was a huge armload of flowered plants. "Night Light, if I remember what you taught me, this should be lobelia and yarrow, in my language. I don't remember the names in your language. We found it last evening just before full dark. I had the men pull it up, roots and all. Can you make a tea from this to help?"

Night Light picked up a small handful of the herbs and held them to her nose. With a smile, she answered. "I make."

Gwyneth expressed in strong terms the need to have sanitation and for everyone to wear a mask. Summer had taken on the task of handing out masks torn or cut from clean bed sheets, not the best material for masks, but all they had. Night Light plucked the herbs into smaller pieces while Daniel built her a fire. Summer dug around in the small mountain of supplies and came up with the coffee pot. The ranch men gritted their teeth when Summer scrubbed the coffee stains from the pot, believing it would take many pots of their favorite beverage before they could expect drinkable coffee again. Daniel called people from the village in small groups, holding them a good distance from the ranch camp. Presenting freshly cleaned cups, each was given a hot drink.

In rapid-fire Ute, Night Light told them what they were drinking and showed them the pile of herbs on the ground. They were all familiar with the treatment and knew what to expect. The lobelia, prepared first, would bring about vomiting. Each one drank their portion and then walked quickly away, having been told to stay away from each other and deal with their stomach cleansing far from the teepees. The yarrow would be prepared later, hoping it would do the magic of reducing fever and swelling.

Wyatt had mounted his horse and gone in search of the men handling the steers. One animal was probably killed by that time, and the women would be butchering the carcass. They had all been given masks and told how important it was to be clean and to put some distance from each other. He might find something he could do to help, if nothing more than handling the meat carefully. Before he rode out, he spoke quietly to Gwyneth. "Don't worry about me. I speak Ute. I lived with them for a couple of years. That was further north. I don't really want them to know I speak the lingo. I might hear something if they don't know I understand."

"Thank you, Wyatt. It was generous of you to come. There is some chance that we are all risking our health and, perhaps, our lives. You didn't have to do that."

"Actually, yes, I did. It was a White man's disease that took my Ute wife and son. She woke up sick, and by noon, she was gone. I'm hoping that never happens again."

# Chapter Twenty-Five

Spike was glorying in the beautiful spring morning in Pueblo. The sun was shining, warming the earth after the night's coolness, but there was still a slight dampness in the air that he could almost taste. The westerly winds dropping down from the snow-covered Sangre de Cristo Mountains had drawn the moisture with them. But that time was past, and Spike had the whole new day ahead of him. The enthusiastic and faithful runner and general handyman for the Wycome Medical Clinic in Pueblo had made his usual rounds of the town, acquiring a letter at the postal service.

Letters were rare in Spike's life. This one, seeing the return name and address, somehow seemed more important than the few other sealed envelopes that had come into his hands. With excitement and great enthusiasm, he rode his bicycle up the gravel driveway, shouting for Sky, who had been alone in the clinic, now into the second week. She had faithfully maintained the clinic to the best of her knowledge and ability, explaining to each patient that the doctor was away on a visit to Bessie Creek and that she was a nurse only. In addition, she promised that she had considerable experience and that she would do her best.

If the medical situation was beyond her experience,

Gwyneth had instructed her to suggest that the patient move on to the hospital or one of the other available doctors. The result was that only two patients were beyond her knowledge, one an accident from the mill, where again, molten steel had caused damage to a man's legs. This suffering man was not removed from the wagon that had carried him from the mill. At a call from the teamster, Sky had rushed out to the driveway, taken a quick look, and advised the driver to get him with all speed, directly to the hospital, apologizing for the doctor's absence.

The second patient had needed immediate care, and probably surgery, to repair an arm with a compound break. The skin had opened in two places, with shattered bone fragments showing in both. Sky carefully wrapped the arm with gauze bandaging to keep it clean and sent the man to the hospital. She held the door for him as he left the clinic. When he struggled to mount his horse, she asked, somewhat in amazement, "Are you alone?"

"Yes ma'am, no one here but just me and ol Pal here. But he's a good old horse. He'll get me there."

"Hold on."

Sky rushed to the shed where she knew Spike was cleaning up around. "Spike, saddle up. Be quick about it. There's a man here needing an escort to the hospital. I'm afraid he may pass out and fall from his horse. Be quick now."

Spike focused intently on Sky's eyes. "I do believe you've already told me to be quick. There's no need to give directions, only but the once to Spike, ma'am. You need to be in remembrance of that, just in case ever another situation should come up."

"Spike, you could have saddled that horse in the time you've been advising me of your merits, and here you haven't even started. I could do it myself more quickly."

"Now, ma'am!"

"The horse, Spike. Saddle. Remember? Quick, quick."

As she left the shed and returned to the suffering man who

had somehow mounted to the saddle, she remarked, "Spike's a good boy and he'll do right by you, but he does like to gab. Don't encourage him. He can bring your gelding back here for boarding if you wish. God bless."

Now, on this remarkably beautiful morning, with Spike again agitated with excitement, he rode the bicycle to the clinic door, hollering all the time for Sky. He dismounted in a flurry and leaned the bicycle against the clinic window, something he had been told many times not to do. Sky turned from bandaging a small girl's badly skinned knee and sighed in resignation. She had put three small stitches where the deepest tear had occurred and a simple bandage over it all, after daubing a disinfectant on the skin. Under her breath, she said, "Our errand boy. He's been told many times that one day he's going to break that window. But does he listen or pay attention?"

The girl's mother laughed. "Well, at least he's enthusiastic about his errands."

"You weren't really meant to hear that. Just me, talking to myself. He doesn't work for me, and it's not my place to criticize, I suppose. In any case, with the doctor away, Spike has chosen to follow my wishes, but only at his own speed. That's better than outright rebellion, I suppose."

Both women laughed at the thought, while again, with a chipper attitude, the young mom, leading the little girl toward the door, holding her hand while the girl sucked on a penny candy Gwyneth kept in a glass jar for the younger patients said, "When you get a child or two of your own, you'll either gain patience or tear your hair out."

Sky couldn't form an answer before Spike interrupted with the slamming of the opened door. The excited words burst from him. "A letter from the doctor."

"Spike. I'm busy, and you know not to come in here without washing up first. Wait outside. The news can wait a few minutes."

The mother and daughter left after much thanking of Sky

and paying the small fee. Sky washed her hands carefully and returned the items she had used in patching up the girl to their proper places before opening the door into the sunlit backyard. She held out her hand to the pouting Spike, who wordlessly passed over the sealed letter.

Turning her back to the sun to make reading easier, Sky opened the envelope and unfolded the enclosed single sheet of paper. She read silently while the eager Spike looked on. Knowing she would have no peace if she didn't share the news, she looked up at Spike and said, "The doctor has been called away to an emergency in a Ute village. She wrote this just before she left the ranch she was visiting. I'm supposing the rancher passed it along to the stage driver, who delivered it to the postal clerk. She says she has a couple of things to talk about when she returns, but she could be gone another week or more. She gives no details. That means you and I will have to carry on. I'm hoping we won't be having to replace that window as one of our chores."

# Chapter Twenty-Six

By the third day in the village, the people were adequately fed and resting, at least as much as possible. Children were again running here and there, playing their games. Two of the stronger men had left on the hunt. The two beeves sent along by Billy from the B4 weren't going to last very long. With Walks A Lot's help, Gwyneth had explained the need for cleanliness, both personal and their campsite. She leaned heavily on the dangers human waste carried.

All the teepees had been abandoned, their flaps left open to welcome the clean, drying winds. All the bedding and animal robes were spread out in the sun to dry after being washed as thoroughly as possible, considering the conditions. The few less-ill women boiled a large pot of water, added soap brought from the B4, and scrubbed clothing, hanging it from branches, draping it over low-growing plants, and spreading the rest on the ground. The worst of the clothing was burned. The people had separated themselves into family groups and made temporary camps wherever a bit of shelter could be found.

Charles had settled in to work with the two men caring for the one remaining steer. They didn't really need the help, but he accepted the situation, mostly keeping tabs on the animal during the hours of darkness of night. There was nowhere else he was needed either, which was a bit of a comedown from being part of the G4 ranch, where there was work enough, and more, for everyone. He had said nothing before riding away from the ranch, mostly to avoid an unnecessary discussion, but his primary reason for joining the expedition was to protect his sister and the doctor. Even though there was no obvious threat, and the women exhibited no fear, he was constantly on horseback, well armed and ready.

Gwyneth had trouble convincing the healthy to allow themselves some distance from those who were showing the worst of the illness, especially their own families. She and Walks A Lot settled for a partial victory on that matter. The issue causing the most objection was the wearing of masks. Gwyneth was again trying to convince Walks A Lot of the mask's importance but was met with stubborn resistance.

Wyatt, who had been standing by, finally broke his silence, speaking in more fluent Ute than Gwyneth could come up with. Walks A Lot turned in surprise to Wyatt, rattling off a string of Ute that left Gwyneth's poor understanding of the language behind. All she could make out was a question of where this White man had come to know the mother tongue. The back and forth appeared to answer that question to Walks A Lot's satisfaction before the matter of masks was addressed. Wyatt spoke with both his tongue and his hands, making signs of spitting and sneezing. When he finally lowered his mask and faked a sneeze and then a cough into the palm of his hand, showing Walks A Lot the moist result, adding words that, to Gwyneth's ear, sounded like *very bad* or *big trouble*, the Ute leader's eyes lit up in understanding.

Walks A Lot asked another question before nodding, putting on a mask, and, with a good supply of torn bed sheet masks in his hand, walked among the Ute, telling them to wear the mask. One by one, they obeyed.

Gwyneth and Summer seemed to be everywhere, helping

the sick where they could, and silently praying for those who looked as if they were likely to die. Wyatt, now that he was free to speak the Ute tongue, kept himself busy encouraging the people and showing how to best tie the masks, putting the filthiest of the masks in one of the several fires, and getting new masks to distribute. When he wasn't with the ill Ute, he was in the saddle, hunting for herbs that may prove helpful.

Riding beside him and giving directions as she pointed out plant after plant was an elderly woman, a temporary replacement for the shaman or native doctor, who had died early in the epidemic. Gwyneth had lost track of all that was happening with the herbs, but she saw Daniel carrying samples to Night Light, who was adding her wisdom to that of the older woman. Understanding that she had little knowledge in the use of native plants, Gwyneth asked no questions, feeling she had done all she could with masks and hygiene advice and the delivery of the B4 steers.

Late in the afternoon of the second day following the people's agreement on the masks, several riders approached from the north. Charles saw them immediately and hollered at Wyatt, who, in turn, got Walks A Lot's attention and then Daniel's. Together, the men rode to intercept the arriving group, intent on holding them away from the camp. They immediately ran into a bit of a firestorm. A self-important man dressed in the uniform of the US Army rode forward when the others stopped. He looked at the three non-Utes facing him.

"I am Major Josia Remple, commander, US Army. Word has reached the reserve north of here of these breakaway renegades. And now I'm told there is sickness among them. If you have any authority over this bunch, have them pack up their belongings and gather their horses. I'm moving them to the reserve where they can get proper medical attention." As he was talking, the group of seven soldiers spread themselves into a short skirmish line, as in a show of power to back up the Major's words and intentions.

While this was going on, Daniel was trying to decide if anyone from the village was missing. There would be no way the news of the small band could reach the reserve unless someone had carried it. But he could think of no one who couldn't be accounted for. He decided it wasn't all that important. He may discuss it later within the group but would not bring the subject up with the military.

Walks A Lot rushed in with, "No reserve. No army. We stay here. We no more sick. You go."

Daniel, hoping to say something that would calm the anger on the major's face, said, "Major. I'm sure we can work this out to everyone's advantage. There's been typhoid in the village. Some have died. Most have survived and are fully on the mend. We hope the threat is over, but with typhoid, it's difficult to know for sure. A very good doctor from Pueblo is here, helping. The army has known of this small bunch of Utes for many years and has left them alone. They are a quiet, nonviolent people who just wish to care for themselves and live their lives in peace. We thank you for coming when you heard there was illness, but there is no more need of your services."

"And who are you, sir, and how do you come to speak for the Utes?"

"My name is Daniel, sir. My blood is half Native. I live with these people. Have done so for many years. My wife's name is Night Light. We have three children. We had another, but he is no more because of the typhoid. Hopefully and thankfully, we will lose no more people."

A disheveled man, displaying a dirty black suit, complete with tie and vest, and topped off with a much-used black bowler hat, and pompous to a comical degree, said, "I am the appointed physician for the Ute. Who is this so-called doctor who has been treating these people without my advice and permission?"

Gwyneth, ever inquisitive and somewhat suspicious, had walked across the camp toward the visitors. She arrived just as the reserve doctor had made his statement. "Good day, Major. Doctor. I am Dr. Gwyneth Wycome."

She was interrupted by the black clad doctor snidely saying, "A woman doctor? Never heard of such a thing this far west. The frontier is no place for the weaker sex. Get back to your knitting, woman. You're best off in some big city where the men can look after you, keep you safe. Whatever you've been taught or told doesn't make you an able doctor. You are out of your depth here."

Raising her voice above that of the scorning man, she continued, "As I was saying, Major Remple, I am Dr. Gwyneth Wycome, honors graduate of the medical school in Chicago, several years on staff at Lakeside Women's and Children's Hospital, and later, on surgical and medical staff at Chicago General Hospital. Now owner and head of the Wycome Medical Clinic in Pueblo. I am here because I had come on a visit to some old friends in the area. My husband and I were cattle ranchers in the area some years ago, when, in fact, it was a true frontier.

"When news of illness among these people, many of whom I had known from before, reached the ranch I was staying at, I knew I had to help. Now, with a combination of our most modern knowledge and the long-known attributes of native plants and herbs, the worst of the illness has dissipated, and I and my friends are free to return home, leaving these people to their privacy. I suggest, Major, that you do the same."

Gwyneth had sensed the mistake it would have been to confront the reserve doctor, asking for his credentials. She strung out her own record of training and service in the hopes that the man would have no comeback. So far, it seemed to be working. The soldiers in the skirmish line appeared to have settled back in their saddles, and even the major was less tense. No one seemed to want to be the first to break the silence. Finally, knowing that to arrive back at the reserve with a ragtag bunch of loner Utes, still showing signs of illness and, perhaps, carrying typhoid with them, would not be well received by the reserve Indians or the army. He sat rigidly at attention, but his eyes roamed over the hillside, taking in the situation. Everything in him was screaming, *Leave these people alone*. Still, he had his orders.

Finally, the major focused on Walks A Lot. "What is your name, sir?"

"I am called Walks A Lot."

"And are you chief here Walks A Lot?"

"No chief. Son of chief, who is no more."

"Then are you the head man?"

"Village work together."

Daniel interrupted with, "Sir, this small group has learned some of the ways of Westerners. Although Walks A Lot is not formally chief, he is the one to be consulted and relied on. If he says something or makes you a promise, that promise will be kept by the village."

Boring a hard look into Walks A Lot's eyes, as only a military officer of some experience could do, Major Remple said, "Walks A Lot, do I have your promise that your band will live in peace and that you will do as Dr. Wycome instructs, and that, later, when you are all well again, you will come to the reserve?"

Walks A Lot, as intelligent as most Westerners, had taken note that the major had avoided putting a time frame on *later*, answered, "When people have no more illness, later, sometime, we come to reserve. Live in peace now. No trouble."

Holding back a grin, the major wheeled his horse around and lifted him into a slow trot. It was a long ride back to the army post. They had best get started. The doctor sat for another few seconds. Gwyneth could see the questions forming in his mind. When he too turned his riding animal toward home, everyone breathed a sigh of relief. There were now just a few last-minute matters to clear up in the slowly recovering village before Gwyneth and the others would return to the B4 and then, for Gwyneth, on to Pueblo and home.

THE VISITORS' last afternoon in the Ute village was easy and generally happy. There was still sorrow and grieving, of course, as some had not survived the typhoid. The teepees had all been taken down and moved to a clean, sun-bright location about half a mile away. Only the best of clothing had been washed and saved for use. Much had been burned. The hunters brought in enough meat to care for the needs of the people for a week or more. They were almost back to their old ways. Wyatt had talked with Daniel and Walks A Lot about bringing out some cattle to raise on the abundant grass in the area. With their promise to give consideration to the thought, he let the subject drop.

Gwyneth and Night Light visited away the last few hours together, enjoying the sunshine that warmed the hillside, until late evening drove Night Light back to her children, and Gwyneth to her bed. They had sometimes laughed like schoolgirls, and sometimes entered into serious, private discussion, covering many topics. Although Night Light was living as the tribe had always lived, except for its smaller number of people, she had tasted enough of the settler's ways to, from time to time, find herself leaning in that direction. That brought on a discussion of mixed marriages and half cast children and their acceptance in a village as small as Bessie Creek or a city like Pueblo. Gwyneth had some doubts about first-generation Utes mixing in, so she made no suggestions or promises, except to say that Billy would more than welcome them back on the B4.

When darkness fell, the camp settled down. Most slept, although the Ute had always posted guards. They would do no less on this night. Charles had felt underused during their time in the village, finding that his sister neither asked for nor accepted much of his protection. He too, saddled up and spent the night on guard.

When the B4 bunch rode out the next morning, they led no heavily packed horses as they had on the inward trip. They carried no bedrolls, and they had only enough food for a skimpy lunch that could be eaten in the saddle as they rode. Everything of use to the Ute had been left behind. Daniel rode with them. He would ride to Bessie Creek, and perhaps to Pueblo if he couldn't find the items the tribe needed in the smaller village. He drove three pack horses before him. It would take all of them to carry the bounty of replacement blankets, clothing, and other items back to the people, paying for it with a small, tanned hide sack of nuggets some of the people had picked from the bottom of streams from time to time.

GWYNETH ARRIVED BACK in Pueblo tired and with much on her mind. The question of expanding her medical services into Bessie Creek, which had been the original reason for her trip, had not been answered. Night Light's knowledge of the herbs was much on her mind. How to make the best use of her nurse, Sky, was an unanswered question. The girl reminded Gwyneth of herself when she was younger. Sky was very capable, able to handle many of the simpler situations that presented themselves to the Wycome Medical Clinic.

Gwyneth was convinced that Sky was near her own equal at delivering babies. But Sky had expressed no interest at all in following Gwyneth's path to college, stating she was happy as a nurse and was looking forward to marriage sometime in the future. Could she be stationed at Bessie Creek, handling the cuts and scrapes, the broken bones, the colds, and seasonal ailments of the small population and the surrounding area? Would such a clinic cover its own costs in collected fees?

As a last, almost humorous thought, Gwyneth admitted to herself, *I've never once thought about Clayton Bonifare during the past couple of weeks.*

Even with all the man's overtures and the pleasant dinners they shared, could anyone she cared about so easily slip from her mind? She contrasted that with her first meeting, years before, with Trent Wycome. Even lying on the stretcher in the doctor's office, fresh from the cattle trail and stinking of campfires, cattle, and man odor, and needing a badly broken arm cared for, he still captivated her with his grin and his determination to get to know her, a determination that led them to having dinner together that evening, and eventually to marriage. My, how she missed Trent. Would she ever get over him? But Clayton? Although she was sometimes lonely in her beautiful home and often thought of the comforts of companionship, there wasn't a single thought of having Clayton fill that gap in her life in anything but a casual, totally platonic relationship.

Gwyneth arrived home late in the evening. The house and clinic were both in darkness. Sky was not there. That would mean there were no critical issues needing attention. There was no one bedded down in the recovery room. Gwyneth had the hired hack driver drop her near her front door, where she would only have to lift one weary and aching foot at a time to rise up the stairs to the veranda and the front door. She hadn't ridden so many miles on horseback for years. Or lost so much sleep as she had during the time with the Ute. Although she rode regularly and enjoyed it, she wasn't as young as she used to be. The miles from the B4 to the Ute village had been long, the hillsides the trails led up and over were a challenge for horse and rider both. But they offered beautiful vistas of the western country, which had been shrouded in darkness on the trip to the village but were seen in the bright light of day on the return trip.

The venture to Bessie Creek and onward had been satisfying in many respects, especially in seeing most of the tribesmen recover from the dreadful disease. She would never be sure if the masks and the cleanliness had been the key to their recovery or if the native herbs and plants had played a big part. But considering the limitations of the current medical knowledge, and with the little she had on hand to work with, it was the best she could do. Trying to be honest with herself while at the same time admitting her inward rebellion and disgust at the lack of care for hygiene and the lives the Ute lived, including their sparse diet, she hoped they might have sparked some interest in cleanliness, at least.

All in all, home could not have looked more welcoming. She felt as if she had been in some foreign land. A land she might never be able to understand. It might take a day or two to work the sights and smells out of her mind and get back to her own life. She unlocked and opened the door, closing it quietly behind her. The small lamp she kept on the foyer table was where it was supposed to be, as were the matches. She lit the lamp, set it down, adjusted the wick, and looked around. How she loved her home.

Of course, Trent was missing, and she had no other to talk with, someone who would respond when she said, *What a wonderful sunset*, or *What should we have for dinner this evening*? That, and a couple of other vagrant thoughts, went through her mind as she looked over the house while she carried the lamp toward the kitchen. There had been a temptation to take her dinner in one of the restaurants near the depot, but her weary bones had seemed to be crying, *Go home.*

After a satisfying night's sleep, Gwyneth enjoyed a casual breakfast in her own kitchen, where she could look into the rear yard, past the neighboring homes and to the far-off mountains, to the northwest of the city. The living room and veranda offered an almost unobstructed view of the snow-capped western hills. She had risen early, luxuriating in her bath, reveling in the choosing of clean clothing in which to face the day, looking forward to the continuing adventure of the Wycome Medical Clinic. In the back of her mind floated the years of ranching, bathing in the snow-melt creek water, washing clothing and bedding in the big wooden tub, after heating water on the stove, and sharing the workload that included milking the cow and caring for the chickens. She had loved it at the time, but was not eager to return to that way of living.

Even with her casual start to the day she was still stepping down the back stairs to the clinic before seven. To her great surprise, Sky was already there. They both spoke their greetings at the same time for the first few seconds, before Sky began laughing, saying, "You first."

Taking turns, they were caught up to date within a few minutes. Sky then asked, "Did you notice the letter on the desk?"

Gwyneth turned to the desk and found the wrinkled, much-traveled envelope lying neatly beside the paid billings and Sky's daily report. Sky had always impressed Gwyneth with her neatness and attention to order. Fingering the day journal that she would read later, she picked the envelope up, knowing who it would be from. She received little mail, and she knew the handwriting of Helen Wycome, her former mother-in-law. She was the single connection Gwyneth had with the years gone past.

Helen was a faithful friend and communicator. Gwyneth had probably written even more than Helen had, but no one was keeping score. Helen never failed to bring Gwyneth up to date on hers and Abe's lives, and the lives of the two daughters who now lived close to the Texas Wycome family. Gwyneth had never met either of the daughters, but she felt as if she knew them, their husbands, and their children, knew them from the writing in Helen's newsy letters.

The letter was written in the ordinary pattern Helen had established years before, updating Gwyneth on the happenings of the family and the country around their home until Gwyneth turned to the second page. She read the first few words, then, without taking her eyes from the page, reached for the chair that was forever by the desk. Turning the chair to where she could sit on it, she slid down and rested.

What she was reading was news of Abe and Helen's new neighbors. It was news of Cob Fleming, their old friend who had stood beside Trent and Gwyneth through every minute of their struggles with a small ranch in a new country. He had been a friend like no other. Into Gwyneth's mind flashed the remembrance of the last time Cob helped her clean up after the ranch hands left the house, leaving dishes to be washed. Cob had been strangely quiet as he dried the dishes. They were to part the next day, Gwyneth to college in the big eastern city, and Cob to Texas and the family ranch. This could be their final time together. There was no doubt they could both feel the tension in the air.

Gwyneth knew, or at least suspected, where the evening's conversation was headed. She had known from the start how Cob felt about her, had known even as he was standing by as Trent married the girl Cob loved. She knew, oh yes, she knew. That nothing had been said over the years was a testament to something, she wasn't sure what, perhaps respect for the now-dead husband and friend, perhaps fear of refusal if a proposal were to be put forward, perhaps something altogether different, something Gwyneth was unaware of.

This was Cob, the tough, no-nonsense cowhand and rancher, the man who was never without his Colt 44, a tool of the western cattleman. Cob was practiced and adept in the weapon's use. Sitting there in her medical clinic office, she smiled privately at the remembrance of the man who was always first to step toward trouble, the man, of all the men she knew, whom she would always trust.

When this man, standing beside the stove drying dishes, inelegantly stumbled into an expression of his love, Gwyneth could have cried for him. He was being such a gentleman, so caring, so unsure of what to say next, it was tempting to simply say yes to a marriage, although she didn't have feelings to match Cobs. A great many frontier marriages thrived on far less than what Gwyneth and Cob had between them, but the lifelong desire to attend medical school couldn't be so easily cast aside.

Now, a thousand or more miles away, in Texas cattle country, Cob Fleming, one of the third-generation sons of the Hat, or Sombrero brand, was expanding the family ranch on new property recently purchased near the town of Burnt Lake, the town where Abe and Helen had established their general store.

# Chapter Twenty-Seven

GWYNETH WAS JUST SETTLING IN TO READ THE letter again when a buggy, carrying a single passenger, pulled into the driveway, needlessly moving forward all the way to the shed at the back of the lot. That brought Spike from the shed, yawning as if he hadn't quite faced the day yet. "You can leave the animal, sir. I'll care for him. If it's the doctor you're in need of, just make your way back to the house. The clinic entry is that door with the white trim and the sign showing."

Smiling to himself, as the stableboy repeated the obvious, the driver spoke his thanks, laid a double twist of the reins around the small snubbing post built into the dashboard of the buggy, and stepped carefully to the ground. With equal care, he made his way to the clinic. A one-knuckle wrap on the screen door brought Sky. "Come in, sir. The doctor will be with you in just a moment. If you would care to tell me what your ailment is, I may be able to prepare the clinic for the doctor."

"My ailment, my dear, is that I have lived too long. And don't you go to offering solutions to that problem for me. I'll accept my fate until the Good Lord decides I've caused enough misery here on this earth and it's time to remove me from His creation."

Sky smiled at the man and said, "Please take a seat here, sir. I had not thought of digging my pistol out of its hiding place, if that was your thought. The medical profession has not yet sunk to such solutions, although there are days and there are patients... But I must not talk of that."

"No, indeed, we must not talk of that."

Gwyneth entered through the inner door in time to hear the last of the man's statement. "What is it we're not to talk about, sir?"

"Good morning, Doctor. This pleasant young lady and I were just discussing the options facing the elderly and their many aches, pains, and limitations. Although that subject is one that is worth philosophical exploration, and I would dearly love to spend part of the morning on it, that is not why I intrude upon you on this lovely sunny day."

Struggling to his feet, he removed his hat, saying, "Please, allow me to introduce myself. I am Dr. Silas Grant. And you, lovely lady, must be Dr. Gwyneth Wycome, of whom I have heard many encouraging reports. And your very pleasant young nurse, Sky, whose name is so often adjoined to yours, Doctor, on many of those reports. I have not come seeking medical advice, although I admit to having given myself questionable counsel over the years, where I might have benefited from a second opinion on occasion. No, what I'm about today, is business. The medical business, to be sure, but still business."

Sky quietly slipped through the door into the recovery room, closing it behind herself.

Turning a chair to where she could sit facing the visiting doctor, Gwyneth sat and invited Dr. Grant to sit also. "We can talk here, sir. I have been away for the past two weeks. Sky has been caring for the clinic. She has a couple of things that need doing if you'll pardon her absence."

"Of course. My visit today won't take long. When I referred to age, that was more than idle chatter. The pure fact is, Doctor, that I have come to the age of retirement. I can no longer keep up the pace. Further, I feel inadequate in my medical advice and practices. I have found it difficult to even comprehend some of the advances in the practice of medicine and am not sure how much I really care anymore. Gathering all that into a simple statement, I have come to ask your permission to direct my patients your way, since I will no longer be available to them, and to advise them of your superior services.

"In addition to that, I wish to publicly recommend your clinic for my patients' further medical needs in my retirement notices. I intend to close my practice in one week. Letters from the east have built in me a desire to know my grandchildren. I am a frugal man, not wealthy, but with adequate set by for whatever remaining time my maker has in mind for me. I offer you, Doctor, at no cost or thought of remuneration, the few files I have kept on special patients, along with the furniture and equipment weighing down the floor at my offices.

"I have been advised by others that my book of patients might be worth a sum of money to someone taking over the practice. I am uncomfortable with the thought. The practice of medicine has been good for me, financially as well as personally. I have met and interacted with a great many wonderful people. I'll not try to gain from the sale of their loyalty. So it is yours for the taking, good Doctor. What say you to that, Gwyneth Wycome?"

Gwyneth could have answered Dr. Grant's question immediately, but that would have spoiled the morning for the old man. He had come to talk and reminisce a bit and perhaps exchange stories with his much younger replacement. When, in answer to one of his questions, Gwyneth talked about how she had originally been attracted to serving in the Civil War medical tents, she saw a tear escape one eye. It trickled down his cheek without any attempt from him to try to stop it, or the several that followed. The second eye mysteriously remained tearless.

"Horrible. Ugly. Stupid. Inhumane. I was there every minute of those dreadful years. I lost track of how many fine young men either died or entered into their new lives mutilated and disfigured under my care. That is, if I dare call it care. Always and forever understaffed, underequipped, we had no time for the practice of medicine as it is described in the college journals. Couldn't even take time to wash our hands, even if there had been water to wash in. It was hack and sew and move along, more are waiting.

"And my, the work you nurses did, and most of you with not a whit of training or previous experience. If the patients were to sense any love or caring at all in that hell hole, it was to come from the nurses. I'm pleased to meet one of them here in this remote place. It's late in the game but perhaps not too late to say, *thank you*. Thank you for all you did, you and the hundreds of others like you. There were no adequate ways of showing thanks at the time.

"When the final bugles sounded, it seemed as if we were scattered to our many homes before even a goodbye could be said. I'm so glad you survived, Doctor, and have moved ahead to really make something of yourself. Something to be proud of. Something important. I'm more than ever confident that I leave my patients in caring, competent hands."

There was more said as the morning slipped away, but finally the old man stood to his feet. "Doctor, I don't know what your personal beliefs are, but I leave you with this thought. Every person, man, woman, young or old, who comes to you for assistance, is a child of the living God, made in His image and deserving of the best you have to offer. You are working on the very representation of the Creator. Treat your patients with that in mind and don't be afraid to ask that same Creator for wisdom in caring for what He has made. Now I bid you adieu, fair lady. And wish you success upon success, and a long life."

By way of agreement to Dr. Grant's offer, Gwyneth simply said, "You are a generous and thoughtful man, Dr. Grant. I would find it a pleasure, an honor, to work with your patients. Thank you."

Gwyneth and Sky stood together in the clinic window as the retiring doctor hobbled up the slightly sloping lane and approached the buggy. Spike, with wisdom gained from who knew where, saw the need and gently helped the doctor into his buggy. He unwound the reins and laid them in the man's hands before standing back to allow space for the horse to make the turn onto the rear laneway. He stood watching until man and buggy turned onto the road and disappeared.

THAT EVENING, settled into her wicker chair on the veranda as she often did, Gwyneth read and re-read the letter from Texas. It brought many remembrances into her mind, as each of Helen's letters tended to do. The letters were a reminder of both the good times and the not-so-good. The travails and the long miles of travel from Eastern Kansas to their remote valley in Colorado. The shaky start of the Mirrored W Ranch. The hours worked. Some days seeming as if the men worked more hours than there were on the clock. The dreadful news Cob brought of Trent's accident. And on and on, the years of working, wondering, wishing, praying. Privately weeping when she and Trent were not blessed with a family of their own. Struggling with decisions on matters that seemed to shift each time she mentally addressed them.

Finally selling their beloved ranch. The few weeks in Bessie Creek. Splitting from Abe and Helen. A friendly and loving split to be sure, but still a split, enforced by distance and desires. College, hospitals, learning, doing, living. And now, here she was in Pueblo with the responsibility of a medical clinic demanding her time, and a letter from Helen, lying on her lap, awakening thoughts and temptations that might have been better left to their sleep.

~

With the shutting of the Grant Clinic, Gwyneth had instructed Spike to locate and hire a drayage hauler to clean out the old office. Gwyneth went first to gather up usable supplies, tools of the trade, and whatever she might find useful. As she and Sky rummaged around in the old clinic, finding lost or forgotten journals and boxes of fee statements, along with no longer used medical tools, scalpels, and a variety of items that could be the beginnings of a medical museum, somehow a hush fell between the two women. Gwyneth backed from under a low shelf and straightened to her feet. Sky stood with a box of mysterious, unidentifiable suture threads. She was looking at it quizzically when Gwyneth asked, "What have you got?"

"I don't know. Some kind of thread. This place is like a time vault."

"It's that and more, Sky. It's the story of a man's life, even the medical profession's life. Although he is still among the living, I almost feel Dr. Grant's ghost, and ghosts of other ghosts looking over my shoulder, saying something like, *Take care, you are benefiting from the work of others.*"

Sky shuddered at the thought and carefully placed the box on the *to-be-kept* pile.

Gwyneth's big house boasted a partial basement, not meant for living space, but handy for storage, and sometimes used to keep firewood dry. A door to the backyard gave access. It was into this space that Spike and the drayage driver carried the desk, chairs, two stretchers, and three recovery beds, along with all the smaller items from Dr. Grant's clinic, storing them against future needs and growth in the Wycome Clinic.

By the third week after Dr. Grant's visit, Gwyneth was having difficulty sorting out the retired doctor's patients from those who were simply coming to her for the first time, although some eased the mystery by mentioning their former doctor. Not that it really mattered. She and Sky did their best, no matter who walked in the door or sent a message requesting a home visit. Dr. Grant hadn't kept extensive records. But the one box of files on patients who had cumulative or repeat problems that had complicated their care, and the variety of treatments used, along with the results, had been set aside in Gwyneth's small office. At least one of the notes from the past had proven helpful.

Pueblo, like most settlements in the west, was peopled primarily by the young. By contrast, many who found their way across town from the Grant clinic, or who had requested a home visit from the doctor, were older. Smiling to herself at the balance of patients' ages, Gwyneth wondered if, in the selecting of Dr. Grant, those who had watched more years pass had sought the care of someone more like themselves. They brought with them the ailments of the aged or aging, men looking for relief from the ravages of a lifetime of hard work, aching joints, out-of-place, crooked spines, arthritis, especially in the hands and fingers, an ailment also known to be common to women, failing eyesight and hearing, and a general tiredness and lack of energy.

Gwyneth always felt some of the pain people suffered when she had to tell them that medical science had not found a cure or relief for the particular ailment they suffered under.

With the guidance of one particular doctor at Chicago General, a well-traveled and knowledgeable man with a drive for careful experimentation, she had learned something of the benefits of exercise and diet control. Being careful to explain that the advice offered came with no guarantee, and the caution to stay within their physical limits when exercising, she demonstrated a few movement tricks that sometimes helped put the joints back in their proper places while keeping the entire body somewhat limber.

With the elderly especially, stomach and bowel ailments were common. Here, she relied periodically on the knowledge passed along by Night Light. Among other plants, yarrow, oregon grape, and aspen leaves and bark were known to have salutary effects on such human problems. Gwyneth had brought a small amount of several helpful plants home with her after the visit to the Ute village. She offered it sparingly to her patients, thinking she would have to write a letter to Daniel asking Night Light to gather more and send them to Pueblo.

Castor oil, Senna, and Magnesium sulfate were all available at the Pueblo apothecary shops. Each had been shown to be helpful, and none were as harmful as some of the mysterious bottled liquids being peddled town to town by the itinerant medicine men whose offerings were known to contain cocaine, snakebite whiskey, and other toxic ingredients. Gwyneth wrote out the names of products she thought might help her patients, advising them to speak further with the chemist at the apothecary shop.

Constantly seeing the limitations of her profession, Gwyneth had been forced into acceptance of those limitations, while still reading the medical journals, looking for new discoveries.

The issue of who her patients were and whether or not they came from Dr. Grant bothered her less and less over the weeks. What did rise to the surface was her workload. Hers and Sky's.

Again, as had happened whenever Gwyneth did something noteworthy, the Wycome Clinic received public commendation, suggesting that the retiring Dr. Grant had left Pueblo only after coming to the belief that the Wycome Clinic offered the best care for his patients. She was not sought for an interview from the paper that spread that news, nor did she pay for any such coverage. But the results, shown in the number of patient visits, was almost immediate, following each write-up. Gwyneth, cognizant of age and distance traveled for many patients, hired Spike on a full-time basis, holding him and the buggy ready, for a small fee, to carry patients to and from the clinic, or driving for Gwyneth when a home visit was unavoidable.

Even with the extended work hours for both women,

Gwyneth couldn't get Bessie Creek out of her mind. She still had considerable available cash held in the bank account, and her fees were increasing steadily with the rush of new patients. Financing an extension of services into the small town wasn't the problem. The problem was threefold. First, the additional demands on her own time, second, available space for a clinic in Bessie Creek, and third, getting an accurate picture of the real needs. She would need all of that before broaching the subject with Sky. In the back of her mind was Summer Wilmore. She was young by city standards, although many a frontier bride was no older. She had said nothing during the trip to the Ute, but Gwyneth had watched her and made a mental note.

HER THINKING PLACE HAD BECOME, almost right from the start, the quiet evening hours on the veranda. It was there she finally hatched a plan. It would require another rushed trip on the train, but this time she was not going beyond Bessie Creek. She was sure a single day would accomplish her goal. She booked off one day, leaving Sky in charge. Spike drove her to the train, with the promise to be waiting when she stepped off the evening return run. She was in Bessie Creek before lunch, welcomed by a drizzling fall of rain, which did nothing at all toward making the place more attractive. She went immediately to the small general store, the one Betty's new husband had worked in. Betty had supplied the man's name and the information that if anyone had a handle on village matters, it would be him.

The door banged shut with a shaking of window glass, startling her as she entered the store. A genial fellow standing behind the counter smiled and welcomed her with, "Please pardon the door banging. I fixed it yesterday. Looks as if I'm going to have to fix it again. Anyway, welcome. I remember you from your trip here a few weeks ago, although we didn't meet. I'm Emery Radcliff. What can I do for you, Doctor?"

"I've come on a bit of a search. My earlier visit was meant to do what I aim to do today, but there was a small matter of my Ute friends and a visitation of typhoid. I'm afraid I got side-tracked."

"Yes, that matter with the Ute is the talk of the town and the entire district. You left a long trail of positive comments behind you as you traveled, Doctor. Well done with the Utes. We never see them in town, but I had occasion to make a wagon trip to their small village just last week. Your friend Daniel was in here, emptying the shelves of almost everything I had in stock. He then left a list of additional items the Ute were in need of. I decided to go to Pueblo myself to pick up the order and do some banking. Daniel had said to send a runner to the village, and he would return for the order. He had left good directions, and I always enjoy a day away from this counter, so I commandeered my wife to stand in. With my wagon loaded to the railings, I set out. I got lost a couple of times, but I did manage to find the Ute, following the rise of cooking fire smoke there at the last.

"Daniel left me in trust of a hide sack of gold nuggets and some dust, as you most likely already know. The bank in Pueblo valued them for me, as I know nothing at all about gold. All in all, it was a successful adventure in business. The band received their supplies and a small balance to boot on the gold transfer. And they all lived happily ever after, as the nursery rhymes say."

"We'll I'd say we both had an adventure, Mr. Radcliff."

"Emory, please, Doctor. Bessie Creek stands of few formalities."

"What I am in need of today, Emory, is advice. I am considering opening a clinic here in town. I'm not at all sure of the need, so I'm thinking one or two days each week. Or I may open as a nursing station at first. Either way, I would require a small space to rent. Do you know of any such space?"

With a sly grin on his face, he said, "Come with me."

With just a few steps, the grocer crossed the floor, slipped sideways behind a rack of ladies' clothing, and opened a door into a small but adequate room. "I don't know what the original builder had in mind, but he never used this space. And neither have I. We could cut a door into the side for access between this building and the one next door, or we could cut it in front, directly off the boardwalk. What do you think of that?"

A FEW DAYS LATER, back in Pueblo, smiling to herself, the doctor admitted she had never done such a thing before, always holding work and social matters separate, but, just for this one time, she had arranged for a private table at the restaurant she and Clayton Bonifare had found to be to their liking. She and Sky had changed into street clothing after a long day at the clinic. Sky was full of curiosity, but Gwyneth had simply said, "We've something to discuss. We're too busy to do it here."

Spike escorted them to the care of the maître d' before turning the buggy toward a simpler restaurant to take his own dinner, also at Gwyneth's expense. It was a noteworthy event for the stable boy and clinic runner of the Wycome Medical Clinic.

Sky was fascinated by the lush interior of the restaurant. She had little experience in the social side of the more affluent. Gwyneth ordered a small glass of wine for each of them, although such beverages were a rarity in her life. Sky couldn't decide from among the offerings on the extensive menu. She lifted her eyes from the menu and said, "I'm such a rube. I'm totally out of place here. I'm afraid to look around for fear that I'll see everyone staring at me, knowing I don't belong. So I don't make a fool of myself in front of the waiter, how would it be if I let you choose something, perhaps a beef dish?"

Gwyneth smiled, saying, "I had much the same feeling about myself when I first ventured out among the who's who. I only relaxed when I realized that we all put our shoes on one foot at a time, and there is nothing but attitude separating them from us. So I changed my attitude since I couldn't change theirs. Relax and enjoy, knowing you are as good as any here, that you do valuable work, and that wealth is a poor marker to judge a person's merits by. Now, take a look at the prime rib plate, about halfway down on the left. You might like that with a baked potato. And Sky, if there are folks staring at you, it is not because you don't belong, it is because you do belong, only not with me. You belong here with a young gentleman escort at your side."

The blushing Sky held back any retort she might have had in her mind.

The ordering was done in a satisfactory manner and the menus were removed. Within moments, the waiter returned with the small loaf of sourdough bread, which was the customary hors d'oeuvre in the establishment, one of the fixtures the establishment was known for. Gwyneth leaned forward and folded her arms on the table before her.

"Sky, we need to talk about our future. You've never told me if you have aspirations for a career other than nursing. I also know nothing at all about your family, where you're from, although you have mentioned Denver, or if there's a man in your life. Or if you have responsibilities beyond what work you do at the clinic."

Sky filled the next few minutes with her personal information, none of it startling. Her family lived in Denver. She didn't see much of them, although she didn't explain why. Nursing was her life's goal. She had no other. The two years she spent in the Denver hospital, under the instructions of a rather serious and unapproachable matron, were the light of her young life before she came to work at the Wycome Medical Clinic. And no, she had no plans for further study.

There were no men she had any interest in, although there were invitations enough coming her way.

At the end of the evening, the two women had made a deal. An experimental arrangement to be sure, but one filled with hope. Sky had assured Gwyneth that she had no fear of what a small village might offer, and the thought of traveling by horse and buggy to remote farms and ranches to deliver her medical help wherever it was needed would be exciting, an adventure, rather than threatening.

To Sky's inquiry about a nurse for the Pueblo clinic, Gwyneth answered, "We're going to continue to grow, Sky. The country is growing. The city is growing. The entire west is growing. Nothing can stop that growth until the vast populations of the east are finally moved west and settled in among the hundreds of small towns and cities that will yet be built. People will continue coming from faraway lands, but at a slower pace.

"Start-up villages like Bessie Creek are a risk. My prediction is that there will be dozens, perhaps hundreds of towns shuttered and unpopulated when the mines are no longer producing or when bigger towns close by drag all the businesses their way. Then, too, much will depend on where the railways spot their terminals. Pueblo is well past that stage. Our efforts in Bessie Creek may not last, but we have no such fear in our current clinic. As to nursing assistance here in town, I have a young lady in mind but haven't spoken to her yet."

Gwyneth was purposely including Sky in the *we* and *our* statements to give her confidence in her importance to Gwyneth and to the medical practice.

In further and more direct answer to Sky's question about her replacement, Gwyneth said, "I have decided to write to an old friend from Chicago. A nurse, and a good one. Smart, confident, knowledgeable. And with much practical experience. We worked together at Chicago General. Her name is Beatrice Brodrick. She prefers to be called Bea. We became friends when she asked me to teach her to ride. It took a while, but she became a competent horsewoman. In exchange, she guided me on my clothing choices and introduced me to the world beyond my ranching experience. Bea would not be a replacement for you, but an addition to the clinic. Even if Bessie Creek fails as a business, there will always be a place for you in Pueblo.

"I intend to get a letter off on the evening train if I find time tomorrow to write a short note. I may be too late, of course. Bea is an exceptionally attractive girl. Men flock around her, but mostly at a distance. To approach a girl like that, a man would have to be either her equal socially or a fool. And, if I may offer an observation, Sky, you might be experiencing a similar problem. You too, present a strong and confident, and attractive image in public. Men are attracted and cautioned away at the same time."

As if forcing a new thought to life, almost to herself, Gwyneth whispered, "For all I know, Bea could be married by now."

THE NEXT DAY, during a lull in patients, the two women took a careful look at the furniture and equipment that came over from the Grant operation. To start in Bessie Creek, some purchases would have to be made. They wrote out a list and sent Spike to the appropriate outlets to place the orders.

With the daily rail service to Bessie Creek, an exchange of letters had become a satisfactory method of communication. Gwyneth sent a note to Emery Radcliff advising that the offer on the small rental space was accepted. With the note, she sent a list of work to be done to make the space usable, and asked Emery to try to find a tradesman to tackle the matter.

A second note was sent to Mrs. Wilhelmina Radcliff, who was widely known as Willow, the operator of Bessie Creek's only rooming house for ladies, a modest venture the tall, painfully thin woman established as an aid to the modest income of Eli Radcliff, her husband and station master, as well as telegrapher at Bessie Creek. Sky would be safe and well cared for by the matronly woman.

She then sent a separate letter to Eustice Ward advising him of the happenings. Specifically, she asked him to look in on Sky and see to any needs she might have. She would have to remember to tell Sky about Eustice and that she had written him.

While she was in a letter-writing mood, she turned to a clean page in the notepad and, writing more carefully, using the best penmanship at her disposal, she headed the letter, *Dr. Brandy Gilcrist, Chicago General Hospital.* In the carefully worded letter, she told of the happenings in Pueblo and the Wycome Medical Clinic. She explained about Dr. Grant. She told Dr. Brandy how busy the clinic had become, and with no intention of exaggeration, suggested a bright future lay ahead in Pueblo, Colorado. Because the Chicago doctor would not be familiar with the west and had never practiced outside a hospital, she explained how many of her patients requested house calls, and that some of those calls required travel of many miles to reach a mine site or a ranch, or a small farm. Carefully, she made her case for the addition of a second physician. She buttered him up just a bit without being too obvious about it.

Gwyneth was tempted to add that she'd had a preliminary discussion with the Pueblo hospital, at the hospital's request. The discussion had potential for the future, as an on-call surgeon, but at the time, the demands of the Wycome Clinic alone were filling all of Gwyneth's available time.

The note to Dr. Gilcrist closed with an offer to pay his way for an exploratory visit to Pueblo, if he had any interest in joining the clinic as an associate. Because she knew the wage scale at the hospital, she was able to promise to match, or perhaps exceed, his current salary. She delivered the letters to the postal clerk personally to keep her inquiries private. She had known since the beginning that Spike, meaning no harm, but unconscious of the risks to patient confidentially, had a problem with secrets. He had been warned more than once, but some doubts remained in Gwyneth's mind.

There were yet a few late summer weeks ahead, but the heat of July and August had passed. A single letter arrived from Bea. She had quit her hospital job, given up her rental suite, packed all the personal items and clothing she thought she might need, and was heading west as soon as she could secure a ticket that included a private bedroom and, somehow, figured out how to get her three suitcases and her single trunk to the railway station. The abruptness of Bea's decision startled Gwyneth, but soon a smile formed on her lips as she harkened back to the self-assured young lady who had mastered the nuances of saddling a horse after a single demonstration and had reduced the hostler to a willing servant, if not a slave, with her smile.

Sky was established in Bessie Creek, with a modest but satisfactory beginning toward a growing clinic, offering nursing services, with a physician available on alternate weekends, when Gwyneth would make the trip down on a Friday, staying over until Sunday evening.

The rented room joined to the general store had been divided into two spaces. The door from the boardwalk opened into a modest office space, with Dr. Grant's small desk separating the space from the larger room behind, where patients would be seen and treated. As was expected, most of the patients still requested a home visit.

There was a horse and buggy at the Bessie Creek livery, purchased for the clinic with the guidance of Eustice Ward.

That same gentleman, cowhand and part-time pastor of the Bessie Creek Community Chapel, had taken Sky on several trial runs with the horse, utilizing his weekends in Bessie Creek to the best advantage, as he privately thought of his time with the comely nurse. She saw the fussing as being unnecessary, as she had much experience with similar rigs. But she enjoyed the time with Eustice, suspecting all along that he may have more than buggy driving in mind, but she said nothing, offering neither complaint nor encouragement in the matter.

As could have been predicted, Sky's first call out was for the delivery of a baby. The patient was a rancher's wife living in rough hill country, a little more than nine miles to the northwest. The child was welcomed into the world with some fanfare from the young couple and their firstborn, a three-year-old boy. A neighbor had come in to put a meal together and do some clean up of the recently neglected cabin. Night fell before the baby was settled in his mother's arms, and Dr. Grant's old black bag, which Sky had expropriated as her own, was repacked.

As Sky was determined to return to town rather than stay the night, the rancher harnessed the horse and brought the buggy to the cabin door. He went back for his saddle horse, intending to guide Sky through the darkening hills. Sky objected. "You already had the long ride getting me here. I'll have no trouble on the return."

Obviously weary but still feeling the obligation, the rancher said, "If you insist. I'll just ride the first way with you, get you out of these hills, and then, if you still feel sure, I'll return home. Are you at least armed?"

"Sir, I learned this from the doctor. She is armed at all times, and so am I. I have come to be comforted by the heaviness of my pistol."

She said nothing about where she kept the weapon, nor of the loaded carbine secreted beneath the seat, much as Clayton Bonifare had secreted his.

~

Bea arrived in Pueblo to a great flurry of excitement, as it seemed every man at the station had somehow found the time and desire to assist in her disembarking the train and in the arrangement of her baggage in the clinic's buggy. When a business-suit-clad gentleman attempted to push Spike aside as Bea was intent on rising to the buggy seat to join Gwyneth, he somehow found himself suddenly out of breath, all bent over and gasping. It seemed that no one was watching Spike closely enough to notice when his elbow, with serious intent, made a quick move back and then forward, to again hang at Spike's side. With a grin, the observant Bea said quietly, "Thank you, sir. Let us make some haste to get away from here."

~

Dr. Brandy Gilcrist wrote, agreeing to visit, with no promise attached. Not long after, the good doctor, nattily dressed, as any big city professional would be dressed, handsome, financially well off, debonaire, and comfortable in the upper strata of society, single and the heart throb of more than just a few nurses, stepped off the train in Pueblo, Colorado. He carried a single polished leather bag that cost more than most working men would make in a quarter year of hard labor. He would have looked perfectly normal as he boarded the train in Chicago. But in Pueblo, he stood out as Bea had stood out, only this time it was the ladies who were discreetly watching as the disembarking crowd formed and then slowly dissipated.

There were also a few cowhands stepping carelessly to the wooden plank landing, lithe and surefooted. These were riders who had accompanied a herd to the eastern markets. A single glance from one of these cowboys was enough to dismiss the likes of Dr. Gilcrist as being a city sissy who would be totally useless in a man's environment. Put to the test, they would have discovered their error in judgment. Fortunately for all, the test wasn't forthcoming.

When Spike stopped the rig beside the door to the Wycome Medical Clinic, the doctor sat, looking carefully around the area, from the house and yard to the beautiful mountains on the western horizon. And the many other large and intricately planned Victorian-style homes. When he finally brought his eyes back to the clinic door, he addressed Spike. "I'll be staying at the Rimfire Hotel, which I'm told has borrowed its name from the sight of the rising sun on the mountain tops, and not, as I first suspected, a tribute to buffalo hunters or such like. It's not the best in town, but it's close by. I weighed that as being the greater advantage. If you would take my luggage there and have the porter place it in my room, I would much appreciate it."

With Spike's, "*Righty Ho,*" echoing in his ears, the visiting doctor opened the clinic door and stepped across the sill to find he was needed. Not later or sometime, but right at the moment.

Standing a discreet distance from Gwyneth and the patient she was treating, he said, "Good afternoon, Doctor. I see you're busy. I'll just step out and make myself comfortable on one of those benches in the yard. Soak up some sunshine."

Without turning from her work, Gwyneth answered, "No, you won't. You'll take off that fancy jacket and tie I suspect you're wearing, have a good scrub, and get in here to help me. Bea is here, but she's delivering a baby in the other room."

Without asking foolish, time-wasting questions, Brandy Gilcrist turned back to the little waiting room where he hung his jacket over the back of a chair, laying the tie over it. Re-entering the clinic's single working space he found that the once hot water was cooling but he saw no facility for re-heating it, so he rolled up his sleeves, lathered to his elbows, used the little brush lying there to give his nails a good workover, turned back to Gwyneth and asked, "What have we got, Doctor?"

"As happens all too often, what we have is another man

injured at the steel mill. We've had a couple that were burned from contact with molten steel, but not this fella. He had a rolled iron bar, fresh from the furnace, fall off a conveyor. It knocked him onto his back and lay across his legs, burning away coveralls, canvas pants, skin, and a considerable layer of meat below, almost reaching the bone. His workmates managed to grapple it off, but not before considerable damage was done. He's suffering the worst burns I've ever seen, on top of a broken femur in his right leg. I'm ignoring the burns for right now until I get this bone back in place. I think I've got it, but it would help if you could take a grip on his foot and pull just a bit."

Dr. Gilcrist did as he was bid, pulling and then twisting slightly until the right foot, pointing to the ceiling, was at ninety degrees to the stretcher. Gwyneth responded, "Good, good, now hold. I'll dig out a couple of splints. The burn prevents me from wrapping it firmly or even thinking of a cast. Perhaps a cast later if we get the burns under control."

She said all that while finding what was needed and returning to the patient. Knowing she had a well-experienced doctor doing what a nurse would normally be doing, she moved ahead quickly, leaning on Brandy Gilcrist's competence.

With the break dealt with, Gwyneth was making the last wraps with the gauze bandage, testing the tautness with each lap. Speaking under her breath as she so often did, Dr. Gilcrist heard her say. "Tight enough to hold the splints, Gwyneth, but no tighter. We're not creating a tourniquet here. If we cut the blood flow, the leg will rot and fall off and we'll have wasted all this time and effort."

Smiling at both the self-delivered advice as well as her bit of humor, the visiting doctor asked, "Is that how you train your nurses? They listen as you talk to yourself? A bit strange, but to the point I will admit."

"Never mind that. Pass me yonder roll of tape and then grab that bottle of ether. It wouldn't do to have this fella wake up now, would it? Go gently. The goal is to have him sleep a while longer without putting us to sleep at the same time. Ether has no conscious, as you well know, unless you forgot it all on the trip out here. It doesn't care who breathes it in. Nasty stuff, really. This will be an all-around better profession when some of the new anesthetics I've read about prove their usefulness."

The remainder of the afternoon was busy with treating the seriously burned legs.

The hours slipped away as the two doctors worked together, one caring for each leg. All the remnants of cloth and burned flesh were carefully picked out, and the wounds sanitized as well as they could be with the antiseptics available. When that part was completed, Gwyneth prepared and applied a soothing balm of honey and olive oil mixture. At the last, the wounds were carefully wrapped with gauze soaked in Sulfur and vinegar.

Looking up from the patient to Dr. Gilcrist, Gwyneth said, "Oh, how I wish we knew more. What we've done is in no way adequate, but it's the way it is. We'll keep him here for a couple of days before passing him over to the hospital. I'd prefer to keep our patients here until they're well, but we lack the space. We also lack the staff for round-the-clock care, and we have only my personal kitchen upstairs for food preparation. The hospital has all those needful things already. For me to duplicate it would be costly and unnecessary."

Dr. Gilcrist, a man not given to much talk, moved to the patient's head, looking into his eyes and then measuring his pulse. "He'll be waking up soon. Let's pray he doesn't come up sick to his stomach. Jerking his limbs or rolling over could undo a precious lot of work."

Gwyneth was too tired to answer. Instead, she said, "Welcome to Pueblo, Brandy. I'll look around in a bit to see if there is anything I can find to keep you busy."

"I look forward to that, Gwyneth. I'm getting bored just sitting around with nothing to do."

They were both showing tired smiles. Dr. Gilcrist, partly

from the long miles on the train, and Gwyneth from an early start that morning with a visit to a home where two of the three children were suffering from whooping cough.

While they sat watching the patient stir a bit as the effects of the ether wore off, the door to the inner room opened. The cry of an infant assaulted their ears. Bea stepped out and went immediately to the washstand. As she scrubbed, she glanced over her shoulder, saying, “Who’s the visitor?”

Brandy Gilcrist replied, “Oh, how soon they forget. And here I had hoped I had made an impression on at least one of the nurses I’ve worked with over the years. But I see it was not to be.”

After a short pause, he continued, “It’s good to see you, Bea. By the sounds of that cry we just heard, I’m assuming all is well in the other room?”

“As well as it can be with a young mom whose milk doesn’t want to come down. The child seems to have gotten the colostrum, but nothing since.”

“Oh dear,” said Gwyneth, jumping to her feet and heading for the other room. The day’s work was in no way finished at the Wycome Medical Clinic.

# Chapter Twenty-Eight

After their long day, too tired to delve into deeper matters, Brandy Gilcrist suggested that he and Gwyneth delay their business meeting at least one day. Gwyneth responded, "If you hadn't suggested it, I was going to."

Bea put in a long night at the clinic, caring for the new mom and her little one, and then sitting close beside the burn patient, at times holding his hand as he winced bravely at his surges of pain. The young man spoke only once. Rolling his head toward Bea, struggling for words that sleepiness and pain worked together to disguise as mere whispered slurs that Bea had to have repeated before she sorted them out, he asked, "Am I going to be able to walk again?"

The family had been in to see their son and sibling the afternoon before, so Bea knew the patient was a single man. Her response to his question was, "You'll not only walk again, you'll be fit and well, dancing at your wedding, come by and by."

"Will you be holding my hand as we dance?"

It wasn't the first proposal Bea had received from her patients. "By the time we're finished with you, you'll never want to see me again."

The patient had no more to say. With the two patients settled down, and the young burn patient strapped to the stretcher, Bea left the door open between the two rooms and moved to the upholstered chair kept there for the comfort of new mothers. She eased into it and laid her head back, dozing off while her subconscious was attuned to sounds that would indicate she was needed.

SPIKE PULLED the buggy to a stop beside the clinic, wishing the visiting doctor a good day as he stepped to the ground. The door opened just once, allowing the weary Bea to step out and Dr. Gilcrist to enter. Spike would deliver Bea to her rented room and return to the clinic to await his next call.

Telephone services were becoming more available in the small city as they were in larger, grander centers. In Pueblo, it had become reasonably common in the business centers for communications to depend on the mysterious black box that hung on the wall. Just once had Spike managed to worm his way, uninvited, into the telephone exchange office. He stood in wonder, staring at the banks of switchboards, with a woman operator sitting before each one, wearing some kind of a thing on her ears and plugging wires here, there, and everywhere, into little holes in the boards. Spike stared enraptured until a man dressed in a tailored suit, lending an air of authority to the occasion that frightened and overwhelmed Spike, demanded that he explain his intrusion into the room.

Stumbling for words that never quite became audible, knowing that no explanation would suffice in such august surroundings, he turned and, ignoring he man, slipped outside, making his way to the buggy, something he fully understood and had some control over. But that day had stuck in his mind, and frequently he wished the Wycome Medical Clinic had one of the convenient machines. He could save many trips and more miles on the horse and buggy, or on occasion, on his bicycle.

The lines were only slowly being strung to the outer limits of the residential area. Gwyneth had made inquiries, but no one at the city offices had been able to offer any encouragement. For the time being, they would run written messages, delivered by a host of messengers like Spike, to communicate within the town, and use either the postal service or the telegraph for communications beyond the city limits.

Dr. Gilcrist was examining the burn patient when Gwyneth entered from the house, carrying a tray laden with two plates of breakfast. She set the tray on the side table. Her method of greeting Dr. Gilcrist a good morning was simply to say, "Patrick said he could eat some scrambled eggs. There's also a bit of toast here and some strawberry spread. In the Wycome Medical Clinic, Doctor, we all do a bit of everything. This morning we're feeding our patients. I'm sure if you ask nicely, Patrick will allow you to assist him. I'll see to our new mom."

As Brandy Gilcrist picked up the plate of eggs and a fork, Patrick, showing amazing strength on the first day following his accident, grinned, "She didn't seem to leave you much choice there, Doc."

"I can't argue with that, Patrick. There might be a lesson in there somewhere about allowing a woman to be in charge, but we'll lay that one aside for now. Do you think you can handle this on your own? I can help you sit up a bit with pillows, but don't move your legs. Want to give it a try?"

In the other room, the new mother was nursing her baby when Gwyneth walked in with the tray. "Breakfast time, Mom. Are you hungry?"

"If I told you how hungry I am, Doctor, you'd accuse me of exaggeration."

"No, I wouldn't. Being hungry is a good sign. As soon as baby comes up for air, I'll help you into that chair. Then I'll fix the bed up for you and you can have your morning nap."

"I'm thinking this is going to be a boy who spends half his time searching the kitchen for food. But he's had enough for now."

Forgetting about the chair, she continued, "You pass me that tray and I'll trade you for the baby."

Gwyneth delivered babies, cleaned them up, and wrapped them in warm blankets, taking it all as natural and a big and necessary part of her business. But holding them as they burped away the air drawn in with the mother's milk as they lay on her shoulder or cuddled them in her arms as they slept, were small tasks she avoided if at all possible. On this morning, with the mother eagerly tackling the full breakfast, the choice for Gwyneth didn't exist. She sat in the chair Bea had so recently been napping in and burped the child. Then, lying the child on her lap, she rearranged the blankets and lifted him into her arms. The baby seemed to snuggle, even in sleep, reaching out with his mouth for more nourishment. As his head turned just a bit, finding Gwyneth's well-clothed breast, he moved his lips, slobbered a bit, and slept.

The mother, noticing all this from her recovery bed, smiled. "Do you have children of your own, Doctor?"

"No, no, I haven't."

"You should. I'm watching you. You're a natural. Anyone could see that."

Gwyneth didn't answer. Silently, where only her heart could hear, she was sternly holding back tears while she thought of what might have been if only Trent...

WITH THE PATIENTS fed and the clinic as cleaned up as Gwyneth had time for, and with the new mother having been carefully loaded into the buggy for the slow, cautious ride home, Spike being as conscientious to his job as the situation called for, it was time for Gwyneth and Brandy Gilcrist to get to their business discussion. Brandy's previous idea of a dinner discussion was set aside when the badly injured Patrick was imposed on the clinic. He couldn't be left alone, and other patients were calling in, demanding more of Gwyneth's time. As an alternative, they took seats in the somewhat disheveled garden area behind the house. As Gwyneth took her seat, she looked around and said, "I hope the previous owners don't see this garden area. I'm afraid it's on a downward spiral since I opened the clinic."

Ignoring all that, Brandy Gilcrist asked, "Exactly why are you here, Gwyneth? Here in Pueblo, Colorado, I mean?"

Almost as a slip of the tongue, Brandy added, "Here, on your own. And single."

Dropping her eyes to the overly long and trampled grass beneath her feet, Gwyneth repeated, "Yes, and single." Brandon could sense the great melancholy in the two words, *and single*.

"I apologize, Gwyneth. I don't even know where that thought came from. It was unkind and unnecessary. Please forgive me."

Her answer to his bigger question was slow in coming. Finally, she said, "I could write out a short list of reasons for choosing Pueblo. But the couple at the top of the list would be, first, I'm at heart a country girl. I was never really settled or content in the big city. You could say I'm still in the city, and that would be true, although in a much smaller city. But the horse that you've seen on the buggy is also an excellent saddle animal. I ride often. It takes but a few minutes in the saddle and I'm in the countryside. Trails and streams and semi-desert growth. Birds in abundance, and occasionally a deer or other wild animal. I love it.

"And then there's the fact that my old ranching friends and neighbors are only a short train ride away. Further, I've always wanted my own operation. My own private practice. The big hospitals were great for a novice doctor, but as you know, a junior physician, and especially a woman junior, is going to be a long time finding any freedom in that environment. Anyway, I'm here. And I'm enjoying it. And I must add that the western culture has made my introduction to the medical world much simpler than it would have been in the east. I have had only a small number of male patients turn away from being treated by a woman."

Ignoring, rather than responding to Dr. Gilcrist's plea for forgiveness, Gwyneth raised her eyes and suggested, "You're probably wondering why a small, single surgeon clinic has been sent several of the more serious cases to have arisen in Pueblo. May I suggest that you have Spike drive you down to the hospital? Introduce yourself and ask for a guided tour. Look around. Ask some questions. Then go over to the mill. Go in at the main office and ask for Mr. C. J. Benton. Mr. Benton is the mill manager. He's also the former owner of this house. It became available when they were moving into their newly built home. The connection is purely a coincidence.

"Again, ask for a tour of the mill. See the conditions these men work under. Without overtly criticizing the mill operation, contrast the needs, such as you saw with Patrick, who still lies inside, hovering somewhere between life and death, with the facilities and surgical talent at the hospital.

"Also coincidental is the fact that I have gone for dinner a few times with Mr. Benton's assistant manager, Clayton Boniface. Clayton is a friend and a pleasant companion at dinner. Nothing more. Nor will he ever be anything more. At those dinners, we studiously avoid the topic of mill accidents, which I believe to be beyond what might be acceptable dinner conversation, as I see it, given that my clinic is profiting from the results of that same mill carelessness.

"The first mill accident victim came to me almost immediately after I opened the door for the clinic. The hospital was already overcrowded with some kind of multi-injury railroad accident and couldn't offer care for more people than they already had on site. The other doctor offices in town are one-man affairs, focusing on family matters and are ill-equipped to deal with serious injuries. Someone had heard of this clinic, so they rushed him over here. I'm pleased to say the man survived, although it was nip and tuck for a while. Since that time, all the mill accidents have come here except for a couple that needed immediate care while I was away. Fortunately, until Patrick, the accidents resulted in relatively minor injuries, easily cared for. The burns that often accompany the injuries are another matter altogether.

"Of course, there is the constant challenge of new patients with new ailments. I believe I have seen every possible childhood disease now. Of course, the babies keep coming and will keep coming in this young population. The problems that have arisen sooner than I expected are a lack of space and the need for more nursing help. I especially need overnight care for young moms, and once in a while, overnight supervision for serious cases of injury or illness. Another full clinical room is also a priority."

"Picturing the facility you have now, Gwyneth, makes me think you're in for a move to a larger space soon, if not immediately."

"And you're correct to think that. I've called the man I purchased the house through. He's supposed to be doing a search for me, but I haven't heard from him in a couple of weeks. He may not have taken my request seriously, or there may be nothing available. I sure haven't got time to go on a search myself."

Brandy smiled and said, "If I may make a suggestion, you might consider sending your buggy driver, Spike, is it, on the search. He already knows this town like few others, if I am to guess correctly. He'll scour the city and tell you where everyone keeps their secrets, as well as any open spaces available. I know from his talk, as he drove me to and from the hotel that he's your bonded servant. For him, the sun rises and sets on Dr. Wycome and the clinic. I speak quietly because he is not far away, doing something or other in the shed. And while you're letting that idea run freely in your mind, may I request the use of the buggy, and Spike, of course, to carry me to the hospital and the mill?"

"Of course. When do you wish to go?"

"Right now."

# Chapter Twenty-Nine

Dr. Brandy Gilcrist was due back in Chicago. His time in Pueblo couldn't be stretched any further. He had taken a tour of both the Pueblo hospital and the steel mill. He had returned to the hospital for a serious talk with the hospital's head of administration. He had taken a buggy tour of the city itself with Spike pointing out the features. He had enjoyed a private dinner with Gwyneth and another with Bea. He fully understood that Gwyneth was anxious to hear his thoughts after all this activity. But he had purposely left their discussion until there was little time left.

Finally, early on the morning of his planned departure, he and Gwyneth met on the veranda. With coffee cups at hand and with the wicker chairs moved so they faced one another, Gwyneth sat expectantly, while Brandy settled into a comfortable position.

"Gwyneth. Dr. Wycome. You are one of the most talented and best-trained doctors, man or woman, I have ever had the privilege to work with. It is an honor to be invited to visit and look over your operation. You have amazed me at every step. That you and Bea are a great team is beyond question. You told me once, when we were still back in Chicago, that your goal in the medical field was to work with the best and to become the best.

"There are those who would argue that there are great hospitals and teaching institutions all over the nation, and that would be true. When we stand up for Chicago General, we are probably showing some bias, but not without reason. And, of course, there are great strides being taken in other countries and other universities. The truth, in my opinion, is that it is a discussion that will never end, and that declaring a winner would be a mug's game. Medical advancement belongs to no one particular place or generation. We will never know it all, and discovery will never end.

"Having seen what you're doing and what Pueblo has to offer, I have come to this conclusion. To reach those life goals you laid out before me in Chicago, you need to be in a large facility where you have support staff, financial backing, and follow-up procedures available. You are a marvel with the scalpel. You're creative. You're determined. Most times, you're correct in your judgments and procedures. You are as knowledgeable on current matters as anyone I have ever known. You have medical journals at hand that I had never seen or heard of. You study constantly.

"Gwyneth, you are one of a kind. I greatly admire you. But as I'm sure you already sense, working in a small private clinic is not for me. Again, I am honored that you thought of me. My visit has clarified some things in my own mind. But Gwyneth, my very dear friend, I must return to Chicago. For the time being, at least, that is where I belong. I will tell you, just so there are no secrets, that I was offered the job as chief of staff during my hospital visit here. Of course, I turned that opportunity down. I promised to think more about it, but at this time it is a closed door.

"I have probably hurt you in saying all of this. I hope you know I mean you no ill will. And if you were to ask for my recommendation or opinion, it would be that until you know more precisely where your career is headed, to continue running the Wycome Medical Clinic as professionally and as dedicated to the well-being of your patients as you now are. Put off growth until the situation demands it. Dig in and remain the top private medical offering in the area. I believe that one day, and perhaps soon, you will look at your work and the town of Pueblo and find that it cannot satisfy your skills or your longer-term goals. Or perhaps your more personal wants and wishes, matters we have never discussed, and which are none of my business. Only then can you make the decision that will someday have to be made.

"If you ever wish to take up a specialist position in a larger center, or consider teaching future doctors, there will always be a place open for you in Chicago, and, I am sure, in other locations as well.

"But now, Spike will be fidgeting, knowing I must bid you farewell or miss my train. Thank you again, Gwyneth. Please keep in touch."

With that, he stood just as the buggy arrived at the front corner of the house. He hesitated but finally took the single step necessary to give Gwyneth a hug. She didn't really hug him in return, but neither did she repel him. His travel bag was already under Spike's care. He had but to step aboard and, with Spike putting the animal into a trot, in a matter of seconds, Dr. Brandy Gilcrist was out of sight. And Gwyneth was left alone, with her head struggling to sort out all that had been said.

As she looked at the chair so recently vacated, its emptiness somehow shouted a message she preferred not to address. Knowing that Brandy was more correct than he ever could have imagined, she tried, as always, to avoid admitting to the truth of what he had called *your more personal wants and wishes*. That single matter was the only thing that frightened brave, forward-looking, but single, Dr. Gwyneth Wycome. She thought of it constantly. She, at times, recalled one of the elderly matrons she had met along the way. Excellent people, caring for their work and the people under their charge, normally youthful nurses. Excellent and caring women, but turning sour with age. No matter how good one was at their jobs or how much they cared about others, an empty room to return to at the end of the day was still just an empty room.

When was it too late? Could someone enter into that empty room and fill a portion of the heart's desire at 40? 50? 60? She didn't know. But she knew she was at times dreadfully lonely. Admitting that to herself was not easy. She often turned to remembrances of Trent. Trent, so suddenly thrust into her life. A decision taken so quickly. Marriage following a mere few weeks together. And then, all that had come from that good decision. But her Trent had died and was buried. Could she... Was it possible... No, she must keep those thoughts, those dreams, buried. There would be no addressing disturbing matters this day. She would stick to medicine and all of its possibilities. Her patients needed her.

THE NORMAL WORK of the clinic had not paused because Gwyneth was struggling with her future. She returned to the house, taking the two coffee cups to the kitchen washstand. She entered the clinic from the inside stairs, with a somewhat melancholy mind, to greet Bea, who was busying herself with putting the clinic into its rightful order and making a list of supplies that needed replenishing.

Bea studied her friend for a moment, seeing conflicting emotions in her actions and speech. Gwyneth's *good morning* was as bright as always, but the look on her face shouted a totally different message.

"And good morning to you too. May I ask, or is it too soon?"

"It's too soon, and it always will be too soon when you've heard something you don't wish to hear."

"That bad, huh?"

"No, not bad. Disappointing and a bit disheartening, but not bad."

"Disappointing and disheartening sound bad enough for me."

"Yes, I suppose. But when you know you've heard the truth you weren't willing to admit to yourself before, it kind of takes the edge off the disappointment. What's on for today?"

Bea glanced at the open appointment book lying on the small desk. "A runner brought this one in. A family with three sick children. The mother suspects mumps. Would appreciate a visit. I'll take that one if you wish."

"No, it will be good for me to let the wind blow through my hair and listen to Spike's nonsense on the ride over. We've had a few extra busy days. You finish cleaning up and then take your ease. The lull will end soon enough."

# Chapter Thirty

In truth, putting it all together, nothing had changed at the Wycome Medical Clinic. Dr. Brandy Gilcrist wasn't there and never would be again, with his decision to return to Chicago. But he had never really been there. His presence was more of a short-lived mirage. That he assisted with the work on Patrick, the man so badly burned at the mill, was a coincidence of timing. So nothing had really changed. Dr. Gilcrist had floated in and, in a couple of days, had floated out. Life would continue as before.

But beyond the clinic itself, even if the change was primarily in Gwyneth's mind, there was still a change. To deny that would be to deny the emotional depth of Gwyneth's long-held plan and wishes—plans and wishes that had been in danger of being buried under the busyness of the immediate. Although slightly painful, it was good to be forced to reacquaint herself with the truth.

With the arrival of Dr. Gilcrist, Gwyneth had allowed her hopes for the future of the Wycome Medical Clinic to soar, and now they lay on the ground, smashed and dead. No, not quite dead, but certainly gasping for breath and light. She knew she could face the truth and build another plan, perhaps a better plan, but that would be a lot of mental and emotional work. As a consequence, Gwyneth admitted she might have begun the day with a bit less enthusiasm than she normally did, a previously unknown, and temporary trait she tried to hide, unsuccessfully, from Bea. The two women worked side by side through that day and into the next with no mention of the departed Chicago doctor, although neither woman thought of much else, each for their own reasons.

Bringing her busy days to an end, resting on the veranda, had become something Gwyneth looked forward to even as she was working throughout the day. A time when she analyzed the treatments each patient had received, always wondering if there was more she could have done. Were there new or improved treatments she was unaware of? But tonight, her mind went in a different direction, an unplanned and not altogether welcome direction.

*At the start, I thought I was quite content with my nursing. I'm not exactly sure when or why the idea came that I should study to become a doctor. That progression was all so long ago that the details have become blurred. And then for several years, I was content to simply be a doctor. Where did the idea of creating a multi-doctor clinic come from?*

*Was it simply my desire for personal independence, built into my mind and heart almost from birth, it seemed, and expanded during my years in the west? And how did I land on the idea that Pueblo was the place to build the clinic? It's much like the Mirrored W. We could have made a good life on grass in almost any area we chose if we had known the contentment of having enough. But Trent and I pushed each other to grow, to build, to find open grass country, where we could claim and graze all we could hold, as if a better life could be found in bigness. Fortunately, Trent fell on the idea of holding fewer but better beef animals. That had been a good change that saved the Mirrored W.*

*Did the multi-doctor clinic idea grow out of the same thought pattern as the original big ranch idea? I'll never have a clear answer on that. But I am in Pueblo and that's a fact. And I do have a clinic in operation. That is also a fact. And the facts are what I'll have to deal with. Dr. Gilcrist or no Dr. Gilcrist, there is little doubt that the clinic could grow, but... Yes, there is always a but.*

*And now, I had better stop this thinking and get to my bed before I start talking myself into something. Or out of something.'*

A couple of mornings after Dr. Brandy Gilcrist's departure, Bea, with less of herself invested in the multi-doctor clinic idea, was as bright and aware as ever. However, she only had to glance at her friend to know she needed a break. Perhaps some time to think. A quiet time. An alone time. Reading her friend's mind in a way that would have surprised Gwyneth, she thought, *perhaps a break from a dream to allow reality to speak.* Cautiously, she suggested, "Except for a few Sunday mornings, you haven't taken a decent break since I got here. It's time you did.

"You've invested your time, your energy, and your knowledge and talents, to say nothing of the money, in the experiment at Bessie Creek. There's little happening here right now. Go. Get on the train. Go see Sky. Have a heart-to-heart with her. Don't hurry back. Take a fresh look at that village and make a logical decision. Sky will make out no matter what decision you come to. Most days, we could use her here. And the good news is that there's still time this morning to make the train."

~

GWYNETH STEPPED DOWN at the Bessie Creek depot, moved a short distance from the noise of friends greeting friends and the chuffing of escaping steam, set her bags down, and looked around.

She had seen it all before, and with the normal busyness of

her mind, the temptation that rose unbidden was to take a quick glance and move on. But she pushed that temptation aside. The mountains were there. Of course they were there. Where else would they be? The mountains had been there to greet her when she first drove the ranch wagon over the unbelievably difficult trail that brought them to the valley. The mountains had been there each morning to greet her as they built their Mirrored W Ranch. The mountains would be there when she, herself, became just a memory, if there was anyone left that cared enough to do the remembering.

Checking her impulses, she reminded herself of her mission, to analyze the settlement and surrounding territory, assessing it all from a medical services perspective. Determined to see. To really see. Perhaps to see as Brandy Gilcrist had seen the Pueblo clinic, clearly, without the dreams, just the reality.

And so she took her time, standing there after everyone else had vacated the platform, and the little narrow-gauge engine had dragged its few cars off to the west.

The mountains to the north and west were, as always, beautiful, almost beyond compare. At least when contrasted within her limited experience. It was true she hadn't seen the European Alps, nor Asia's Himalayas, and it was unlikely she ever would. But the Sangre de Christo range was glory enough for her. She dragged her eyes from the mountains, which would never need her medical assistance, turning toward the village itself. To view the main, or, in truth, the only business street of Bessie Creek, she had to step to the edge of the platform, beyond the depot wall.

Setting her bags down again, she gazed along the dirt road, identifying from memory the various businesses, trying to decide if any had been added or taken away. Judging by the signs visible from her vantage point, the village was about the same as she remembered. And then, feeling foolish, she smiled to herself. Her last visit was only weeks ago. How much could it possibly change in that short time? That last visit, which was greatly extended due to the typhoid crisis, was spent mostly at the B4 ranch and with the Ute, with little time spent in town.

To look for growth as some kind of confirmation that medical assistance was needed and could be made to at least cover costs might be expecting too much. Or was she, for the first time, being a bit cynical about the village she had watched form itself from barren semi-desert into a railway whistle stop with its single strip of somewhat graded and leveled land on which the village was located. Even though one side of her mind was saying she had gone away to the east a long time ago, in truth, she had seen its birth, not many years before. That sense of ownership, after a fashion, may have slanted her original thinking about establishing the clinic.

Had she taken on a bit of pride in ownership that she would have trouble releasing? Her Mirrored W had been the first ranch to purchase supplies from the tiny general store that was half wood and half canvas at its beginning. Did the town owe her something? Foolish question. The village relied more on mining than on ranching, if she cared to admit it. She had sold the Mirrored W years before and moved on herself. There was nothing left of the hopes and dreams that had drawn her, and others, to the valley in the first place. Everyone had moved on. And of Trent, her much-loved husband, who had dreamed the original dream? Only a lonely grave in the forest that surrounded the site of the Mirrored W, now the B4.

It was doubtful if anyone in town, beyond Emery Radcliff, who had rented her the space for Sky's small clinic, even remembered her name. So why did she feel an allegiance to a collection of buildings that would probably die when the mines died, or be reduced to one general store and the depot? And the people who hoped to gather a living from the little collection of businesses called Bessie Creek? They would be forced to face the facts and move on themselves, leaving months or years of effort and hopes behind them, to be weathered to near nothing and blown away by the wind. Perhaps razed to the ground by some careless traveler's untended campfire.

*Stop thinking that way, Gwyneth. You're here to see Sky, not fill her heart and mind with a melancholy you yourself can't rightly explain. But perhaps even if your thoughts were wrong, if the village managed to survive and grow and prosper, was not the thought part of the whole? Of seeing? Seeing the truth?*

Picking up her bags, one that held a change of clothing, the other her battered, black medical bag, she started to walk. The small space rented for the clinic was about halfway along the street. The door was locked to her touch. A handwritten note, dated just that morning and tacked to the door, stated that the nurse was away on a call, expecting to return late afternoon. Moving on, Gwyneth stepped into the small hotel, which was as crude and poorly constructed as it always had been. There was little sign of effort at improvement unless one were to take in the big, colorfully-printed calendar on the back wall or the oversized, inaccurate, and unrealistic painting of Indians chasing and taking down buffalo with spear and arrow.

But the clerk who finally looked up from the magazine he was reading reckoned that he could spare one room fit for a lady, at the exorbitant cost of one dollar for the night. She signed the register, leaving off the Doctor title, paid the fee, accepted the key, and took her bags up to the room, locking the door again as she left.

With no particular plan, now that she was unable to connect with Sky, Gwyneth decided to walk around the town. At a decent walking pace, Gwyneth could have circled the village, leaving out a few far-flung cabins visible through the light forest, in an hour. But she wanted to see, had prayed, sitting on the train, that she would be able to see. So she strolled, a city-clad woman wandering the crooked roads of the tiny village, stopping often to look around her. That she was noticed was no surprise. Once, a woman puttering in her struggling flower garden looked up with a wave and a quiet, "Good morning."

Gwyneth responded in kind, then turned to stand outside the picket fence. "I always loved flowers and wished I could grow them, but they seem to up and die if I even come close. Yours are lovely. What do you call them?"

Coming erect and stepping toward Gwyneth, the woman smiled. "Well, my husband calls them a waste of time. The kids call them a nuisance, especially when they have to carry water for them. Their proper name is geranium, and that's good enough for me. They're a very adaptable flower. Pretty much grow all around the world. This soil would never support a vegetable garden, but I keep these few flowers alive with a shovelful of aged droppings from the stable now and then, plus regular watering and just a bit of care. They're my one spot of beauty among all the drabness. They don't make a good bouquet, that's their one shortcoming. I'm Mary Gladstone, by the way," the gardener said, holding out her hand.

"And I'm Gwyneth Wycome. I'm very pleased to meet you."

As they shook, Mary said, "You're welcome to wander our dirt roads until you're old and as gray as the roads themselves if you wish, Gwyneth, but I'm willing to guess that you're the first to ever do that. There's little enough to see."

As Gwyneth was forming a response, she noticed two neighbor ladies walking their way, with a third lagging behind. Instead of speaking her response to Mary's hinted-at question, Gwyneth said, "It looks as if I'm drawing a crowd."

"My neighbors, of course, as curious as am I. We've never had a lovely lady such as yourself, all decked out in town clothing, casting your intelligent eyes over our modest dwellings. Questions form unbidden. Out of politeness, we'll probably leave the question unasked."

Mary didn't bother introducing the neighbors, but her statement alone was an invitation for Gwyneth to volunteer information. She would have to carefully consider her answers. To say much at all would surely lead to comment on the small doctor's office, Sky, and the future of a nurse or doctor on site. Gwyneth wished to avoid that discussion with all but Sky herself. Instead, she stated the truth but left out the doctor part.

"The name has undoubtedly passed from local lore, but I was part of one of the very early cattle operations in the valley. I've been away for some years and was curious about Bessie Creek's growth. That's about all there is to it. I live in Pueblo now, so I caught the train this morning and came down, just to satisfy my curiosity."

An elderly woman, by frontier standards at least, perhaps in her mid-fifties, the one who had been lagging behind the others, said suspiciously, "I'm among the early ones too, me and mine. Town didn't amount to hardly nothing at all when me and my man walked out of the brush, lost for the most of a week, and saw this place with just the two buildings, and them mostly canvas. Followed the smoke of that coal-burning blight on the landscape they call a railway. And mighty glad we were to see folks. Might still be wandering through the brush without we saw that smoke.

"Man's a miner. Found himself enough of the shiny stuff to keep body and soul together and a bit to lay aside. So we stayed. Now tell me your name again. My memory ain't what it once was."

"My name is Gwyneth Wycome. I'm happy for you that you found the place. I wouldn't likely have known you, or you me. We were ranchers south of here. We seldom came to town and then, only for supplies. I didn't often come myself. Usually, my husband came with the wagon. Our ranch was the Mirrored W."

"I knowed that ranch. Sold 'er out some years back. That big, boisterous Irishman's got er now. And I know you too. You were the nurse what traveled wherever needed."

Knowing the cat was out of the bag, Gwyneth laughed.

"Yes, that's me. But I really didn't want to be recognized here today. Promise you won't spread the word around?" she asked with a conspiratorial grin. "Anyway, ladies, I must move along. Nice to have met you."

She sped her walking pace up enough to complete the task of surveying the town in time for a late lunch.

# Chapter Thirty-One

GWYNETH RECEIVED A FRIENDLY WELCOME FROM THE somewhat rotund cook who was taking his ease with a cup of coffee, after serving the ten men who had shown up for lunch, in the Bessie Creek Eating House. The only advertisement posted anywhere on the premises, inside or out, was the simple, single word FOOD, sloppily hand-painted on the window.

The term *eating house*, Toby and Jessie, who had shared their table with Gwyneth on her last visit to Bessie Creek, advised her, was a verbal contribution from the clientele, who had held a straw vote one lunch hour some time before. Amid much laughing and teasing of the cook, several possible names were presented aloud. By popular choice, *eating house* was determined to be the best representative of the establishment. One of the local miners shouted out. "Ain't no one com'n here fer the ambiance. Only reason to be here is to eat. So it's the eat'n house."

In response, the small crowd held an impromptu discussion on what exactly ambiance meant.

As long as the people kept coming, the cook didn't care what his establishment was called. And the ambiance, good or not so good, had never once entered his mind.

"Come in, Doctor. You're getting to be a regular, both in town as well as in my humble establishment. I've got beef and spuds quickly available, or, depending on your preference, I've got eggs and freshly baked ham I can whack a nice slice off. Coffee's reasonably fresh. By that I mean it was made today. Help yourself."

Gwyneth moved to a window seat so she could watch for Sky in case she chanced to walk by and grinned at the cook. "I haven't had two breakfasts in one day for ages. I believe you've talked me into ham and eggs. Perhaps you could lay of scoop of those potatoes on the grill and fry them up a bit."

"Easy as pie. Just give me a few minutes."

As Gwyneth was sipping on her second coffee, Emery Radcliff, the general store operator who had rented the small space for Sky's office and clinic, stepped into the café. As he turned to close the door, his eyes fell on Gwyneth. "Why hello there, Doctor. Welcome to Bessie Creek. Again. So soon after your last visit. How is that nurse you stationed here doing?"

"Good afternoon, Mr. Radcliff. Probably I should be asking you how Sky is doing. She apparently is out of town today, and I haven't had a report from her for a week or more."

Radcliff poured himself a mug of coffee before asking, "May I join you, Doctor?"

With a simple nod and a gesture with her raised mug, Gwyneth indicated the chair opposite her. Picking up where his question to Gwyneth left off, he said, "I'm not sure Sky has had time to file a report for you. I seem to hear that office door opening and closing regularly when she's in residence. Of course, she's often seen pointing her buggy toward one of the far-flung ranches or into that little mining settlement just to the west, along the tracks. Keeps herself busy, she does."

~

SKY DIDN'T RETURN to Bessie Creek until near dark that evening. The coming night air was pleasantly warm. Gwyneth had taken a chair outside the general store, near the medical clinic, to watch for her. The livery man was cleaning up around the big barn doors, with rake and shovel, his wheelbarrow on standby, pausing from time to time to stare down the trail to the west. His actions spoke as clearly as if he were speaking aloud. He was ready to close the doors and settle in for an evening of coffee and reading in his tiny room. He was clearly waiting for something.

That something turned into the clopping of a single horse, and the light grinding of steel-rimmed wheels on the rough trail. He carefully placed his rake and shovel inside the barn and stood waiting. In another thirty seconds, the buggy became visible, slightly backlit by the sunset glow behind it. Gwyneth assumed the driver was Sky. Even that was made clear as the liveryman said, "Long day, Sky. Drive yourself off to the rooming house. I'll follow along and bring the rig in."

"Thanks, Mr. Dreyfus. But I'm all right. The horse needs rest more than I do."

"Rough trail out that way, is it?"

"Rough enough, for sure. Person could break a wheel with no trouble at all. But we're back, none the worse for wear."

"And the child?"

"Rough place to come into the world, but he's a big strong lad and the mother is doing all right. Climbed out of her bed and made dinner for her husband and their other two little ones. I offered, but she was determined it was her job. You ever get wondering what true pioneer stock looks like, you go see to those folks or others like them."

"I've seen them a-plenty. Know their looks. I also know the looks of a tired young lady and a horse that needs a rub down. You take care for the one and I'll see to the other."

"Good night, Mr. Dreyfus, and thank you."

Sky had taken a few steps toward the boarding house when

Dreyfus said, "Come near to forgetting Sky. The doctor is sitting yonder there by the store. About wore out her shoes, I'm guessing, pacing the town, waiting for you. Best you go put her wondering about your welfare to rest."

Gwyneth and Sky did little more than greet each other when Gwyneth said, "Sky, the liveryman was correct. You look absolutely weary. Take yourself off to bed. We'll meet at the café for breakfast. I'll be ready around eight. You come when you're rested."

WHEN THE BREAKFAST CROWD, which consisted of a maximum of ten people, left for their day's work, the little café was redolent with the rich scent of cigar smoke over the background of the greasy aroma drifting off the hot grill. Gwyneth pushed the door open and gasped. Taking a liberty, she pushed the door fully open and stepped back a couple of feet. Somehow, the smoke and aroma were almost tolerable in the evening, but first thing in the morning was another matter altogether. Watching the top of the doorframe, she could see a small whiff of gray smoke drifting out. She allowed a full minute to pass before stepping inside.

In truth, her actions didn't really do much for the space. It would take more than one or two minutes of mountain breeze to clear the air. The best she could do was take a table near the door and leave the door open until someone objected.

Sky bounced into the Eating House full of energy and excitement, anxious to tell Gwyneth all about her weeks in Bessie Creek. While the morning's fare, a choice between overcooked rolled oats or ham and eggs, were decided on and consumed, a time period of barely one-half hour, Sky hardly ceased talking. Gwyneth listened with a mix of pleasure and amusement. Pleasure in that the gamble at Bessie Creek showed signs of life, and amusement at Sky's enthusiasm. But the big surprise wasn't disclosed until they were back at the clinic, seated in the tiny office.

Sky squirmed on her chair, seeming to seek a comfortable position, but what she was really doing was buying time while she searched for just the correct words. Finally, thinking of no other way to say it, the simple truth popped out of her mouth.

"I've met an old friend of yours, Gwyneth. He says he helped some, bringing your original herd over the trail. He's a Texan, but he's settled in here as far as I can tell."

Before Sky could go on with the story, Gwyneth interrupted. "You're speaking of Eustice Ward, of course. Have you been attending his church here?"

"I have. And oh, Gwyneth, he's the most wonderful man. Kind and generous and a thorough gentleman. He's so sincere in his teaching, and his heart is really in helping those who need help. He's cowboying during the week just to make enough to live on, but really, his heart is in ministering and teaching the truths of God's word. He's, well, he's just the most wonderful man."

"Does he know you're in love with him?"

"I didn't say anything about being in love. Where would you get that idea?"

"Oh, just kind of reading between the lines."

There was a pause of a few seconds before Sky plaintively said, "Gwyneth. What am I going to do? If you saw through me so easily, others will too. And poor Mr. Ward, He'd be so embarrassed."

Gwyneth leaned back in her chair, tapping her teeth with a pencil she found lying on the desk. Hating to give personal advice but easily seeing that the young nurse was in a quandary, she asked, "Have you spent time with him alone, where you might talk and get to know each other?"

After receiving a shy *no* for an answer, with Sky seemingly forgetting about the trial rides in the buggy as Eustice was helping her choose a horse and buggy to purchase, Gwyneth suggested, "I'm willing to bet that Willow Radcliff would be happy to help you put a picnic basket together. You have the horse and buggy. Suggest to Eustice that a perfect way to relax after a busy week is to find a pleasant spot for a picnic and a ride through the countryside.

"If he's too thick in the head to grasp our meaning, you don't want him anyway. But I'm thinking he'll grin and accept. He might even shave and wash behind his ears. And don't give me that helpless look. Sometimes a lady has to look out for herself. You'll probably have to help him see how much he cares for you. Cowboys can be a bit dull when there's more than horses and cows involved. But now, we must change the subject."

Sky nodded in agreement before saying, "I have to make another out call. One where your help will most likely be needed. Message came in late yesterday. Perhaps you'd like to come with me. We can talk along the way."

THEY WERE a couple of miles along a dim trail with Sky chattering all the way about the various cases that had come her way. She mentioned that three patients could have really benefited from Gwyneth's knowledge and skills. "But they couldn't wait for your help, so I went ahead, doing what I thought you might do if you were there. Somehow, hearing you speak into my ear, I managed to bring satisfactory results."

"How far are we going this morning, and what's the problem?"

Sky lifted her right hand, pointing off to the north. "There's a small group of mines and miners' shacks about five miles into those hills. Up along the tracks. I don't know what mineral they've found, but whatever it is, it's enough to keep them living in virtual hovels, doing little more than working and sleeping, so far as I can tell. Living poor while they plan and dream of a better tomorrow. Twelve-year-old boy from up there rode to town yesterday afternoon, asking for help. Said it was urgent. Left the message in the store because I had already gone off on the other call. The boy said a rock had fallen on his father's head. 'Knocked him silly,' was what the boy said. His mother managed to stop the bleeding, but she called for help anyway. It's probably a good thing you're here."

The buggy rocked and bounced over the rough trail, with the horse having to dig his hooves in to gain the top of one rise after another. Hoping to break the bone-jarring monotony, Gwyneth said, "We should have brought a jar of cream with us. We'd have butter by the time we got back to town."

They finally entered the small gathering of slab-built cottages but didn't know which one held the injured man. It was only when the same twelve-year-old boy ran into the road waving his arms that Sky turned the buggy toward the correct home. She pulled the horse to a halt in the only shade available and called the boy. "Is this where your father is?"

"Yes, ma'am."

"Can you unhitch this horse and rub him down some, take him to water after he cools down, and picket him on some shady grass?"

With the boy's assurance, the doctor and nurse both gingerly stepped to the ground and lifted down their black bags. By that time, the door opened. A weary and bedraggled-looking woman stepped out. She said nothing at all, simply holding the door and waiting. Sky walked up to her, saying, "I'm Sky Whitely. This is Dr. Gwyneth Wycome. I'm a nurse working with the doctor, down from Pueblo today. And what is your name, please?"

"Folks just call me Gert. That'll do."

"Thank you, Gert. Now what's the problem?"

"Problem is my Tennison, he got his head in the way of a falling rock. Had a sharp edge to it by the looks of things. Hasn't woke up or said nary a word since."

Gwyneth was reminded in that moment how much Sky differed from her in her approach to the emotional situations they were regularly confronted with. That difference had been clear during the time they had worked together in Pueblo. To Sky, it was simply the natural order of things, and Gwyneth had thought little of it. Sky's first impulse was to befriend and comfort the troubled wife. Whereas Gwyneth stepped through the door with her mind focused solely on the patient.

Even as she was moving toward the cot where the man lay, her busy mind was telling her that Sky's actions took little more than seconds but might hold benefits as the day progressed. But with long-held habits and determination, she pushed aside any thoughts of the wife's needs and knelt down to manage a closer look at the wound. The light was so poor she couldn't be sure what she was seeing. Regaining her feet, she said, "Gert. Let's open the door and whatever windows will open. And let's set a lamp here so we can see better."

"We've no lamp, Doctor. Just some tallow candles I pour myself."

"Then let's see if we can move this cot closer to the door. In fact, it would be good to take the cot outside. Natural light and fresh air will do the patient good. Could you track down a couple of men who might help us move it?"

Gwyneth added nothing about the benefits of an open door and some air movement, but she had come close to gagging as she first stepped into the home, which was clearly kept shut tight. The odors of wood smoke, cooking, dampness from the dirt floor, unwashed bodies, and just plain living hung in the air like a cloud.

Two men were found and ushered down to the home of the injured man. The cot was soon outside. With the injury now exposed to the full noon sunlight, Gwyneth was able to see the damage. That the situation was serious was clearly obvious with just a glance.

Sky had put Gert to work heating water. She started to ask

for some towels but thought better of it. "You heat two big pans of water, Gert, and have some soap handy. I'll bring in the few other things we'll be needing."

From the box containing supplies that was kept in the buggy for immediate use, she brought in clean white cotton towels, a large roll of bandage material, and a small roll of tape. She returned for the wooden box containing the few surgical instruments Gwyneth had left with her. Gwyneth, in the meantime, was assessing the wound and the overall condition of the patient.

With the assessment completed, which hadn't taken long, Gwyneth stood and spoke to Gert. "Gert, the first need here is to wash your husband's hair and cut a lot of it off. We'll be wanting to shave his head all around the wound. I'd like it if you could assist Sky with the washing. That would be easier if you cut most of it off first. Before you begin, I'm going to put a bit of a patch over the wound. We don't want water entering the damaged area."

WITH THE HAIR washing and rough cutting completed, Gwyneth knelt beside the patient again. A pan of hot water, a bit of soap, and the straight razor from the wooden instrument box in hand, she removed the gauze and tape patch she had applied to hold the water off the injury and slowly, very carefully, shaved the area. Sky was watching intently, trying to learn all she could. At the same time, she was passing items to Gwyneth, and taking away and cleaning those that the doctor was finished with.

With the injury seen clearly, after all the cleaning and shaving was completed, Gwyneth hesitated, rocked back on her heels just a bit, and then stood to relieve the pressure on her knees and hips. Speaking only to herself, she said, "Not good. Not good at all."

Having thought it through, she turned to Sky first and then to Gert. "Sky, we'll be needing the cutters and the tweezers."

"And Gert, we're going to do all we can do here with what we've got to work with. But I won't try to fool you. Your yard is a far cry from a proper hospital operating room. Your husband is seriously injured. It looks as if the rock that fell was shattered to a point, or near enough to a point. It was certainly heavy enough to break the skull. You did well in getting the bleeding stopped. There's just a bit more blood now, but that's only because I've been digging around in there. I'm going to trim the shattered bone as much as I can and clean up around. I'll then put a mild disinfectant around the area to hold off infection. I'll bandage and cover it, and we'll move him back inside.

"Whether or not he'll heal and recover, I couldn't guess. But he would have his best chance if you could have him brought down to town and loaded onto the train. Take him to the Pueblo hospital. Or even up to Denver. They have the ability there to do what I can't do here. He's also going to need round the-clock care. Feeding, cleaning, and so forth. You might find that to be a burden beyond your ability, along with the care of your family. I'm sorry I can't offer more hope. We know little about the brain or how it functions. The skull is broken, and a small bit of the brain is exposed. Your husband needs hospital care, and you need to prepare yourself for a lengthy stay in the city while he heals."

Gert stood in silence, wringing her hands—twisting one into the other and then slowly undoing the knot—as Gwyneth bent to her work.

Sky hovered close enough to see as Gwyneth very gently picked out small fragments of bone, bits of ragged skin, and hair. Anticipating the need, Sky passed over the bone cutters as she retrieved the tweezers. Gwyneth, with about all the strength her fingers could apply, trimmed off the single piece of bone that was sticking awkwardly past the surface of the skin. Where the bone was broken, a loose piece was embedded in the brain.

Just a tiny leak of blood eased past the bone shard. Gwyneth hesitated and then gently pulled it out, in no way sure she was doing the right thing.

Disinfectant and bandaging completed all they could do in this makeshift, open-air operating theater halfway up the mountain, where the miners lived in the roughest of conditions. Wishing she could do more but knowing she couldn't, Gwyneth silently prayed for the man and rose to her feet.

After a bumpy, silent ride, halfway down the trail, where neither woman spoke, they arrived at a level spot with a small stream flowing alongside. Without consulting Gwyneth, Sky turned off and hauled the buggy to a stop under the shade of a row of poplars. She stepped down and, reaching under the seat, lifted out the lunch bag brought from the boarding house. They ate in silence, with Gert's Tennison on their minds, each buried in their own thoughts of injuries, love, contentment, and their own futures, and death, which could sometimes not be avoided, no matter the training of the medical people.

# Chapter Thirty-Two

COMMUNICATING BY LETTER, GWYNETH CONTACTED Summer Wilmore, inviting her to join the medical clinic staff in Pueblo. She worded her message as carefully as she knew how. So far, none of Billy and Gladys's family had left home. But as the family, one by one, reached toward their twentieth year, there would be no holding them on the ranch. She wasn't sure how the big, loud-speaking, boisterous, but good-natured father of the Wilmore tribe would take to the idea of his beloved daughter leaving for the city, being, in fact, the first to leave the nest.

Even with other daughters, he held a special relationship with this one, the one he saw as special, the one he insisted on calling Sissy, an adlib from Summer, her true name, sparring with words and enjoying the doing of it. This was all clear to Gwyneth. Whether it was clear to the others in the Wilmore family, she had no idea, nor would she inquire.

She had no doubt the invitation for Summer to join the clinic in Pueblo would challenge Billy's thinking. She had to tread carefully.

During their recent time with the Ute, Summer had been a great help, showing compassion and determination in equal shares, sacrificing her own sleep, risking her own health, and doing more than could ever have been expected of a girl her age. Gwyneth had no objection to being a ranch wife. She had been one herself. But whereas Summer's older sister saw nothing but ranching in her future and would probably end up being the wife of Ty Cameron and matron of the B/C Ranch, Summer seemed to be destined to take another path. What that path would be was not for Gwyneth to decide but getting her off the ranch to where she could survey the options might be a good beginning.

Fearing the young lady was wasting her youth on the isolated ranch and was likely to waste her life if she didn't break free, Gwyneth offered her a training position at the clinic. She also offered to pay the expenses for an exploratory visit to Pueblo.

The return letter arrived just about as quickly as any message that depended on train and stagecoach delivery could be expected to. The answer was an eager *yes*. Gwyneth could expect Summer on the train the following Monday. She would stay with Gwyneth. There was ample room in the big house, but several of the rooms sat empty. Gwyneth would have to purchase a bed and bedding to accommodate her guest. She smiled at the answering letter, wondering again what Summer's father had to say about the matter. Wondering too if her older brother Charles would accompany her as guide and protector.

It had been a different situation when Bea came to assist in the clinic. Bea was a mature woman, familiar with big city ways and well-able to take care of herself. Believing that too much togetherness could become a problem for friends who spent their days working together, right from the start, Gwyneth had encouraged Bea to take up residence in a local boarding house. It had worked out well. But seeing no harm in a limited amount of socializing, the two friends, doctor and nurse, had enjoyed several dinners together.

Wishing to have a private talk, Gwyneth arranged for

another dinner with Bea. This time, they met on Gwyneth's own veranda.

The meal was simple but tasteful, leaning heavily on the recipes and style Gwyneth had found much to both the cowboys and the women's taste during her ranching years. Earlier in the day, she had sent Spike to the butchers with a note and to the bakery with another note. She had fresh vegetables in her icebox and baking supplies enough in the cupboards. Spike returned with two nice fresh steaks, carefully wrapped and ready for the flame that would turn them into the succulent treat she knew they could be. The apple pie from the bakery would be a seldom enjoyed surprise ending to the feast.

Not wanting to build an open fire in the yard, Gwyneth improvised. She cleansed a cast-iron oven rack till it shone. She then retrieved four clay bricks that were lying carelessly beside the back shed. When all was ready, she would bake two smallish potatoes in the oven, lightly boil two servings of fresh carrots, and prepare the dough for a spread of biscuits. Thinking carefully about the timing each piece of the meal would require in order to arrive on the table hot from the stove, she laid it all out. She placed the bricks on the top of the cast-iron kitchen stove, ready to hold the oven rack close enough for the steaks to feel the heat, and perhaps just a lick of flame when the firebox lid was removed. Checking the big mantel clock against Bea's planned time of arrival, she decided to wait another quarter hour before starting the meal.

The potatoes went into the oven first. Then the pot holding the carrots was slid across the stovetop until it rested above the rear of the firebox. When the time came to start the meat, she laid the two steaks on the rack, powdered with salt and pepper, and rubbed with an opened and crushed garlic clove. She removed one stove lid, allowing the heat and just a touch of flame from the burning wood to tease the bottoms of the steaks and for the smoke to swirl around the meat before escaping out the opened window. The biscuits were the last to go into the oven beside the almost-baked potatoes. A small bowl of whipped butter was laid out, ready to melt into and enhance the taste of the buttermilk treat. The last item to feel the heat of the stove was a small cast-iron pan with a load of sweet onion slices waiting to be lightly sauteed.

Warming on the back of the stove was a pot of refried beans, which Gwyneth had made the day before, richly flavored and spiced as the Texans among their rancher friends had liked them.

Gwyneth decided the meal would be worth the small cloud of smoke gathering under the kitchen ceiling and slowly leaking out the open window.

Spike had been kept late to drive Bea to her home and return her after she had a chance to rest and put on what she considered to be proper party clothing. Bea would never do less than her best, presenting an image of near perfection.

When the time came to lay out the feast and settle in for an evening's enjoyment, Bea carried out the dinner set Gwyneth had chosen for the occasion. Her ordered and precise mind worked its magic in the setting with dinner plates, bread plates, water glasses in lieu of wine goblets, which neither lady would use, silverware, and white linen napkins. The veranda table was small and the settings tight to each other, but somehow Bea made it all appear as it would have in the dining room in the fanciest eastern hotel.

While Bea was setting the table, Gwyneth was laying out the food in matching serving dishes. Bea returned to carry them out. Last to come were the steaks, sizzling and crispy on the edges, succulent and slightly rare in their insides, and with the name of the maker of the oven rack seared into the meat. As an explanation mark on the feast, Gwyneth, careful not to burn her fingers, set the biscuits in a covered bowl. She let them sit for just a moment as she pushed the lid back into place on the stove and closed the oven door.

Sitting in the wicker chairs across from one another, Bea

said, "My dear friend, I have never seen the better, as Spike might have worded it. Perhaps you missed your true calling. Good chefs are hard to come by."

Folding her hands, Gwyneth responded, "I think we'll just settle for saying grace."

A short half hour later, Bea gently laid down her dessert fork, slid her pie dish carefully to the center of the table, leaned back, and said, "Hmm-m. I'm guessing it would be out of order to have a nap now."

"Have a nap if you wish, but first, I have a question."

"Ask away. I have been thoroughly and well bribed. I can tell no lies."

"My question is simple, and the meal not a bribe. The meal is actually more of my reminiscing. Imagine, if you can, holding a steak like that over an open fire, speared on a sharpened stick, with the heat threatening to scorch your brow, and the smoke swirling first here and then there, so as not to miss fouling everyone's eyes. On another close-by fire, someone would be watching over pots of beans, potatoes if they were available, whatever vegetable hadn't gone bad in the back of the wagon, and mountains of biscuits. And often enough, the steaks would be from whatever wild game the men were able to bring down."

"I take it you didn't use your best crockery and linen napkins."

"More like a tin plate, a single fork, and the camp knife hung from your belt, with your pant leg for a napkin. And often enough you'd eat with your fingers."

Bea leaned further into the wicker chair, closed her eyes, and said, "When the Lord made some of us, He had city living in mind."

"Yes, well, to my question. Have you heard from Brandy Gilcrist lately?"

The question caused Bea to open her eyes, study her friend for a moment without lifting her head, close her eyes again, and say, "What makes you think I would receive a letter from Brandy?"

"The same thing that makes me believe you are struggling right now to hold back a grin."

"My, what a vivid imagination you have."

"What am I imagining, the letter or the grin?"

"And if I plead no contest?"

"Then you will be doing nothing more than supporting the thoughts I have held to myself since his visit."

"Aw, well. You always were too smart for me, always a step ahead. So what do you predict will come next, my brilliant friend who can see through the mysteries of the darkness and tell the future?"

"Sadly, I predict that you will be leaving me. Returning to where your immediate future appears to lie. Have you planned a date for your return yet?"

"I can't. I have never faced such a dilemma. Never have I enjoyed my work more, nor felt more useful and needed."

"But. This is where the but comes in."

"Yes, the complicating and ever-present but."

"So tell me, Bea. Tell me honest. Do you love him?"

"I'm hesitant to admit it, Gwyneth, but I fear I do."

"And is he being forthright with you, or is he playing with your feelings?"

"You know the answer to that. If nothing else, I know how to stand up for myself. To your certain knowledge, you know that I have not lacked for interest from the opposite gender. In those matters, the matters of a lifetime companion, I may face judgment from some, but I admit to thinking of my own self first. Protecting myself. When I am sure, I will have no problem surrendering myself to the right person, but I must be sure."

"Which is a long way of avoiding my question."

Bea opened her eyes, looking directly at her friend of several years, leaned forward, and said, "Brandy has made his proposal. By letter only, to be sure, but he hinted at the same when he was here. Just sorting out the situation, I suppose. Wondering if there was anyone else in the picture. There isn't, and I have answered his proposal with a yes, contingent only upon meeting each other's families whenever that can be arranged."

"I'm very happy for you both and, I will admit just to you, a bit envious. Not over Brandy, you understand. Just the situation in general. Will you stay just long enough to point Summer in the right direction or for me to find another nurse?"

"I'll stay until you don't need me anymore. I've told Brandy that, and he has encouraged the same thing."

# Chapter Thirty-Three

SPIKE HARNESSED THE DRIVING ANIMAL, BUT Gwyneth took the reins herself when the time came to meet Summer at the train. The young lady was full of excitement at her first sight of the city and the general hubbub of activity around the arriving train. Gwyneth knew she would be wearing her best, which on the ranch was perfectly acceptable, but she stood out a bit on the railway platform. Not that the situation was abnormal. Pueblo saw many ranchers, farmers, miners, and travelers. But for Summer to work in the clinic, Gwyneth would have Bea take her shopping. There was no one quite like Bea to know just the correct dress or blouse to lift off the rack.

Summer stepped down from the buggy and stood in awe of the grand house Gwyneth had purchased. At the same time, Spike, waiting to take the horse to the shed, was standing in awe of the beautiful young lady guest. It was doubtful if Spike could have studied and passed a higher education exam, but he had street smarts and instinct to compare to anyone. The wisdom of the street warned him immediately to look away, take the horse, and move on. He loved his job at the Wycome Medical Clinic. He'd do nothing to cause the doctor concern. Doing anything to put that relationship in jeopardy would be foolish. But perhaps just one more quick peek as the girl was lifting down her bag.

Gwyneth got Summer settled into her own room with the new bed and the modest chiffonier with the mirror attached. The first time she had ever had her own room. The young ranch girl seemed to see another new wonder in every direction she looked. She finally realized that she had used all the expressive words in her limited vocabulary, most of them more than once. But she was also fatigued from the early morning start at the ranch and the stagecoach run, followed by the excitement of riding a real train. Gwyneth put an easy meal on the table and suggested that Summer might benefit from an early night. The next day, she was to get her first experience in the clinic.

MORNING CAME with a rush of patients, two coming to the clinic and another sending a messenger to request a home visit. Summer stood by while Gwyneth attended to a boy of about ten years who had fallen out of a tree in his backyard. The young fella pridefully fought back tears as the doctor gently maneuvered his broken arm into the proper position. Even though neither Gwyneth nor Summer had ever broken a bone themselves, it was as if they could feel the boy's pain, adding an extra level of care and gentleness to their ministrations.

When Gwyneth instructed Summer to cradle the arm in position as she prepared, and then began applying a light cast, the boy's eyes locked on Summer's and held until the cast was well enough formed that she could remove her hand from the arm and simply keep it steady with a grip on the wrist. When the eye contact broke off, Gwyneth looked at Summer and smiled just a bit. Summer's mind swayed somewhere between wonder and confusion. The boy's mother, seated on a chair off to the side, noticed her son's rapt attention on the pretty girl and was also smiling. Summer had just turned eighteen. The distance in years and maturity separating patient and student nurse were wide, but perhaps not so wide at that moment.

Spike harnessed the gelding and Bea, with a light jacket covering her shoulders against the morning's chill, and with her well-stocked medical bag lying on the floor of the buggy, took her seat and tried to relax as Spike drove with one hand on the reins, and the written directions to the patient's home held in the other. If the competent nurse found herself in a situation where she needed Gwyneth's assistance, she would send Spike back immediately.

When the boy and his mother left the clinic, Summer, instinctively seeing what had to be done, stripped the white sheet off the stretcher and carefully laid out the clean sheet. She then picked up the refuse from the making of the plaster cast and carried it to the trash can set there for the purpose. When Gwyneth returned from scrubbing drying plaster off her hands, all she could do was look at what the ranch girl had done and congratulate her, before saying, "Scrub your hands again. Then we'll go into the other room and see how our about-to-be-a-mom is doing."

Summer's first day on the job was turning into a crash course in human nature, with the expectant father pacing the backyard while coming to look in the window every few minutes. That the windows were blocked out with a curtain halfway up seemed not to influence him in the least. Perhaps he thought the curtains would magically part and celestial trumpets would blow when the happenings inside were completed.

In Summer's previously small world, the matter of procreation and childbirth were taboo subjects, hardly mentioned and most certainly kept private. The conversation between her and Gwyneth on the ride up to the Cameron Ranch, several months before, was her only personal discussion of intimate matters. From her ranch life, Summer was aware of the basics of the proceedings. But it was doubtful if she had ever before considered how the intimacy of personal privacy and modesty were set aside when it came to medical necessity. She was unprepared for the openness once a patient submitted herself to the medical world. Her education in those matters began rather abruptly and grew over the next few hours.

Unprepared and suddenly shocked, she actually took a step away from the bedside, her heart suddenly a-flutter and her cheeks flaming in embarrassment, when Gwyneth folded the covering bed sheet back to examine the pregnant woman. She wasn't at all sure what Gwyneth was looking for, but she would ease into that question in the privacy of the clinic at a later time. Her mind and emotions were weighted down with all the newness she could manage for this one morning. But there was more to come, whether she was ready or not.

As the young wife struggled through labor that seemed as if it would never end, she thrashed about on the bed, while occasionally sliding her feet to the floor to pace slowly around the room. She suffered and sweated, her hair becoming limp with moisture. She soaked through her nightgown and the sheet she lay on. Summer quickly replaced the sheet while the patient was on one of her walks and helped her out of the soaked nightgown and into another she had found in a drawer. She was acting totally on instinct, but Gwyneth was in the other room, within easy call if she was needed.

While the struggle went on, the patient's eyes, not quite glazed over but also not fully aware of her surroundings, held no sight for anyone else or anything beyond the child she waited for. Noon came and went. The woman was near to exhaustion. She had borne more pain that morning than she had believed possible. But finally, with Gwyneth and Summer both in attendance, while Bea was in the other room writing up her report for the home visit, the morning's hard going finally produced a fine, healthy little girl, along with much startling education for Summer.

Gwyneth allowed Summer to take the news to the father,

adding still more to her education. She was shocked when the young man let out a whoop-de-doo and then, for some strange reason, hugged Summer and twirled her around in a circle. Seemingly unaware of what he had done, he again rushed to the window.

Straightening her dress and fluffing her hair as she attempted to put herself back together after suffering through the impromptu twirl, Summer was silently thinking back to the ranch. She had never seen such excitement from her own father except when his favorite Clydesdale mare dropped a set of healthy twins, a rare happening indeed, a couple of years before. When she returned to the birth room, Gwyneth was ministering to the baby.

Summer straightened the bed as best she could, removing a couple of soiled towels. Then Gwyneth gently lay the baby on her mother's breast. At Gwyneth's request, Summer gently wrapped mother and child in a stove-warmed bed sheet. Feeling just the beginnings of some confidence, she said, "If it's all right with everyone, I'm going to open these curtains. That man is going to burst at the seams if I don't."

With the curtains opened and the man's nose coming close to being pressed against the glass, Gwyneth smiled and said, "Summer. Gently and carefully lift the baby and hold her so her father can take a better look."

Frightened half to death, and with extreme care, Summer did as Gwyneth suggested."

On her first day as a nurse in training, she had built more memories and learned more than she ever thought possible. She had trouble convincing herself that just thirty-six hours before she had stepped aboard the stagecoach, leaving the home ranch with all of its familiar and predictable daily tasks.

~

Bea had no problem with the home visit. There was an elderly lady who had a bad cough and was concerned about pneumonia. Bea advised her to keep warm, gargle with salt water, drink hot lemon and honey tea, and get lots of rest. She promised to have the doctor come out the next morning as a precaution against the much-feared pneumonia.

As Bea was preparing to return to her rooming house that afternoon, Gwyneth called Summer from her place by the young mom. The room had been cleaned up and the laundry dealt with, fit for company. The father was sitting by the bed holding his daughter. Summer doubted he would ever quit grinning as he studied the little hands and feet, and then again stroked the bit of hair she had been born with.

Gwyneth spoke to Summer and Bea together.

"We have nothing on the calendar for tomorrow, except that one visit, although that could change. But right now, we'll assume I'll be able to manage on my own. You're both to take the day for shopping and fixing. Summer is in your care, Bea. Don't lose her in the crowd. In the morning, I'll have Spike bring Summer to your place. She is yours for the day. Take her shopping. Guide her around a bit. Purchase several day outfits for work and one or two for church or evenings out for dinner. Get some good, solid work shoes. Do whatever else you think needs doing. And, Summer, my best advice is to trust Bea's judgment. I know of no one anywhere with more clothing or style sense than Bea. You'll be kept busy after tomorrow, so make the most of the day. I can't give you Spike for the day, so you'll have to hail a cab to get back here."

When the hired buggy pulled into the side driveway that evening, to deliver Summer back to Gwyneth's home, the young ranch girl alighted, loaded down with bags in her arms and with more bags and boxes yet in the buggy. The driver stepped down, gathered up what remained, carrying it to the front door, laying it on the table. With a finger to the bill of his cap, he bid good night.

Gwyneth opened the door and literally gaped at the girl standing there. She had sent Bea out with a young ranch girl to purchase some city-appropriate clothing, but what stood before her was something else altogether. Standing taller than she ever had before, taller and straighter, Summer was decked out in a dressy, slate-gray skirt and a light blue and white, high-neck blouse with a wide lace trim. The narrow-waisted blouse flared slightly over the skirt, which seemed to float downward into more fullness where it draped over the black shoes with heels that matched Summer's riding boots for height. Her sun-bleached blond hair had been washed and set in a series of waves and ringlets that fell over the blouse at the back.

Gwyneth smiled and said, "I'm not at all sure who you are in all your fancy duds, but you can't just stand there. Come in and introduce yourself."

Summer couldn't hold out any longer. After carrying in the remaining parcels and setting them on the one couch in the big room, she turned to her hostess and mentor.

"Oh. Gwyneth. I never in all my life dreamed of such clothing as Bea showed me today. Why, even that big Montgomery Ward catalog that comes to the ranch by the mail looks old and plain by comparison. I do believe I've tried on most of the women's clothing in town, with Bea saying several times how she wished we were in Chicago so she could do the job proper. After what I've seen here, I can't imagine any better, Chicago or no Chicago. She even had me try on and purchase unmentionables. I was never so embarrassed.

"And such a thing as was never heard of before. We went to a shop where a woman forced me to lie back on a chair with my head in a big basin. She ran hot water over it from a fancy porcelain jug and soaped it all up. Hot water right from the reservoir on the little stove they had lit there. Have you ever heard of such a thing? Why she washed and rinsed and then washed and rinsed again. She was primed to start in cutting until I stopped her. Had her scissors all set out and a big comb such as I'd never seen. Bea laughed and told me it was just for styling. She wasn't going to cut it all off.

"And all the while that's going on, another woman is doing I don't know what-all to my hands. Rubbed some kind of smelly oil into them. Made them all greasy and slippery. You'd think I'd just been delivering a calf, such a mess they were. Cut and filed all the rough edges off my nails. That was all right, I guess. Cleaned and scraped under the nails until the last of the evidence of the ranch was gone. But Gwyneth. You just won't believe. Another woman pulled my shoes off and did the same to my feet as what was done to my hands. Why, I never!"

Wanting Summer to enjoy this moment that would probably never be repeated, she made no comment except to say, "Summer, you look lovely. Stunning. Like any young man's dream. But let's see what else you have in the bags. You're not going to be able to work in those clothes."

Summer opened the bags and the two boxes. Each box held a hat. She held the first one up and said, "For out or church and such, so Bea says."

She opened the second box and lifted out her ranch hat, badly used and a bit weather-worn, but the original beige color still showed through.

"Silly woman asked if she should throw my hat away." I was all set to reach for my pistol until I realized it was still in my satchel upstairs. "I don't know where these city women growed to be adults while still knowing so little."

Summer finally got to the bags that held the work clothing. And here Bea showed her versatile judgment. The clothes were stylish but practical. As washable as the available fabrics allowed. From the final bag, Summer withdrew an assortment of high-neck aprons to wear in the clinic to protect the street wear from the assortment of hazards of nurses' work.

The two women took a cup of coffee each and settled into the veranda chairs. It was time for a wind-down after such an exciting day for Summer and a difficult workday for Gwyneth. The clinic had become busy by mid-morning, but Gwyneth wouldn't talk of that for fear of spoiling the outing Bea and Summer had enjoyed so much.

# Chapter Thirty-Four

TWO MONTHS HAD GONE PAST. BEA HAD STAYED ONE month tutoring Summer while assisting Gwyneth. Considering her short time at the clinic, she had learned a lot. She was still a long way from being a qualified nurse. But by anyone's standards, she had come a long way. She had a breakthrough of sorts the first time she observed as Gwyneth made an incision to remove an infected appendix. Even with the warning from Bea, Summer stiffened as the scalpel slid across the skin, leaving behind it a short, bleeding wound that would allow the doctor access to the problem. She got a bit dizzy and nearly collapsed when she seemed to lose her balance.

Bea was sympathetic but showed nothing but professionalism as she said, "Come on, girl. Take a grip on yourself. This is the work, and you're studying under the best doctor you're ever likely to see. You have a job to do. Gwyneth needs you, and so does the patient."

That was to be her sole display of weakness until a man came in with a knife wound high on the inside of his groin. He confessed to having slipped and fallen on his own knife while attempting some minor repair to his house. The wound was serious. He had pressed a folded cloth against it in an effort to stem the bleeding, but he was only partially successful. His underwear and pants were soaking up more blood than the folded cloth.

Gwyneth had him remove his shirt, pants, and underwear. He lay on the stretcher with only a folded bed sheet covering him to the waist. Summer blanched at the very thought of what might be coming. She stood resolute but off to the side, where her vision was blocked by the doctor. When Gwyneth called her, she didn't respond immediately. Gwyneth looked over her shoulder and understood what the problem was. Quietly, she said, "Summer. I need you."

Summer took the few steps to place herself across the stretcher from Gwyneth, never looking down. Needing to stop the bleeding as quickly as possible, the doctor decided to prepare the needles and suture thread herself. But Summer was going to have to help too.

"Summer, bring those cotton pads over. Good. Now take one and press it where I'm holding this one. As soon as I pull away, you take my place. I'll bring a larger towel over and show you what you will be doing in another case such as this one."

Gwyneth had the man roll onto his side, bend his one knee a bit, and spread his legs. Summer was mortified, her face blazing pink from embarrassment. But Gwyneth insisted that she watch carefully. A short few seconds later, with the towel wrapped and snugged in place, the injury was exposed, but little else.

As was normal, Gwyneth had Summer wash the injury area while she attempted to stem the blood flow, which thankfully, was slowing. Summer again held a pad against the injury while Gwyneth prepared the needle and suture thread. Once more trading places, Gwyneth lifted the cotton pad and searched through the wound as best she could in the tiny space. She picked out a small bit of cloth but decided there was no more. The man's knife was sharp. It cut through the pants and underwear cleanly, leaving little residue.

She dribbled a bit of disinfectant over the wound, allowing some to flow into the gash. That brought a rise from the patient, but he soon settled down. Four sutures were all the small opening required. With another cotton pad held in place with several wraps of gauze bandaging, the job was done.

"All right, sir. That's the best that can be done. Remove the bandage in a couple of days. I'll give you a small supply. You can re-wrap it yourself or come back here if you need help. I'm tempted to warn you about climbing ladders holding a knife in your hand, but I'm guessing you already know. If you see any sign of infection or reddening around the sutures, come here immediately. Come back in one week anyway and I'll remove the sutures. Summer, you untie that towel and we'll let this man free."

Summer's task had been made easier with Gwyneth's assistance. But once taking up the challenge, she had stuck with it, earning Gwyneth's praise when they were finished.

Each new situation was proving to be a critical learning experience in nursing. Taken together, they confirmed for her that she really could do the work and wanted to do the work, no matter how uncomfortable it occasionally was.

SUMMER AND GWYNETH found they could continue living together without getting in each other's way, after the working day was over. They both relished time in the evening to unwind and do what one wished, but they found different interests that kept them out of each other's way.

Compared to the ranch, where there were always people around and never a time without something to do, to Summer, this was new freedom, never before experienced. She learned to manage for herself, going shopping for simple items that she and Bea hadn't bothered with during the first big foray into the wonders of the fashion world, Pueblo style. Gwyneth gave her full freedom with the horse. That alone filled many evenings for the ranch-raised girl. The two women cooked together most evenings. But Summer awakened early to the fact that Gwyneth treasured her alone time on the veranda in the evenings. She seldom encroached on that time.

Billy and Gladys, Summer's parents, surprised her one weekend when they arrived at the house unannounced. Arriving on the evening train and spending the night at a hotel, they had taken a hired rig to the clinic. A joyous reunion took place outside the clinic door, but Summer had to get right back to work assisting with a small surgery. Billy and Gladys puttered around in the back garden until the work at the clinic was completed. They stayed over Sunday but took the train back to Bessie Creek Monday morning. At first startled by the change in Summer, Billy finally admitted to himself that his lovely daughter was a better fit in the city than she had been on the ranch, although she could always ride and work like the best of those on the B-4.

Summer was left alone for only one day in the month following Bea's departure. Sky and Eustice had announced their marriage to be held at Bessie Creek. Summer would hold the fort but would do little other than promise that the doctor would return the next day. A minister from Pueblo arrived at Bessie Creek on the same train Gwyneth rode in on. The service was simple and short, similar in all ways to the one that had joined Trent and Gwyneth in holy matrimony so many years before. Gwyneth relived that time in her mind as she watched the exchanging of vows. Silently, she wished much happiness to the happy couple while holding deep, private sadness in her heart for herself. She seldom thought of herself, introspection not being one of her gifts, but during the ride home on the train, her mind was focused on little else.

It was only a few weeks later that a letter arrived from Chicago. Telling herself that the clinic was too busy for her to stop and read a letter, she set it aside until her veranda time. Seated in her big wicker chair, Gwyneth slowly, cautiously, slit the envelope open as if she feared something was going to jump out at her. In truth, there was no surprise once she did slip her fingers in to retrieve the paper folded inside.

Enclosed was a posed photograph of another happy bride and groom. Bea Brodrick had become Mrs. Brandy Gilcrist. The photo was lovely, as was Bea herself. Bea's description of the wedding was poetry itself. This news, although expected, hit Gwyneth much harder than Sky's wedding. Gwyneth and Bea had a lot of happy history between them. As she studied the photo and glanced again at the note, an overwhelming aloneness came over her. She felt the tears welling up in her eyes as she hurried to her own room, not wishing to embarrass herself. There, she closed the door, leaned back against it, and cried.

Summer heard the weeping through the thin wall but was wise enough to say nothing.

From that time, as awkward as she found the process to be, Gwyneth began a thorough examination of herself, her accomplishments, her dreams, her future. She had fulfilled her two main wishes in life, one to be a doctor, the other to marry a good man. Yes, that had been her reality, but it was no more. Her dream of a lengthy, happy marriage had vanished on the Colorado grass, leaving in its place a hollowness she seldom allowed to surface but often had to fight down. Periodically adding to that hollowness was a bitter aloneness and loneliness that Gwyneth had trouble admitting even to herself.

She had her clinic. And that was an accomplishment, to be sure. But beneath her composed exterior, an unsettling truth had become noticeable to both Bea and Brandy Gilcrist, although they were cautious about mentioning it. She had to admit that bitter truth. She was alone. Was there no one else for her? Trent had been wonderful; all a woman could want. For years, she had been telling herself that one good man in a lifetime was all she needed. Even if that was true, it didn't help during the long, lonely nights. And she couldn't logically claim that the clinic, as much as she loved it, was any comfort either.

She couldn't talk to the clinic. She couldn't turn to the clinic and say, "I love you." She couldn't...well, there were so many things, so many needs that the clinic couldn't satisfy. She'd been so sure. One Trent was enough in her life. The world of medicine would fill and challenge her mind while she was doing good in the world. Yes, okay. But was that her final answer? Perhaps her life was going to require a complete rethink.

# Chapter Thirty-Five

THE UNWELCOME AND SOMEWHAT MYSTIFYING NEWS came by way of the community paper. In a blaring headline, the citizens of Pueblo were informed that the Western States Iron Mill had funded the addition of a specialized burn unit at the Pueblo hospital, along with the hiring of a physician proficient in the treatment of burns and the issues arising from them.

Summer read the headline while looking over Gwyneth's shoulder. The doctor was clearly staring at the page longer than it took to read just the words. But Summer had little knowledge about how much the work from the mill had impacted Wycome Medical Clinic. After waiting a discreet length of time, Summer said, "Did you see that coming? I know you have a friend at the mill."

"No, Summer. I had no knowledge of this until right now. It's strange that they would do this. They fought the paying of my modest billings at the first. And they were a pittance compared to what this will cost. They must have their reasons.

"This will take away a piece of our work, but not a major piece in terms of time involved, although quite significant in terms of our billings. Dealing with burns is complex work. I was able to bill more for that than for simpler work that makes up most of what we do. The clinic will miss that income. And I don't know where they're going to find a doctor to fill the bill unless they go searching through the big eastern hospitals.

"Thankfully, the incidents of accidental burns and mill accidents in total appear to be tapering off. That's all for the better."

Venturing into untried territory as only the young can sometimes do, Summer asked, "Would you want that job?"

The answer was slow in coming, as if it required much thought. But finally, Gwyneth replied, "No, I wouldn't. If I can't have the clinic, I would probably look beyond Pueblo. I've worked in big hospitals. Two of the very best. And among top surgeons and physicians. I don't want that again either.

"Have you ever considered Summer, how free we are in the west? The big eastern cities can be stifling with their crowds of people, all their rules and regulations, all the restrictions, all their expectations. My years of ranching out here, and now with my own clinic, have spoiled me for that kind of regimentation. Those kinds of crowds. I'm afraid I would kick over the traces and cause no end of trouble for the institution if I were back there again."

Their conversation was broken when a black shiny buggy pulled to a stop beside the clinic. Spike was there immediately to take the horse. Summer needlessly said, "Someone's hear. It's a man in a suit."

"Yes, I know the buggy. And the man."

Although the door was open on this beautiful summer day, with no patients needing care, the visitor gave a one-knuckle knock and waited just a moment before asking. "May I come in, Doctor?"

Wearily, Gwyneth responded, "No, Clayton. I'll come out. We'll sit in the garden."

The visit was shorter than Summer would have thought. A handsome young man coming to visit the doctor. They were on a first-name basis. There must be history here. And perhaps an invitation of sorts. For dinner. For an outing into the country.

Summer was young, often showing a romantic side, as if she could imagine something into reality. Things like the doctor smiling and accepting a dinner invitation. Or perhaps the young man was going to reach into his pocket and present the doctor with a gift. Oh, so many things might be taking place in the back garden. She dare not look, for fear of being found to be a snoop. But even as she puttered around in the clinic, straightening and fixing things that were already straight and fixed, the buggy was rattling over the gravel of the driveway and would be lost to sight before long. Gwyneth sat in the garden by herself for a while before returning to the clinic. Summer continued redoing work she had already done.

When Gwyneth returned to the clinic, she sat, picked up the neighborhood paper again, and began reading.

Assuming a position she knew was potentially hazardous, Summer quietly said, "Talk to me, Doctor. Was that the man from the mill?"

Smiling up at her intern, Gwyneth answered, "Yes. That was Mr. Clayton Bonifare. Assistant manager at the mill. We've had dinner a few times, but I haven't heard from him in months."

Continuing to push her luck, Summer said, "And?"

"And nothing. Nothing at all. All he really came to tell me was that the gift to the hospital has been in the planning stage for some time. It wasn't supposed to become public until the mill approved its publication. And that wasn't supposed to happen until Clayton had a chance to inform me. "Just as a professional courtesy," he said. When I had no response, he added, 'It's nothing personal, just business. The mill can earn a lot of community support by funding the clinic, and everyone will be better off.' As if that would somehow satisfy my every question."

Showing some quiet wisdom, Summer said, "Well, perhaps not everyone."

"No, perhaps not everyone. But don't think I'm missing Clayton personally, beyond the occasional dinner. I'm not and never would. I would not even consider getting serious over him. But he is a pleasant dinner companion, a good conversationist. And he makes no demands I have to fight off. I kind of miss the dinners."

THE CLINIC CARRIED on as before for another two weeks, when a different buggy pulled into the yard. This time with a driver and a passenger. Another man. A smallish, slim-built man who came near to jumping to the ground and then sprightly walked to the door. The buggy horse waited patiently as if it was happy to stop and pick the grass on the edge of the driveway. Seeing him coming, Summer stepped outside. "The doctor is busy, sir. Is there something I can do for you?"

"Unless you speak for the doctor, I am afraid not. I'll wait though, if the doctor will be finished sometime soon."

"She's just closing up. A few more sutures, a bandage, and she'll be done. I can't let you in though. The clinic is not large, and there is no sitting room. There are a couple of chairs under that tree if you would like to take advantage of one."

"Thank you, young miss. I shall do that."

A quarter hour later, Gwyneth came out, still wiping her hands on a towel. "You wanted to see me, sir?"

Jumping to his feet, as if he did everything quickly, in an athletic manner, he responded, "Indeed, I do. Dr. Gwyneth Wycome, I presume. May I introduce myself? Dr. Hollister Peabody. Up here from San Francisco. May we have a private chat, Doctor?"

Gwyneth led the visiting doctor down the driveway and to the veranda. Settled into the wicker chairs, Gwyneth said nothing. She simply studied the doctor and waited. Finally, Hollister Peabody began his story.

"As I said, Doctor, I'm from San Francisco. My wife and have lived there going on ten years. We have two children, ten and eight. I am California-born and raised, although from some distance south of the big city. My wife is from a small town a bit north of Denver, so not far from here. To be clear about the issue that I am attempting to sort out, my wife hates San Francisco. To hear her tell it, it is all crime and violence, steep hills, and bitter summer winds off the ocean. Hardly a civilized citizen to be found anywhere.

"Now I will admit there is some truth in every one of her complaints. But it is not all bad. And as far as the people are concerned, I deal with fine folks every day. Nevertheless, she is adamant. She will not live out her life in a place she hates.

"I was uneasy about what solution to seek, attempting to read my own mind, don't you see, when an advertisement for a qualified physician, especially one familiar with the latest in burn treatment, showed up in our local paper. I had never heard of Pueblo, Colorado, but my wife's eyes lit up the moment I read out the ad to her. She stopped what she was doing and announced that she would go and begin packing. I managed to slow her down by promising to come and see what this job offer was all about. It's a long ride on the rails, but still, we must be thankful we're beyond horse and wagon travel, must we not?

"I received my answer today during an interview at the Pueblo hospital. There are two others applying for the advertised position, both easterners. I am also eastern trained. I doubt if either man would better my training or expertise in the skills the hospital is seeking in the new hire. But none of that matters. I quickly decided that I didn't want their job. The hospital is new, as hospitals go, barely on its feet, trying to find its way in the world. I have no wish to be involved in someone else's growth struggles, and, in any case, I wasn't at all drawn to the folks I was introduced to, if you will allow me that bluntness, without otherwise adversely judging me.

"But during our somewhat dreary conversation, your name was mentioned, along with the information that you had been treating the burn victims from the mill. Silently, I was thinking they might be wise to either recruit you or leave things as they are, but I had no right to say such a thing, so I stayed mum. However, I decided I had to meet you. So here I am. And here you are. And I have several questions swirling around in my head. But before I ask them, perhaps I should allow you to comment on what you have heard so far. Perhaps you think me a crank."

As she had just moments before, Gwyneth sat silently while she studied the man, as if seeking wisdom. When she spoke, she said words that frightened her. But she had thought long and hard about her clinic in Pueblo. She had prayed humble prayers, seeking wisdom, direction, and guidance. Was this dapper little man sitting on her veranda there in answer to her prayers? She had seldom moved quickly, although she had admitted to herself many times that leaving her comfortable childhood home to walk to the battlefield and volunteer as a nurse was ill thought out.

One of the things that drew Gwyneth to Trent in their meetings leading up to the marriage was that Trent, in opposition to the reckless life led by most trail driving cowboys, was a careful, thoughtful, planning man. Following their marriage, they proved the merits of their method when their detailed plans and their careful search for available grass had resulted in the Mirrored W Ranch. Caution was now in her bloodstream, even if it hadn't been in her younger years.

Stepping right into the thickness of the issue, Gwyneth said, "I presume, Dr. Peabody, that you are a stable family man. That you are not here driven by some errant wind. That you have a plan for your life. And that you have worked yourself into a position of reasonable financial security. Am I on the correct path in making those presumptions, Doctor? I'm thinking that to contemplate a move such as the one that led you to the Pueblo hospital, you would require at least a few of those positions."

"My dear and lovely Dr. Wycome. One of the reasons I find the hospital position untenable is the pay scale. My income in San Francisco considerably surpasses their offer. Simply practicing medicine as an individual, with no complicating issues, has afforded my family a comfortable living. Even in the big expensive city we managed to live well below my income level. My wife and I are in agreement on most family matters, setting aside the city we live in, as I have already explained, and we are, as you put it, Doctor, reasonably financially secure.

"There is little room for growth at the Pueblo hospital, and I am one who covets growth. Not financial growth only, but intellectual growth. I have a desire to know. A desire to grow within our chosen life's work. There are medical discoveries being made all around the world. I want to know about them and offer them to my patients. A private clinic such as yours puts the future in the doctor's own hands. Learn and grow or settle in and get stale. Those are the choices. What I have heard of you, Doctor, moved me to wonder if we wouldn't make a good team."

Gwyneth again paused. She was liking the way Dr. Peabody gave her time to think. Still, when she spoke, her thoughts were only half-formed.

"Doctor, you have placed a dilemma right before my eyes. Just weeks ago, I invited a fine doctor, one I had worked with back east, to join me in building a multi-doctor and, perhaps a multi-disciplinary clinic. He didn't find Pueblo to his liking. He is now back in Chicago in a large hospital. I had laid that plan to rest, and now here you sit, challenging me. Please give me the full of a day. If we both take a day to think and pray, we'll be better prepared to face the issues tomorrow evening. You reserve a table at the Southern Belle restaurant for seven tomorrow evening. I will meet you there. Is that satisfactory, Doctor?"

"Done and done, Doctor. The Southern Belle. Seven tomorrow evening. And now I will leave you to your patient. Thank you and farewell."

Gwyneth remained in her wicker chair as she watched the driver maneuver the buggy down the lane. Her mind was swirling with thoughts. Thoughts that were coming from different directions, some of them bumping into others as she worked her way through them.

# Chapter Thirty-Six

Gwyneth left the straightening up of the clinic to Summer the following afternoon. It had been a busy day. Both women were tired. But the doctor had a dinner date, a fact she had shared with Summer, assuring her that she was meeting a married man for dinner with only business matters to be discussed.

Summer, again showing that her perceptions of daily matters were most often correct, asked, "Big changes coming in the clinic?"

"Possibly Summer. There is much to be discussed. Dr. Peabody has a wife and two children in San Francisco. He also has a steady medical practice ongoing. His interest is primarily to get his wife back to Colorado. If joining the clinic in some fashion would work to my benefit, as well as his, perhaps we can work something out."

"You have been unsettled ever since your two nurses were married. I've sensed a change coming."

"Sometimes, Summer, your clear vision frightens me. It's all a part of that freedom we enjoy in the west. Herding cattle in rough country, or riding the night watch, or climbing on an unknown animal from the rough string, requires real men and women. Parlor games just don't make it. The circumstances we live with force us to trust our riding partner. When trust is lost, there's no going back on that person. So it's imperative that we see clearly. You have excelled in that."

"Do you remember, Gwyneth, that time with the Indians? There was so much hurt, so much suffering. So much loss. Even Daniel and Night Light buried one of their children. The first couple of nights there, I lay in my blankets holding back tears. I hurt for the Ute, but I was frightened too. It became very clear to me that I had lived a protected life. Protected by family that loved me and by a father and mother who wouldn't let any harm come to me.

"Really, I was just a child, although my mind and body said I was an adult. But I had never suffered any loss, and there we were among a small tribe who were suffering terrible loss. If ever I had my eyes opened, it was then. Instead of just helping you treat them, I started to see them. Really see them. They had so little, and even most of that was being taken from them. If nothing else came of that, I have learned to be thankful."

"I'm happy to hear you learned those things, Summer. And yes, you're correct. Something inside me is pressing me to re-examine my life and my desires for the remainder of my time on this earth. Meeting with Dr. Peabody is a part of that. One thing I will promise Summer, is that whatever happens with the clinic, I will see that you're cared for."

THE TIME at the Southern Belle was intense and interesting. Dr. Peabody, who insisted Gwyneth address him as Hollister, his given name, was a bright and well-trained physician and surgeon. Perhaps better trained than Gwyneth had been, although she was confident that her time in the two Chicago hospitals, along with her years of personal study, had brought her up to his knowledge level and perhaps even a bit beyond. It wasn't a point worth discussing, so they left it alone.

At the end of the long evening, the maître d' very politely approached their table inquiring if there was anything else the couple needed. Gwyneth looked around, realizing for the first time that they were alone in the grand space. Slightly embarrassed at the length of their stay, she thanked the man with an apology, explaining that they had just hammered out a business deal, that there was nothing of a personal nature in the meeting, and mentioning how the Southern Belle afforded the opportunity to combine dinner with business.

She was hoping the man wouldn't read more into the meeting. He had seen her there with Clayton Bonifare, and later, with Dr. Brandy Gilcrist. And now here she was with another man. The temptation to allow those simple facts to become something more than they were could ruin her reputation and her clinic if the gossip mongers got hold of them.

DR. PEABODY WIRED his wife the next morning using just five words. *Deal made. Stop. Proceed as planned. Stop.*

Their preplanned messaging meant that Mrs. Peabody would move quickly, listing the house with a land agent and shipping their goods. The doctor would be expecting her and the children within two weeks.

Dr. Hollister Peabody arrived at the Wycome Medical Clinic bright and early the next morning, ready for whatever the day would demand. The first thing was to introduce him properly to Summer and then to Spike, explaining the responsibilities of the two young people. She then led him to the collection of furniture, supplies, and instruments stored in the basement after cleaning out Dr. Silas Grant's clinic several months before. It would all suffice until the shipment from San Francisco arrived.

Dr. Hollister Peabody spent his first day as a part of the Wycome Medical Clinic sorting out what he needed and familiarizing himself with the supplies and equipment on hand. Summer would stay near, ready to assist him in whatever came to hand.

Gwyneth had three home visits to attend to. She took the buggy out herself. Spike was given the day off to attend to something his mother needed done. It was a long day of house calls. Gwyneth arrived back to find the clinic in darkness, the door locked. She let herself in and lit a lamp. Glancing around, she could see that between the doctor and Summer, they sorted out the equipment and laid it all out.

Summer had left notes in the daybook on the two patients who had come in and the treatment given, along with the billing amount. Gwyneth let herself into the house and climbed the stairs. Summer had made enough dinner for two before heading for her own room and an early night. Gwyneth had but to warm up the plate and get a night's sleep.

# Chapter Thirty-Seven

THE ADDITION OF DR. HOLLISTER PEABODY WORKED better than either he or Gwyneth could have hoped. The Peabody family was settled into a small but adequate home within walking distance of the clinic. Gwyneth had taken on most of the home visits, leaving Hollister with the clinic work, along with Summer, who was advancing well as a nurse. Gwyneth was handling most of the births, as the mothers were making it plain that they preferred the female doctor. Summer had become competent enough that she could have handled the simple births herself, although Gwyneth always stood by with a steady eye on the situation. The hospital had been unsuccessful in enticing a burn doctor to Pueblo. They had instead contracted with the Wycome Medical Clinic to treat mill injuries and serious burns. It was a good choice for both parties.

With Gwyneth out of the clinic for a big part of each day, Dr. Peabody found the existing space to be completely satisfactory. He enticed a qualified nurse from Denver to join the clinic, freeing Summer to travel regularly with Gwyneth.

Feeling it was time for him to move on from the Wycome Clinic, Spike, having wisely saved much of his income, purchased a two-seater buggy. With this, and a sturdy horse, he met every train arriving in Pueblo, picking up fares to hotels, businesses, and private homes. Gwyneth now drove the buggy herself, or had Summer come along if she was needed on the out calls.

Gwyneth was busier, more fulfilled in her love of medicine, and making more income than she had thought possible. But none of that did anything for the gnawing in her heart. She wasn't altogether sure when the gnawing had begun. She admitted to herself that it had started well before the two nurses' marriages that had brought it to the surface. Some days it felt as if it had been there forever.

Night after night, she prayed and thought. Prayed and cried. Prayed and sought answers. She feared her internal pain was dragging her down and she had no idea what to do about it.

Summer watched and worried for her friend.

Dr. Hollister Peabody noticed, of course. Anything that impacted the practice of medicine at the Wycome Clinic was noticed. But of more concern was the welfare of Gwyneth herself. As a student of human nature, Hollister thought he saw in Gwyneth a woman with a decision to make but who couldn't see the way forward. Perhaps she hadn't even identified the choices before her, turning the need for a decision into an impossible situation.

SIX MONTHS WENT PAST. Six months that took Pueblo into, and past, another winter. Spring was late in coming. Heavy spring rains were impacting the city as never before. The streets were a quagmire of mud, water, and the constant overabundance of horse manure. Walking across an intersection was a challenge avoided whenever possible. Dr. Peabody appeared before the town council to emphasize the seriousness and the health risks of the situation. He explained the very real reality of flies carrying typhoid fever, in addition to cholera and stomach and bowel distress. He had made a list of a startling number of avoidable medical problems that had passed through the clinic and urged that immediate action be taken.

Council had acted, but progress was slow.

One more nurse had been recruited. On the evidence of busyness and income, it appeared as if the Wycome Clinic was becoming stronger and better known and trusted with each passing month. The doctors had a contractor visit with a mind to open more of the basement area to clinic needs.

Gwyneth should be content. And, oh, how she wished that were the case.

An unusually fierce late spring thunderstorm was passing across the city and surrounding countryside. The gap between one lightning flash and the next was so thin it was impossible to keep track. And really, who cared anyway? Thunder rattled the windows and caused the horses to lay their ears back, tugging on their tethers. Rain came down in sheets, angled and driven by the northwest wind.

The day had been busy. Lunch was forgotten. Gwyneth had been soaked as she sought out the addresses of the ill, with the buggy top offering only partial protection. But still she soldiered on, driving her rig from one sick home to another. Coughs verging on pneumonia, children with childhood communicable diseases, one sprained ankle that she couldn't do much about except support it with a tight wrap of gauze, reminding the injured young man to keep his weight off it. These filled the long day.

That evening, after bathing a portion of the day's weariness away, she wrapped herself in warm clothing, picked up her favorite blanket, added a cup of hot coffee, and made her way to the veranda. This was her daily habit. A little bit of rain wasn't going to cause her to lose out. She was no sooner settled into her big chair when the storm that appeared as if it would be settling in for the night was interrupted by the clopping of a horse.

Amazed that anyone would be abroad on this night, she raised her eyes to watch the buggy pass. When the buggy turned into her driveway, her first thought was *not now, not tonight*. There had never before been a time she wished a patient away. This was the first for her. But she simply had no desire to move from her comfortable position. She was further amazed when the buggy stopped beside the front walkway instead of continuing on to the clinic entrance. Although somewhere above the black clouds the evening sun would still be shining, little of it penetrated the bleakness of the early evening.

It was dark enough that she knew no one would be able to see her sitting there. Waiting, she didn't move. But as the buggy pulled to a stop, a form wrapped in a big, oiled canvas coat stepped to the ground. From size and demeanor, she identified the visitor as a man. The buggy held its position, waiting. With slow, careful steps, picking out the way in the darkness, the man found the stairs. Unwillingly, subconsciously, Gwyneth counted the steps as the walker rose from where she could only see his hat, to where he stood on the veranda floor. One. Two. Three. Four. Five. Six. She knew the number without counting, but her mind wasn't satisfied with that.

Her habit of always being armed had held true that evening. Rather than being tucked into a pocket in the folds of her dress as it usually was, the .32 lay on her lap, covered with the blanket. Her arm was beneath the blanket, her hand on the pistol. When the man didn't speak right away, she eared back the hammer. The sound was faint, but still heard by her visitor.

"You'll have no need of the weapon this night, Gwyneth."

Startled, Gwyneth leaped to her feet. The blanket fell away. She knew that voice. She hadn't heard it for years, but she would never forget. Of their own will, the words spilled from her mouth. "Cob? Is that you, Cob? My gracious man, what are you doing here?"

"I've come for you, Gwyneth. I've come to take you home. Home to Texas. We're to be married and you're going to open a clinic in Sombrero. That's a town the ranch started a while ago. You'll love it there. Hills and grasslands, and mountain trails leading to the wonders of the world. And not far off, the biggest 'ol' canyon eyes ever did see! Sombrero cattle enough to feed half the nation. My ranch, your ranch, our ranch."

"How did you even find me?"

"I've always known where you were. Did you really think I'd let you get away? Besides through Abe and Helen, who are both fine, by the way, I've kept up a trail of correspondence with Eustice Ward. Him and a couple of others. You've done well here. You can be justly proud of yourself. But now it's time to come home."

"What do you mean home? I've never been to Texas."

"You've had a piece of Texas in your heart ever since you met your own Texan. When you get home, you'll feel as if you've always been there and that you should have never left."

There was silence for what seemed to Gwyneth to be half of an eternity. Thoughts whirled through her head. Uncontrolled thoughts for the most part. Jumbled thoughts. Thoughts of a clinic she had worked so hard to start and build. Thoughts that there were others depending on her, all the time knowing they could get along without her daily guidance. Thoughts of her beautiful home, which, in truth, was little more than a big empty house. These and many other images, a ranch, a husband who she had buried on a wooded hillside, a college she had excelled at, the big hospitals where she had worked and learned, her very few romantic interests, all of which went exactly nowhere, patients, oh so many patients, thoughts, images, then relief. Acceptance. Acknowledgment.

Quietly, almost a whisper.

"All right."

# Teaser: Gwyneth Finally (Frontier Dreaming 3)

TEXAS

*El Paso, Texas*, the sign on the station house wall appeared proud to announce.

After having held to their seats to allow others to vacate the railcar, Cob, followed by Gwyneth, stepped to the pine-planked station platform. They were welcomed by a single shot that sounded to Cob like a .44, followed by another short volley. People started screaming, running every which way, seeking shelter. Cob turned to Gwyneth. “Get Back. Stay inside. Stay low.”

Ignoring that good advice himself, he drew his belted .45 as he scurried along the side of the passenger car, hoping to see where the shots were coming from, and what the danger might be. If asked, Cob would describe himself as a simple cattle rancher. But that didn’t mean he would stand by where danger loomed.

The action appeared to be centered around a heavy, high-sided wagon drawn by a four-up team of strong mules. The well-experienced teamster had the rig backed up to the baggage car door. The train had come to a stop only moments before. Indicating that the attackers had knowledge of where the baggage car would stop. The heavy car door was slowly moving, was almost closed, as if the attendant had opened it on their arrival in El Paso, before Cob had heard the first shot, but was now frantically attempting to close it.

Even as Cob watched, a big-hatted man rose from the wagon bed, rifle leading the way, as he placed one booted foot where it would prevent the closing of the car access. He transferred the rifle to his left hand, rested his right shoulder against the leading edge of the door, and pushed back against the efforts of the baggage clerk. Even as he held the door, two men who had jumped past the opening were lugging a heavy, iron-strapped box out of the car, squeezing past the half-closed door. They dropped the box onto the bed of the wagon and returned to grab another.

Riders coming to the assistance of the thieves raised their Colts. Hot leads slammed through the thickness of the car door. A sharp cry and then a morbid groan rose from the baggage car. When the wounded man holding the door collapsed to the floor of the car, all resistance to its opening was removed. The thief who had been holding the door against its closing easily slid it back, creating an opening wide enough for Cob to see the unmoving attendant. He appeared to have skittered away a few feet and was now lying on the floor with his back leaning against other cargo and baggage. He was holding his shoulder with his one good hand. Blood dribbled through his fingers.

But when the two men who had removed the heavy box leaped from the wagon back into the car, the wounded attendant rolled onto his side, facing the daylight with a double-barreled express gun aimed. The whoomph of released lead from one barrel was followed quickly by the same from the second death-dealing ten-gauge Remington. The two raiders were smashed back, crumpling to the floor of the baggage car, in a pile of blood and gore. Fools, Cob thought. Brave men dying for nothing.

***AVAILABLE FEBRUARY 2026***

# About the Author

Reg Quist's pioneer heritage includes sod shacks, prairie fires, home births, and children's graves under the prairie sod, all working together in the lives of people creating their own space in a new land.

Out of that early generation came farmers, ranchers, business men and women, builders, military graves in faraway lands, Sunday Schools that grew to become churches, plus story tellers, musicians, and much more.

Hard work and self-reliance were the hallmark of those previous great generations, attributes that were absorbed by the following generation.

Quist's career choice took him into the construction world. From heavy industrial work, to construction camps in the remote northern bush, the author emulated his grandfathers, who were both builders, as well as pioneer farmers and ranchers.

It is with deep thankfulness that Quist says, "I am a part of the first generation to truly enjoy the benefits of the labors of the pioneers. My parents and their parents worked incredibly hard, and it is well for us to remember".

www.ingramcontent.com/pod-product-compliance
Lightning Source LLC
LaVergne TN
LVHW091249110826
845146LV00002BA/680